THE WORLD OF DARKNESS

"THINGS ARE RARELY WHAT THEY SEEM"

BY JULIE TÉTREAULT

iUniverse, Inc.
New York Bloomington

This is a work of fiction. All of the characters, names, incidents, organizations, and dialogue in this novel are either the products of the author's imagination or are used fictitiously.

iUniverse books may be ordered through booksellers or by contacting:

iUniverse
1663 Liberty Drive
Bloomington, IN 47403
www.iuniverse.com
1-800-Authors (1-800-288-4677)

ISBN: 978-1-4401-5629-8 (sc)
ISBN: 978-1-4401-5630-4 (ebook)

Printed in the United States of America

iUniverse rev. date: 7/9/2009

"Some people see things that are and ask, why? Some people dream of things that never were and ask, why not?"
George Carlin

"Unless you believe, you will not understand."
Saint Augustine

PROLOGUE

FOR MALERK AND NATURE

In the next galaxy, after the Milky Way, there is another solar system. It is composed of four suns and twelve planets. These planets are called: Linos, Bond, Breathless, Phantom, Escape, Fantasia, Osiris, Aura, Legend, Fidelity, Knowledge and Ocean. Linos is the closest to the suns while Ocean is the farthest. Linos and Bond are twins. They both have a size of 210 650 324 km² and are silver coloured. Linos has two moons and Bond has five moons. Breathless is a hydrogen planet. The hydrogen is held close to the planet's core by gravity. It has a surface area of 306 758 910km². It as eight moons. Phantom is the seventh biggest planet with a size of 460 819 726km². It is made of helium and kept together by gravity just like Breathless. One moon watches over this planet. Escape is a dark green planet of 367 053 120km² surrounded by ten moons. Fantasia as 487 372 198km² of black surface surrounded by fourteen moons. Osiris is a desert planet of 520 178 310km² which has three moons. Aura is the fourth biggest planet with a size of 500 721 327km². Half the planet is of darkness, the other of light and it is watched over by four moons. Legend is a young planet still covered by lava and volcanoes of 541 521 637km² and has nine moons. It is the biggest planet of that solar system. Fidelity is a bronze coloured planet of 521 367 890km² and has eighteen moons to keep her company. Knowledge is a white of 473 197 837km² and as twenty moons. The last planet, Ocean, is a water planet of 423 178 256km² and as five moons. But only one of these twelve planets is inhabited. That planet is Aura. It is the home of 7 641 007 450. The Auriens have lived on Aura for 65 billions years. They are people of great powers and youth. But after all those glorious years, their powers are fading. The four suns and four moons are diminishing in light which makes their powers diminish as well because their powers depend on the strength of their lights. Two kingdoms rule Aura. The north, which is called the black kingdom because their powers are considered evil, and the south which is called the white kingdom because their powers are considered good. The black kingdom is ruled by King Vile and Queen Audrey. They have three children; two boys, Malerk and Rekor, and a girl, Laurie. Queen Peridot and King Oric rule the white kingdom. They have two daughters, Sapphire and Nature. When the rulers of the two kingdoms realized that their powers were diminishing, they knew they had to do something to stop it. They chose two persons to go explore their galaxy and the neighbouring ones to see if they could find another planet that would provide the same amount of power. They decided to send one person from each kingdom. King Vile chose his youngest son, Malerk, who is 18 years old. Queen Peridot decided to send her youngest daughter who is 21 years old, Nature. A small ship was prepared for a two-year journey.

Malerk and Nature explored every planet in their solar system but found nothing. Since only five months had passed, they decided to go explore the next galaxy. The first three planets were too cold to live on. The fourth one was too dangerous because it was surrounded by a belt of asteroids. The atmosphere of the fifth one was poisonous. The terrain of the sixth one was not made for life. On their way to the next planet, they used their last drop of gas. The shuttle went threw the atmosphere and crashed. Malerk and Nature were able to get out of the shuttle unharmed. After realizing that they were trapped on the planet, Malerk and Nature decided to explore the planet. It was perfect for their people. The only sun and moon were more powerful then Aura's four moons and four suns. They sent a message to Aura to tell their people that they were stranded on the perfect planet. The message reached their planet and the receiver told them that they were on their way to rescue them. The messenger left his post to go tell the king of the black kingdom and the queen of the white one. He found King Vile first. After hearing the message, the king bribed the messenger to keep the incident a secret and to instead tell the queen that her daughter had decided to live on the new planet and did not want to return. The queen never learned the truth. Nature and Malerk's message was sent 12150 years before this story or in -10 000. A thousand years passed and no one came to rescue them. Nature and Malerk realized that they were not going to get rescued. To make herself at home, Nature decide to make trees, lakes, rivers, plants, animals, etc. Seeing that Nature was making everything form the white kingdom, Malerk did the same. He created the clouds to hide the sun and moon, volcanoes, ice, mountains, etc. It took them a thousand years to complete their world. Nature and Malerk married themselves in -8527 after realizing, unlike their kinds, that one cannot live without the other. It takes darkness to make light. They had their first children in -8000. Non-identical twins: Lydia, who would later be known as Oracle, and Lumos, protector of stars, who would later be forgotten by his parents for untold reasons. In -6573, Nature made the first Wood-Elf. She thought him to care for all "good" creatures of the world and fear the others. After exploring his land, the Wood-Elf named the planet Melda Cemmen which means Beloved Land. In

-6505, Nature made a small modification to the Wood-Elf. This Sindarin-Elf liked to live in a house instead of a tree. In -5987, she created a small version of the Elves, which she called Hauflin. In -5960, she created the Dwarves to keep watch on Malerk's mountains. In -5245, Nature used a river which she accidentally filled with blood when she made rivers to make the Vampires. They would be born from blood and would die into blood. In -4923, Nature made the Humans and gave them an inventive brain, which would eventually lead them to their doom. When Malerk saw that Nature had created the Humans, he decided to create a species whose only purpose would be to destroy the Humans because he knew what they would do to the same to the rest of Melda Cemmen. They would be called Demons. In -4867, Nature created the Dragons to keep watch over the sky. In -4598, Nature gave away a part of her powers to two new species: the Wizards, keepers of Nature's magic, and the Witches, tamers of Nature's magic. In -1965, Nature created the spirits and the Animal spirits. She created the Spirits to preserve the souls of the greatest people who ever lived and the Animals Spirits to preserve the souls of the peoples who dedicated their lives to Nature's creations.

FOR THE TWINS

It all started in the future, in the year 2150 to be precise. Twins were born in the second kingdom called Yaviere, in its capital called Tindome, from Queen Selene and King Lyco. On their night of birth, the thunder was roaring and the clouds were crying. Only a few people were there to witness their birth. There was Jonathan, Selene's protector, and Ashka, a dear friend of the queen. On that very night the troubles they would never escape started. The trouble began when Lyco first saw his children. There was a boy and a girl; they were un-identical twins. The girl was more like her father who was a Wood-Elf. She had pointy ears, blond hair, blue eyes, would never get sick, she was light-footed, and, like the Vampires, she had fangs and retractable claws. The boy, on the other hand, was more like his mother. He had dark hair, dark eyes, fangs, retractable claws, and, like his father, pointy ears. But these children where not like most children; unlike the others, they had special abilities. They had powers given to them by Nature. The girl could see the future and the boy was able to produce a shield that would come out of his hand and it would protect anyone inside and keep enemies out. Lyco was afraid of their powers so on the same day, he went to the Oracle. He explained his fear and asked to be destroyed. But the Oracle could not destroy him because he was her brother so she separated his soul in two and locked him up in his children's bodies. That way, he would have to live with his fears and eventually conquer them. When he was locked up, a tattoo was imprinted on each of his children's back. It was the body of a demon that was covered with the wing of an angel. Jonathan was also jealous but not of the same thing. He was jealous of the love between Lyco and Selene. When he saw Selene cry because she had learned that Lyco was gone, Jonathan decided to ease her pain. He killed her and because the girl resembled her mother, he took her and sent her to live a human life in the past where she was never to be found. When the council heard the news, they were scared for the safety of the boy who was the only one of royal blood left. They decided to search the kingdom for kids of his age who might be powerful enough to protect him. They found six. They were also gifted with powers. They found: Drew gifted with mind travel and the power to see anyone wherever they may be, William gifted with a mind that knows what strategy to use at any time of danger or war, Essie gifted with hypnotic powers, a knowledge of every languages and an ability to erase memories, Marty gifted with telekinesis and an ability to heal people, Karl gifted with super human physical prowess and invisibility, and Juliet gifted with the ability to control the elements and to see auras. The boy would now be raised by Ashka.

PART 1: QUEEN EOS

CHAPTER 1
A LONELY LIFE

Nineteen years later, the boy, Scott, was still safe and his life had never been in danger since the day he was born. He had grown up ten times faster then he was supposed to like all his friends. In other words, they had grown up like humans. He was now 5'11". He had light brown hair and dark blue eyes like the ocean. He was living in the castle with many guards, servants and his friends. But his peaceful life had been different these past few days. Every night for about five days, he had dreamed of a girl that was his age and looked like an elf. He went to the Oracle and told her about his dream. She analyzed his dream and thought: *"Maybe the girl his only lost and not dead"* but did not pay much attention to it. A couple of weeks past normally but then Drew saw Scott's sister with his powers. Drew was also nineteen years old. He was a pure blood vampire. He was 5'10". He had the same coloured hair as Scott and had grey eyes. He could see anyone one he wanted with the permission of Vira, protector of life, even if they were on the other side of the land. He had been trying to find Eos, Scott's sister, for a week and had had finally found her. He had found her in the past, in the year 2004. The council knew Scott and Eos would have immense powers if they would be brought back together. So, not knowing what to do, they went to the Oracle. Her real name was Lydia. She had been nicknamed Oracle after she had made a general prediction about the future of Melda Cemmen and had been right. She had a castle close to the castle of the council, of Nature and of Malerk on the northern point of this land in the middle of a forest. When the council arrived at the Oracle's castle, they asked her what they should do.

- Oracle please help us. Said the Dragon Spirit.
- What seems to be the problem? Asked the Oracle.
- It's Eos. She has been found. If the twins come back together they will have immense power that could change a lot of things. What should we do?
- If Eos was found then Fate wants us to find her. We have to bring her back. Send Scott, Jonathan and the others.

Fate was the Oracle's little sister. She controlled most of the major events that could change the course of history. Every living being except, of course, for her family had never seen her. The Dragon Spirit then asked:

-Are we obligated to bring her back?
- It will determine if the Vampires are remembered as great or weak.

So that night, the group prepared to go get their lost queen, heir to Selene. The protector, Jonathan, had to think of another way to make himself forget Selene. Ashka, the family friend, came in the room in which Jonathan slept, to ask him if she could help him destroy the chances of the twins reuniting. He replied that any help would be appreciated especially from her because she knew almost everything about the royal family. Before she left the room he asked her:

- Why do you want to help me destroy her? Asked Jonathan.
- Because if she dies, I am the one who gets the throne of the second kingdom, the world of the Vampires.
- I see. But there's just one thing wrong with your plan.
- What is it?
- Eos as to give you her place for you to be able to rule at her place.
- True. How are we going to do it?
- We will make her give us the throne.

Klashka wanted the throne so badly that she was willing to let the "us" pass.

Meanwhile, at the castle of the second kingdom, in the city of Tindome, the rest of the gang: Essie, Scott, Karl, Juliet, Marty, Merrill, Drew and William, were getting ready for the journey through time that would bring them back to the great kingdom they once were. Essie was half-Spirit and half-Vampire. She was 5'9", had emerald eyes and chocolate coloured hair. Karl was half-Vampire and half-Demon. He was 6 feet, had light green eyes and dark brown hair. Juliet was a quarter Wizard and three-quarter Vampire. She was 5'8", had sea-blue eyes and black hair. Marty was a quarter Demon and three-quarter Vampire. He was 5'10", had sea-green eyes and had ebony black hair. Merrill was 5'7", had brown eyes and medium brown hair. She was a Witch by birth but her blood was mixed with Vampire blood at the age of twelve. Since then her family had thought that she was dead so she had stayed with Drew. She had also stayed with him because Witches did not like Vampires very much. William, Scott's best friend, was a pure blood Vampire. He was 5'11", had brown eyes like the earth and light brown hair. At the same time, messengers were arriving at the castle of the 4th kingdom, the kingdom of the Wood-elves, to tell the king, Louisiam, son of Vanyar, that they had found the queen of the 2nd kingdom, the Vampire kingdom, and that they would bring her back for her to grow up as a real Vampire. Louisiam was a nineteen year-old Elf who had been ruling the kingdom since he had been sixteen years old. His eyes were blue and had golden and white striped going from the centre to the exterior of his eyes. His hair was gold with a hint of blond.

The next morning, back in the Vampire kingdom, they had a celebration to bring good luck to the Vampires who would bring back the queen that had been lost for almost twenty years. The sun was shining with all her strength (the Elves, the Spirits and the Vampires consider the sun to be feminine) and was bringing colours to the clouds that were watching them have fun. They were making sure it was a good day for them to leave the comfort of their home. After drinking many glasses of blood it was time to say their goodbyes to their families and past threw a portal that could bring them wherever they wished to go, in whatever time period, if they had the only person that could open the portal in that generation for that kingdom or the key has she was called. They all placed their hands on a brick that had a hand imprinted on it and were sucked in the portal that would bring them to the year 2004.

CHAPTER 2
SEEING HER FACE TO FACE

Traveling to the right time took about a day because they had to calculate the exact day and year in which they had to go. But recognizing her was no trouble for them because every Vampire could feel each other when they were close to them. It was as if they had a special sense. When they entered her school, they found her sitting on a bench with her friends she had made there. She was in university. Their was about thirty-five thousand students at that school. When they got close to her they could sense her. Jonathan was the first to see "the lost one". When Jonathan saw Eos, he began to be nervous. His brown eyes were filled with fear, jealousy and love at the same time. He remembered Selene that he had once loved before. Eos looked a lot like her mother. The rest of the gang saw her shortly after him. No one said anything or made any movements. They just stared at their beautiful queen. After a couple of minutes of staring at her, Jonathan asked Scott:

- Can I go see her first by myself?
- Sure but we are only giving you three minutes alone and that's all.
- That will be enough. Thanks.

Jonathan approached her carefully because now that Scott was close to her she was slowly regaining all her powers and no one knew what they were. His hands were sweaty and he did not know what to say to her. So when he finally arrived beside her, he said the first thing that came to his mind:

- Hi.
-What do you want? Said Eos with a voice that seamed already to tell him to go away.
- To talk to you.
- Why? You never wanted to talk to me before. You always ignored me.
- What!?
- Don't act like you don't know what I'm talking about. Just leave me alone.

Jonathan did not add anything. He just turned around and went back to the rest of the gang. Jonathan, unfortunately, used to be a Human who went to that school in that year and he had seen Eos before. Scott passed by Jonathan with a face full of laughter. He was happy that Eos did not like Jonathan. Scott approached Eos because he knew that because of their blood connection and the connection between vampires that she would recognize him. Eos' ears and teeth were still normal so she could still blend in with the Humans that were having fun with her but that would not last long. Her hair was as golden as the sun and her eyes were as blue as the water in the elfin streams. When he was right beside her he said:

- Hi. (Being a little shy.) Do you know who I am?

Eos turned around to see Scott standing beside her. At that moment, something in her mind told her who he was and the memories of her father and mother on the day of her birth came back to her. Somehow Eos knew who he was but she only had pieces. She got up and said to Scott:

- You're Scott, my brother, I think.
- Yes it's me and now a part of me is back.
- Who's that? Asked one of Eos's friend called Liv.
- It's too complicated to explain. Answered Eos.
- Can I talk to you? Asked Scott.
- Sure as long as you can fill the gaps of my memory.
- Come with me.

They went away from her friends, about four meters, and Scott told Eos who she truly was. He told her who her parents were and how he had come to find her here in the Human kingdom, the 9th kingdom called Earth. In her mind she knew everything he had said to her, it had only been lost in her memory. She also had been dreaming about it for a week just like Scott.

Meanwhile Louisiam was watching their every move. He had also traveled from the future after hearing the news. He wanted to rebuild the alliance between the 4th and 2nd kingdom. The alliance had been broken when Queen Selene and King Lyco had suddenly died. He also had a personal reason to be there. At Eos' birth, the Oracle had predicted that Louisiam would marry Eos. So far, the Oracle had never been wrong. Everything she had predicated had happened. Louisiam believed even more the prediction that the Oracle had made now that he had seen her. His heart wanted her close to him. He wanted to feel her on his chest when they were sleeping or hugging. He wanted to feel her lips close to his. She had stolen his heart.

Scott introduced to Eos all the other Vampires. First he introduced her to Drew. Eos shook his hand and immediately had a vision of what he had once done to betray the Vampires. He had changed a Witch into a Vampire because he loved her. Witches were the enemies of the Vampires. Then she met Essie that she immediately wanted as best friend. Then she met William and Juliet. William did not care about many things. Juliet could ask anything of William and he would do it. Karl and Marty followed. Then she met Merrill the Vampire that wasn't a Vampire by birth. She would hate her from now on. Everyone Eos had met were all 19 years old except for William and Juliet who were 20. Scott then introduces Jonathan and explained that he was the Spirit who had to protect her. Scott asked Eos if she could come to their house tonight for a celebration. It would be to celebrate the finding of Eos. She accepted with pleasure.

CHAPTER 3
PART OF THE GANG

It was the evening of the full moon so Eos knew it would be a night to remember. When she got there, she was greeted by Essie who showed her into an abandoned mansion that they had arranged to live in until they could go back. The mansion was in an abandoned neighbourhood. This neighbourhood was the centre of a city called Edain that the Humans had long forgotten about. Those mansions used to house the royal family and, the Lords and the Ladies of the Human kingdom. When she was inside, they offered her a red drink in a golden glass with elfin design. She didn't want things to go wrong so she took it. The red drink was of course blood. But not Human blood. It was Vampire blood from the blood river that separated the Vampire kingdom from the Hauflin's and the Witch's kingdom. It would help her return to her old self. It would make her ears pointy and her teeth into fangs. She could see a small knife under the fire and wandered what they were going to do with it. When they served the supper, she forgot about the knife. They had prepared stuffed rabbits and mashed potatoes. After a well-deserved meal, they left the kitchen to go to the room that was right beside it. The drink was starting to take effect. A chair was placed in the middle of the room. Essie told her to sit on the chair. Scott went and got the knife. When Scott came back, Essie said:

- You might want to hold your breath.
- Why? Asked Eos.
- Because this is going to hurt.
- What are you going to do?
- Where going to give you your tattoos back.
- Did I have them before I was sent back in the past?
- Yes.
- Won't I have them if we return to the future?
- Yes, but until then people need to know who you are. Lie down and relax.

William was holding a drawing. It looked like tree leafs interlocking each other. In each leaf there was a word. In the first leaf was written "together", in the second it was written "we stand" and in the third it was written "alone". It meant that all the Vampires stand together but in the world they stand alone. Scott started to cut the skin tracing the tattoo. Each time he lifted the knife, Drew would pass a flame over the tattoo so it wouldn't heal and stay in that shape for eternity. As the pain was sensed by Eos, her fangs and claws come out and her ears became pointy. After fifteen minutes, they stopped so Eos asked:

- Is it over?
- No we still have to do your demon. Said Scott
- Relax and breathe because it's going to take a while. Said Essie

After another fifteen minutes the demon was done. The last tattoo was a sideway Demon with an angel wing covering most of his body. Eos was back to her old self. Then Scott gave her a ring. The ring was made of white gold; it had a Peridot that was held by two string-like pieces of white gold, and two diamonds. They also gave her to her a crest of power. One of only five given to the most powerful beings compared to their kind. That painful full moon night was over. Scott explained to her sister that when she was relaxed, she would look like a Human but when she was angry, her true form would be shown. Eos then said goodbye to the gang before going back home.

CHAPTER 4
A NEW LIFE BEGINS

Eos woke up, the next morning, at 6 o'clock as usual. It would be the last time she would wake up at that house. Her adoptive parents' memories would be erased and replaced with something else. She got dressed and then had breakfast. Then at 7:05 left for school, took the bus at 7:20 and again at 7:30. Arrived finally at school at 7:45. She met the gang of vampires at 7:50 in front of her locker. They talked about their kingdom until eight when Liv, a friend of Eos, arrived. She was a 5'4", dark haired and brown-eyed girl who was a year older than Eos. Before Eos had her vampire friends, Liv and Eos used to hang out together every day. When she saw Eos, Liv said to her:

- Hi Eos.

Eos said nothing to Liv and did not turn around to look at her, so Liv said to Eos:

- Hi!?! Repeated Liv, having no answer from Eos like she usually got.

She approached Eos curiously, because she was wondering what was wrong.

She turned the corner and said:

- Eos! I am talking to you why don't you answer?

Liv had turned the corner. Suddenly Liv was standing face to face with Eos and her new friends that did not look happy to see Liv. Eos asked:

- What do you want?
- Aren't we going to walk around the campus like we usually do? Said Liv.
- Can't you see I have some new friends that are more exciting then you?
- What!? Why do you hate me suddenly? You don't just wake up and hate someone.
- You're right! You don't. That's why I hated you for a while.
- What? Since when?
- Since about a year. Now could you leave us alone?
- You'll regret this!
- Sure I will. Maybe in a century or a millennium. Now leave us alone.

Liv went away full of hate but before she was too far and to make her angrier, William said:

- non abes non perfectus cum tu.

Just when Scott was about to tell Eos what it meant, Eos translated it by herself and left everyone surprised:

- Don't go too far, we're not done with you. Said Eos. I know what it means.
- How did you know that? Asked Scott.

- I studied the forgotten languages. The Humans still remember the languages but not the story behind them.

Not so far away was Louisiam, son of Vanyar, King of the Wood-elves. He was also interested in Eos but not for the same reason as the Vampires. After looking at them for a few minutes, he decided that he would go see Eos that night. He would try to become her friend and bring back that alliance between their kingdoms.

CHAPTER 5
CLOSE TO DEATH

The gang of Vampires were having a party. Eos was no longer living with her human family. Her family's memory of her had been erased. They did not know that she even existed. For the night's occasion, Marty had prepared a meal. The girls had put on new dresses that Essie had made herself. They were white decorated with gold strips and elfin words in the gold strip. After the music had started, each guy chose a girl to dance with. William decided to dance with Eos, Karl chose Essie, Drew chose Merrill, Scott chose Juliet and Marty chose no one because he did not like to dance. Everyone was having fun when they were interrupted by Louisiam and Halir, Louisiam's general, entered who had the room. Each guy took their swords and pointed them at Louisiam and Halir. No one had seen their pointy ears that were under their golden hair. Eos looked at them carefully and saw that their eyes were of a deep blue that could never be of a human eye. Eos then said:

- What is your name and title?
- I am Halir, General of the army of the 4th kingdom.

- I am Louisiam, king of the 4th kingdom, son of Vanyar. I am one of the five most powerful people in all the kingdoms.
- That's great! This is my brother Scott, this is Juliet and I am Eos, Queen of the 2nd kingdom and we all have a crest of power.
- That's incredible! There as never been more than one crest of power per kingdom. You must be very powerful and you must be half-bloods.
- Yes we are. Now, what do you want?
- I want you to come back to our time as fast as possible because we need to restore the alliance between our kingdoms. And we have to fulfill the Oracle's prediction.
- What prediction and who his the Oracle?

The Vampires looked at each other. They knew which prediction Louisiam was talking about but they did not think that Eos was ready to know it. Louisiam explained:

- The Oracle is a woman that knows our future based on the events of our past and our present. To you and me she predicted that we would get married.
- I will decide my own future. Said Eos.

Eos left the room and went to her new room down the hall. On her way over to her room, she saw Drew. He had gone away when the Elves had come in because he knew it was going to turn bad. He was painting flowers. Eos went by his side to see what he had done.

- Nice painting! Said Eos.
- Thanks! But I can never get it right. Said Drew.
- What do you mean? It's beautiful.
- Look at my painting and then look at the flowers.

Eos looked at the painting. He had painted white, pink and red roses. Then she looked at the flowers. They were dying as he was painting them.

- How come it does that? Asked Eos.
- It's my curse. Everything I paint will die. I was seven and everyone was jealous of the way I could paint. They asked a Wizard to give me this malediction so I wouldn't paint anymore.
- But you're still painting!
- You made me want to keep trying.
- Why me?
- Because for nineteen years you have been dead to us. I found you. That means that even if you've lost all hope there's still a chance for it to happen.
- Since I was your inspiration, I will try to remove the curse you carry.
- Thanks!

So as planned, Eos went to her room where she though of her future. Meanwhile the other Vampires were preparing Eos' birthday while keeping an eye on the Elves. They thought that for her birthday they could give her something very rare. Louisiam thought that he could offer her the white spirit tiger. He was once a Wood-Elf who adored and took care of every animal so, when he died, Nature transformed him into a tiger. Scott and William decided that they would give Eos the sword named Tari so she could protect herself.

CHAPTER 6
AN UNEXPECTED BIRTHDAY

It was the 30th of January and Eos was still asleep. The gang was preparing a surprise birthday party. The gifts were wrapped up. They were hanging the decorations and preparing the meal. When Eos woke up, the gang yelled:

"Surprise!" Not expecting that moment she screamed in fear. Louisiam wanted to comfort her so he approached her. When William saw what he was doing he took his sword, Yar, and held it under Louisiam's neck and said:

- You move closer to Eos and you die.
- William! Put the sword down. Said Eos.
- Why? Do you like him?
- I am telling you to put the sword down.
- Well I won't.

Eos moved in hyper speed, removed William's sword and pointed it at his throat. All the Vampires could move very fast for short periods of time. If they did it for too long, they would die of exhaustion. With the sword still pointed at William's throat, Eos said:

- I told you to put the sword down.
- Eos please put the sword down. I'm sorry.

Eos pulled the sword away fast and close to his throat so that he would bleed.

- Ouch! Said William and Eos at the same time.
- Why does it hurt me? Asked Eos.
- I'm your soul mate. Said William.

A soul mate was a person that was connected to you. They had to be of the opposite sex and of the same species. If one of them was hurt, the other one felt it but to kill them you had to strike them in the heart at the exact same time or else it didn't work. The Vampires had had soul mates since the day they had made a deal with the Witches. The Witches had given that and the ability to walk in the sun to them in exchange for peace. Most Vampires did not even know who their soul mate was. But every Vampire in the room knew who was theirs. Juliet was the soul mate of Scott, Eos was with William, Essie was with Karl, Merrill was with Drew, and Marty had none. Marty was the exception to the rule. For some unknown reason Fate did not wish for him to have a soul mate.

Marty approached William and Eos. He placed his hand on their throats and pressed real hard. When he removed his hand the wounds were gone. Marty could heal wounds by touch. From that moment on Marty would have a job.

- Now let's go open my gifts. Said Eos.
- I think she got used to her powers fast. Said Scott. Don't you think so?
- I think you're right. Said Karl.

They went to the main room where they gave Eos her presents. Drew gave to Eos the picture of the roses that she had seen before. The rest of the gang gave her the sword named Tari. Its wooden handgrip was covered with leather and adorned with gold leaves. The blade was made of platinum with a gold band in in the middle in which *"Dia Regina"* (Noble Queen) was incrusted. Then Louisiam and Halir gave to her the white spirit tiger. Halir let it in the room. As soon as he saw Eos, he charged at her. Just before the tiger jumped on Eos, Halir said:

- Desinos! Tuus domino est. (Stop! She is your master.)

The tiger stopped right before Eos and went back beside Halir.

- Thank you Halir. Said Eos. See Scott, Elves aren't that bad. (Scott did not listen) Scott! Our father was a pure Wood-elf so why do you hate Elves?
- Because our father left us on the day we were born. Does that answer your question?
- They're not all like that Scott.
- He's the same kind of Elf.
- So what? It doesn't mean anything.
- You love him. I can see it. You protect him. Some day you'll betray us and you will love him for eternity.
- Why would I betray you by liking Elves?
- They let you down when you need them the most.
- Whoever agrees with me place yourself beside me and the others can go behind my brother.

William, Juliet and Merrill went behind Scott while Essie, Karl, Drew and Marty went behind Eos. Jonathan was laughing in his corner because everything was going to plan.

The gang was separating itself in two small groups so killing them would be easier for him.

- Essie, Karl, Drew, Marty, Louisiam and Halir follow me. We're going some place else. Said Eos.
- Don't bother. I'm leaving. Said Scott.
- I don't want to leave Merrill. Said Drew.
- Then change side. Said Eos.

They went their separate ways, which was a big mistake. Jonathan went outside and called Ashka with his mind:

- Ashka! Phase one his complete. Meet me at the park tonight. I'll give you phase two there.
- O.K. I'll meet you there at 8:30. Said Ashka. See you there.

CHAPTER 7
EVERYTHING GOES TO PLAN

- Hey! Said Ashka.
- Hi! Are you sure you're alone? Asked Jonathan.
- Yes. What's phase two?
- We are going to set a trap for our Vampire queen and her friends.
- What do you have in mind?
- We are going to cause a war. The gang against the Demons. They're sure to die.
- Where will the war take place?
- At the end of the 9th kingdom, the kingdom of the Humans. Where no one lives. A complete desert.
- How will you make the Demons come here?
- You'll see, just wait and see.

Jonathan left and went east to the Demon kingdom. There, he killed a member of the king's council in the shape of the body of each Vampire that were with Eos. He then returned to Eos. When he entered, he was greeted by Eos who had a suspicious look and was waiting for him at the door. She asked Jonathan:

- Where were you?
- Just out side watching the sunset. Answered Jonathan.
- It's nine o'clock the sunset was three hours ago.
- I mean I was watching the moonrise.
- The moon rises when the sun goes down.
- I...well I...
- Drew is there a fast way to get to the council?
- Yes. With your ring and the white spirit tiger. But he can only do it once. Look in his eyes and then think of where you want to go. He will bring you there.

She did as Drew had told her to do and the tiger brought her to the council in a second even if it was on the other side of the world. She arrived in front of a big wooden door. She pushed it open and saw one Wood-Elf, one Sindarin-Elf, one Dwarf, one Demon, one Witch, one Wizard, one Hauflin, one Vampire, one Spirit and one Animal-Spirit in the shape of a Dragon. Essie, Karl, Drew, Louisiam, Halir and Marty bowed before the council. Eos stood on her feet looking at them. Eos asked them:

- Who's the boss here?
- We all have the same authority here. Said the Wood-Elf. How can I help you?
- I want another protector.
- What is wrong with the one you already have? Asked the Spirit.
- He's trying to kill me.
- Can you prove that? Asked the Wood-Elf.
- With all due respect sir, I don't think it is a wise decision to wait for a proof. Said Louisiam.
- What a wise comment the Elf said. Said the Witch.
- I suggest we give to her the protector in training. Said the Sindarin-Elf.

- But is he ready to face the dangerous world that follows Eos? Asked the Demon.
- There is no other who is ready enough to protect her. Said the Wizard.
- Then we have no choice but to give her Simon. Said the Hauflin.

The Dragon closed his eyes and reopened them seconds later. After a few seconds had passed, a Spirit appeared in the corner of the room. He had blue-grey eyes, brown hair and looked like he was about 20 years old. The Dragon said to Eos:

- This is Simon. He will be your new protector.
- Thank you.

Everyone bowed before the council before going back to the Human kingdom. When they arrived back at the human kingdom, Eos spoke with Simon to know him better. Simon knew everything about every member of the gang. He asked Eos:

- Where's your brother, Scott?
- We had a fight so we went our own separate ways.
- Why?
- Because I'm a friend of Louisiam and Halir and my father was the same kind of Elf as them so he thinks they will also break my heart and leave me by myself.
- He still remembers every detail from his past. You can't let this separate you. You have to stay together.
- Why?
- If you get too far away from your brother, both of you will loose your powers. That's why you didn't have any power for nineteen years while you were here.
- What?

Just when Simon was about to explain to Eos her loss of power while she was in the human kingdom, Halir entered with a face showing nothing but terror. He said in a trembling voice:

- Eos! You'll never guess what I saw with my foresight.
- What's wrong?
- The Demons are coming to kill us.
- Get Jonathan in here now! Screamed Eos.

CHAPTER 8
FINDING A LOST FRIEND

Eos pushed Jonathan's human body very hard on the wall. Jonathan then said to Eos:

- You know you can't hurt me, right?
- I know I only want to ask you a question. Did you or someone you know invent a reason for the Demons to come looking for us?
- Maybe.
- I want the answer or I will have a pleasure watching you die by the hands of your replacement, Simon. Eos pointed to Simon as she said his name.
- Your replaced me!?
- Yes I did because you weren't doing your job properly.
- Then I did invent a reason for the Demons to kill you.
- Which is?
- I might have killed a few important Demons in the shape of each of your bodies.
- Did you or did you not?
- I did.
- We're in trouble. Said Eos while letting go of Jonathan and

turning to her friends. Unless we find some people to help us fight against the Demons, we're all going to die.
- Eos! Said Halir shyly from a corner of the room. Can I suggest something?
- What's your suggestion?
- You could use my army with the permission of Louisiam.
- You have my permission. Said Louisiam.
- Seriously!? Said Eos.
- I would never lie to a queen or a king.
- Thank you. How fast can you get it here?
- Around 56 hours.
- Leave now and try to get them here faster.

Louisiam and Halir left the room to go get the army they had promised to Eos. They had to travel a distance of 3200 km. The elves could go about 60km/h when they were running and that's why it would take them around 56 hours. Simon then turned to Eos and said not wanting to bother her:

- Eos. Unless your brother is with you, you won't have full power.
- How can I get him back with me in less than two days?
- You'll have to tell him that he will die if he doesn't help you and why he will die.

Eos left the room quickly without looking if someone had followed her. She went to her brother's "hideout" a few blocks away. When they arrived in the front of the right building, Eos felt the presence of her brother. She then knocked on the door of that building. William opened the door and said, when he saw Eos:

- Get out of here.
- Why? Asked Eos starring at William waiting for an answer. There's something I have to ask my brother.

- I can't let you see him.
- It's very important.
- No. William hesitated and then added. I'm sorry.

Eos looked at William as if she was disappointed. Then she pushed him out of the way and said to William:

- I'm sorry too, but I have to see my brother.

She pushed opened the big wooden door, of which the hinges were barely holding on, that led to the main room. She entered the room, sat down on a chair and looked at her brother who was wondering what she wanted. After a few minutes of staring at each other, Eos said to her brother:

- I have something to tell you.
- I told you not to let her in. Said Scott to William with an angry voice.
- Scott! I have something to tell you.
- What is it?
- Jonathan made a mistake for which we are going to suffer.
- What did he do?
- He killed important Demons, well not the king or his family but still important, in the shape of our bodies.
- By our, who do you mean?
- Me, you and everyone else.
- We can't fight the entire Demon army all by ourselves.
- I know. Halir and Louisiam have agreed to help us with the army of the Wood-Elves.
- Then I'm not helping you.
- Then you'll die.

Eos got up and walked towards the door. Just before she stepped out of the room, she turned to her brother and said:

- If you ever change your mind the battle will take place at the end of Earth, the 9th kingdom in 67 hours.
- I doubt that will happen. Said Scott.

CHAPTER 9
THE PREPARATION OF THE BATTLE

Eos got back with Simon, Marty and Essie who had come with her but had waited outside while she spoke to her brother. The rest of the gang that was on her side had stayed behind. Nothing happened for the rest of that day. Two days later, at about 10 pm, Louisiam and Halir came with news from the elves:

- Eos! I have foreseen that the Demons are about eighteen hours from the battle site. Said Louisiam. But the Elves have come to help you.
- Have a rest. We will start preparing ourselves first thing in the morning.

They woke up at about 6 am and Eos started to give the orders:

- Marty sharpened the swords. Louisiam if the elves are hungry, give them something to eat. In two hours we leave for the battlefield.

The gang had a meal with the Elves. Some of them would not join them at the next meal because they were going to meet death. Scott, Merrill, William and Juliet then entered. Everyone turned to them and then Scott said:

- We've brought swords to help you.
- No you've brought swords to help us. Said Louisiam. Come and have something to eat with us. If your swords need sharpening, Marty will do it for you.

After their meal, Marty went to sharpen the swords and some others talked while others prepared their armour. The swords he had to sharpen were called Tari, Vala, Coire, Aire, Maranwe, Vaiwa, Tuo, Elda, Uluk Katumo, Yar and Vanima.

Elda was 34" in length. Its handle was made of silver but its blade was made from an unknown metal. The blade went from silver close to the handle to dark green at the tip. This sword belonged to Louisiam.

Vanima was the same length as Elda. It had a silver blue handle decorated with a blue eye that was placed before the blade. The blade was made of pure silver. It was also made very thin and light so her bearer, Essie, could carry it.

Vala was 36" long. The whole sword was made of silver but on the handle there was a red leather strip where you would place your hands. Vala belonged to the prince.

Coire was 32" long. Its blade was 26" long. The ends of the handle were black and the rest was made of white gold. William had given this sword to Juliet when he was fifteen years old because Coire meant early spring. In that time he thought she was as beautiful as the first flower in spring.

Aire was smaller then Vala but bigger than Vanima. It had a demon like handle decorated with a red stone. This sword belonged to Drew even if he hated its name because it meant eternity. Drew hated the idea of living forever.

Uluk Katumo was a 32". The entire sword was made of silver and there was nothing special about it because Merrill was not a Vampire by birth.

Maranwe was the same length as Vara. It had a gold circle at the end of its wood handle. The blade, like all others, was made of platinum. This sword belonged to Simon.

Vaiwa was 34" long. Her black handle was decorated with a gold circle in which something was written *"Invenit ab tu excessus"* (Death shall come to you). The blade was of white gold and carried the same inscription. This sword belonged to Marty.

Yar was decorated with a pair of golden horns at the end of its black handle. This sword belonged to William.

Tuo was the last sword that Marty sharpened. It was as long as Uluk Katumo. It had a wooden handle decorated with gold lines. This sword belonged to Karl.

When Marty was done sharpening the sword he called out:

- Come and get your swords.

While everyone was making sure their swords were sharp enough, the white tiger entered and he changed into the Elf he once was. His golden hair went to his cheeks. His eyes were two different blues: dark on the edge and pale around the pupil. He was tall like all Elves and as fair as the oldest one of them. While everyone stared at him in amazement, he said:

- I have a gift for every one of you.
- What is it? Asked Juliet being impatient to see what it was.
- I got you clothes for you to wear in battle.
- Can we see them?
- Of course! Wait a minute.

He came back with leather coats. They stopped at the knees. It was the final touch to their dark look. Most of them wore jeans and the others wore black pants. For their tops, they all wore dark red, blue or green shirts with long, short or no sleeves. After putting on her new coat, Eos said to Tiger:

- Thank you for the coats Tiger.
- You're Welcome. But when I am an Elf I am called Gabriel or Gab for short.
- I will remember that. She then turned to the Elves and her friends and asked: Is everyone ready?
- We are ready. Said Louisiam. So what would be the queen's orders?
- I am not your queen so I cannot order you anything.
- This is your war and since you have no army, you command the Elves, but for this war only.
- Thank you. Let's go win a war.

Just when Eos was about to open the door, someone opened the door before her. Eos waited to see who it was. The first face showed itself and then the second. It was Jonathan and Ashka. Jonathan then asked Eos:

- Where are you going?
- We are going to finish the war you started. Said Eos
- Oh yeah, the war Karl started. (Because he had killed the first victim in the shape Karl's body)

Scott already hated Jonathan and even if he was making fun of Karl, who he hated, he had enough of his comments. Scott took out Vala and placed it under Jonathan's throat and then told him:

- You take that back right now.
- O.K. I'm sorry I told the truth to the Demons.

- What do you mean?
- I know your secret Eos.
- What secret? Asked Eos.
- You only go to war to have more power. Deep down you know that's the truth. You know you're a traitor.

Scott lowered is sword and turned to Eos to make sure he was lying. While Scott and Jonathan were turned to Eos, Merrill approached Jonathan and slapped him in the face while he wasn't expecting it. Everyone turned to Merrill in amazement. Then Merrill said to Jonathan:

- What did you say?
- I said she was a traitor just like your boyfriend, Drew. Said Jonathan

Merrill slapped him on the other side of his face and then said to him:

- Be careful what you say I might slap you again.
- Oh no. The Witch is on the traitor's side. Said Jonathan sarcastically.
- Eos is not a traitor and will never become one nor as she ever been one.
- Sure. She only shared secrets about our world to the Humans.
- She didn't know who she was so how could she have shared information about that?
- Let's just go. Said Eos.

Merrill slapped Jonathan again before leaving with everyone else. When they were a short from their temporary house, Eos said to Merrill:

- Thank you for doing that back there. I will never look at you the same way.
- You're welcome and thank you for showing me what it means to show loyalty to a friend.

Eos smiled and they continued their road in silence. A few minutes later, they heard Gabriel's voice coming from behind. They stopped and turned around to see what he wanted.

- Could I come with you? I don't want to be stuck with those creeps.
- Do you know how to use a bow and a sword?
- Bows and arrows sure but don't give me a sword.

They walked another seven hours to finally arrive were the Demons would come to fight against them. Eos then gave everyone their position half the Elves would be on the left side; the others on the right and Scott, Eos, William and everyone else would be in the middle.

CHAPTER 10
SO IT BEGINS

- Eos I see them over the ridge. Said Halir.
- In how much time will they be here? Asked Scott.
- Half an hour, maybe less.
- Clementiam non commonstrare. (Show them no mercy.) Said Eos. So it begins. If we die we lose the future. If we survive, we must keep this a secret for too many things would change if people from this time would know about this.

While the battle was about to begin, the Blackhoods were preparing one of their members to go see Eos and her gang after the battle. The Blackhoods were a group composed of the only Humans who remembered the existence of the other creatures. Those Humans were the descendants of the Kings, Queens, Lords and Ladies. For this generation there were twenty-one members. They all lived in the capital of the human kingdom, Earth, called Edain. The same city where Eos and the Vampires were staying. Their mission was to convince all the Humans that the rest of the world, which they could not see because of the shield, existed. The shield was a magic wall made by the Wizards and the Witches to keep the Humans from seeing the rest of Melda Cemmen.

So the Humans had no knowledge of the Demons, Vampires, Wood-Elves, Sindarin-Elves, Hauflins, Dwarves, Animal-Spirits, Spirits, Wizards and Witches. The member they had chosen to go see Eos was called Neo. Neo wanted to capture one of those "imaginary" creatures to prove to the world that they did exist. He was their leader. He was the king of the Humans.

The battle was taking place in a deserted field at the end of Earth. Eos and her army were standing on a hill, which gave them a better view and an advantage when it came to shooting arrows. Drums were then heard of which the sound resound so loud that it seemed to be coming from the depths of the earth. The Demons then started to appear. They were armed with axes and crossbows. Their wrist were protected with gauntlets that resembled the ones of the Elves except that theirs were black instead of brown and the Demons had a human skull on theirs while the Elves' was decorated with the tree of life and the tree of death. The Demons all placed themselves in a line and prepared to fire arrows. The General shouted:

- Acwellan eall! (Kill them all!)
- Adornatis ab eximere. (Prepare to fire) Said Eos

The Demons started to walk towards the Elves and the few Vampires. When William felt that the Demons were getting too close, he cried out:

- Sagitatis. (Fire the arrows)

The Elves listened to William and fired the arrows at the Demons that were now starting to fire arrows themselves. Eos turned to William and said:

- I am the queen so I give the orders.
- I am your soul mate. I knew what you were going to do.

It was the night of the full moon but you couldn't see it because of the dark grey clouds in the sky. The moon was hiding from the battle that had just begun. The rain would wash away the blood and the red sun would greet them in the morning, announcing the war that would have just finished. If you looked closely, you could see the fear in the eyes of the Elves and the hatred in the eyes of the Demons. While Elves and Demons were falling to the ground because death had caught them, it started to rain. Finally, when the Demons were getting too close, Eos said:

- Comminus sunt. Machaerarum desumitis. (They are too close. Get your swords out.)

As the swords were taken out of their case, you heard the sound of swords hitting their scabbard. The blades reflected the light of the moon. Everyone was ready for the attack of the Demons. The hardest part of the battle had begun. There were 10 Elves and 75 Demons lying on the ground. Marty arrived close to Eos and said:

- How is it going?
- Its going better than I thought it would and you?
- Not bad but I had to kill 5 Demons to get here.
- That's great. Keep going and be careful.

Marty turned around and received a knife in the leg. He fell to his knees in pain. Eos tried to defend him but after a few minutes there were too many Demons and their thirst for blood made it very hard. Marty had removed the knife but the pain was too intense for him to get up. Eos called for help before it was too late. Simon, Gabriel and William answered the call.

Scott and Juliet were also surrounded by Demons. One of them was quick enough to pierce Juliet's stomach. She fell to the ground followed by Scott. Two Demons approached them and seemed to know how to kill them. Their hearts had to be pierced at the exact same time by something made of silver. Juliet and Scott were ready to die. But the king of the Demons cried aloud:

- Aetstandan! Agan fremman dael adlegatio. Mawed beon baec infre. (Stop! We have accomplished part of our mission. We will be back later.)

The Demons departed leaving their dead behind. The rain then came down like the water that comes down from a cliff. William asked:

- Is it over?
- I don't think they would have given up. It's only the beginning. Said Eos
- What do we do?
- Simon and Gab bring back Marty, fast. Said Eos while turning around in the direction of Halir and Louisiam. Halir! Louisiam! Get your army back to the mansion, were going to bring the wounded.
- See you there. May the stars protect you. Said Louisiam.

CHAPTER 11
NEW FRIENDS ARE IN TOWN

They were back in Edain. The wounds had just been totally covered when the red sun lifted up above the horizon. It was now time to go to school. Eos had not slept but she wasn't tired. She went to school with the Vampires, Halir, Louisiam and the Spirits. At school, they waited about five minutes before Liv arrived. But she wasn't alone. A guy, who resembled her a lot, accompanied her. When Liv and her friend were close to the Vampires, Eos asked Liv:

- Who's your friend?
- I'm Neo. Said the guy.
- Neo who?
- Neo Mavros.
- You and Liv have the same last name. Are you related?
- We're cousins. Said Liv before Neo could answer.

Eos knew Liv was trying to hide something from her but she couldn't figure out what it was. She knew she had to find out before it was too late. Liv and Neo left the others alone. William then turned to Eos and said:

- He's different from the other Humans.
- We have to find out what makes him different. Said Eos.
- I'll do whatever it takes to find it out.
- If I didn't know any better I'd say you're trying to win my heart.

William smiled but said nothing. At lunchtime, Neo came back to see the Vampires. He asked all kinds of questions to Eos to know more about her. It quickly got annoying. After twenty minutes, William got tired of the questions so he said to Neo:

- Will you shut up? You're bothering her and us so go away.
- I was trying to know her. Said Neo
- There is a difference between knowing her and knowing everything about her.

That was the phrase that made the friendship of William and Eos grow stronger and closer to love. Neo and Liv left the Vampires alone. Eos turned to William and said:

- Thank you.
- You're welcome.

Scott noticed that William and Eos were getting closer so he said to William:

- I am sorry to interrupt but don't forget you can't fall in love with her.
- We were not falling in love. Said William.
- Good because Eos is destined to be with Louisiam.
- Scott! The Oracle does not control my future. She draws a line in the sand that can be changed at any time. Said Eos.
- Eos take that back or you'll be in danger. Said Simon. A danger I cannot protect you against.

41

- If I have to play with my life to prove that I control my future, that's fine and I don't care about the consequences.
- Eos, I've lost you once I don't want to lose you again. Said Scott.
- You won't lose me because the Oracle or Nature or Malerk are not going to do anything to me.

Nobody said anything. They were too afraid to upset the gods of the world. Eos looked at everyone before saying:

- Come on William, let's go.
- I don't want to put <u>my</u> life in danger. Said William.

Eos left without saying anything. When she arrived at the mansion, she went straight to bed.

CHAPTER 12
A FORBIDDEN LOVE

Everyone was sleeping except for William and Eos. Eos couldn't sleep because of what William had said earlier. William couldn't sleep because he had lied to her about not loving her. After a few hours of lying in bed, William decided that he would make it up to her. He got up and went to get Eos without waking the others. When he arrived in her room, he saw that she wasn't asleep so he said:

- Do you want to go out?

Eos jumped in fear because she had not heard him enter her room. After calming down, she got out of her bed and jumped in his arms. Eos then asked:

- Where are we going?
- It's a surprise.

William grabbed Eos' hand and quietly they went outside. They walked two blocks down to another abandoned mansion. The mansion looked destroyed. It was full of dust because it had not been lived in since the time when the Humans knew about the other kingdoms. Eos asked William:

- Why are we here?
- I can't tell you. It's a surprise.

They entered the building. It was very dark inside but William opened a light. When he opened the light, Eos saw that the living room still looked as if someone was still living here. There was a sofa, a table and, in a corner, a fridge. Eos sat on the sofa and William went to the fridge where he asked:

- Do you want something to drink?
- What do you have? Asked Eos
- Vampire blood.
- William the council instructed us to rarely drink blood because of our powers. We can't drink it every day.
- I know. But don't you think they're only giving us a limit so they can hold us back?
- Yes every day.
- I think they're afraid that Vampires we'll become more powerful than them.

William turned to Eos and looked deep into her blue eyes and said:

- I don't know why I lied about not loving you to your brother and everyone else. Whatever the consequences you are worth it.
- I forgive you.

Eos approached William and they kissed as if the world had disappeared from their lives. Time seemed to have stopped and there were no more rules. But in the dark, two eyes were looking at them. Two eyes that never forgot the image they saw. Two eyes that would bring hate to love. Those eyes belonged to Louisiam. Louisiam was standing outside and was looking through a window. He was accompanied by is best friend name Neliam. Louisiam turned to his friend and said:

- Go tell the council that Eos and William are in love.
- As you wish. Said Neliam.

Louisiam's friend did has he had instructed and came back ten minutes later with the guards of Nature. They were half-Elves and half-Dragons. They had arrived that fast because Nature had teleported them when Neliam had requested them by thought. They had come to capture William. Louisiam opened the front doors and came in the mansion followed by Nature's guard. Louisiam said:

- Well, well, well. What have we here? Could it be a forbidden love? Louisiam paused but had no answer. By order of the council, I arrest William, son of Aruor. You shall suffer in the hands of Malerk for a hundred years.

The guards grabbed William. Eos tried to free him with no success. So Eos followed them, while William was asking for help. Eos said to Louisiam:

- You can't do this.
- Why not? Said Louisiam while turning around to face Eos.
- You can't sentence someone who hasn't been judged.
- Wait. Said Louisiam to the guards. Eos, you can have your court session on one condition.
- Name it.
- If he gets the sentence you must marry me as you were supposed to.

Eos slapped Louisiam in the face for the request he had made. The Elfin-Dragons stopped and looked at Eos. Louisiam returned his gaze to Eos who said:

- Love cannot be forced upon someone.
- The Oracle is never wrong. What she predicts happens.
- She is never wrong because people were taught to never disobey her because she is Nature's daughter. She is considered a goddess. No one wants to upset her.
- Except you.
- That prediction of us getting married was made when I was not even born and when my mother was still alive. Too many things have happened that were not supposed to since then for that prediction to still come true. Now give me back William.
- No. He must at least suffer for 24 hours. See you tomorrow.

Eos approached Louisiam to force him to give her William but before she could touch him, Neliam hit her at the back of the head and she fell unconscious on the ground. Louisiam, William and the guards disappeared in the darkness. When Eos woke up, she found no trace of William. The only way she could save him was by waiting until the court session. Eos went back to the mansion. She made sure she didn't meet any of the Vampires and went to bed. Eos did not sleep that night because she felt every bit of pain that William got. Eos could tell that William had gotten shot at least twice as well as kicked, punched and cut. The next morning, Scott went to wake up Eos and found her filled with wounds. Scott called everyone to the room where Eos was sleeping. When Essie saw Eos, she asked:

- Why is she liked that?

- Maybe she was in a fight last night. Said Karl.
- Wait! Where's William?
- He must have been captured and tortured all night. Said Juliet.
- Should we wake her up?
- Yes. Said Scott.

Scott woke up Eos. When he shook her, she panicked and screamed:

- Let me go.

She realized where she was and saw that everyone was looking at her. Scott gave her a hug to comfort her and then asked:

- Where's William?
- Nature's guards took him. He will have a trial today.
- A trial for what crime?
- Loving me.

Scott helped Eos get out of bed. When she was on her feet, a bullet entered William heart. Eos fell in Scott's arms in pain. Meanwhile at the torture chamber, one of Nature's guards asked William:

- Had enough?

William lifted his head showing his face full of pain and said:

- Is this your best?

The guard got mad because of those words. He pushed William's face down on the floor and prepared to kick him when Louisiam entered and said:

- That's enough. Leave us.
- As you wish. Said the guards while leaving.
- So how are we? Can we stand a hundred years of this or are we too weak?
- Why are you doing this? Asked William.
- Eos is mine not yours.
- Face it she loves me and not you.
- Shut up William.
- Why? Are you afraid to face the truth?
- I would kill you right now but if I do I can't prove to the court that Eos is mine.
- You're so stupid.
- What?
- You think she will stop loving me and love you just because you prove to the council that royalty shouldn't chose who they love.
- It's getting me what I want.
- And what's that.
- Your death and the love of Eos.
- She might marry you, but she will never love you.

Just when Louisiam was about to add something an elfin girl entered. She looked a lot like Louisiam. William could tell they were family. She turned to Louisiam and said:

- What's going on?
- Eona, leave us alone. Said Louisiam.
- Who's that? Asked William.
- My sixteen-year old sister.
- So you have a sister.

48

- Louisiam, stop torturing him. He's in too much pain. Said Eona.
- I can't just leave him alone.
- I'll chain him up.
- I'll see you later. Said Louisiam to William.

Louisiam left the room. Eona chained William to the wall. William was dangling from his arms but he could still touch the floor. Eona then said:

- I'm sorry about all this.
- Why?
- Because you don't deserve to suffer because you love someone. Does this hurt?

William screamed in pain because Eona had removed a bullet that had been in his heart. Eona then continued:

- I'm sorry. I'll get you a wet cloth to clean those wounds.

William was surprised to see how nice Eona was compared to her brother. Eona came back a short time later. Back at the mansion, Drew had gone to his room to try to find William and had been joined by everyone else. He would then use his powers to find William. A few seconds later, Drew had found William. Drew was making everyone see what he could see. Eos asked Drew:

- Can you do a close up on the girl?

The picture got closer and showed only the girl. Drew then asked the spirit of life to identify the girl. The spirit of life was called Vira. She knew everything about every living being on Melda Cemmen. Vira answered:

- Her name is Eona. She is a Wood-Elf. She is 1600 human years or 16 elfin years old. She is the daughter of Vanyar and sister of Louisiam. She is the princess of the Wood-Elves.

- Louisiam has a sister!? Said Scott.
- Can we hear what they are saying? Asked Eos.

The sound went on and they heard William's and Eona's conversation. Eona Started:

- You know, love is a painful thing.
- What?! Said William
- Tonight someone will suffer. You will go to hell or Louisiam will loose Eos.
- Why are you telling me this?
- If you go to hell, Eos will be forced to love Louisiam for eternity. When you come back from your trip to hell, you will be forced to forget her because she will belong to my brother.
- That creep. Said Eos. Whatever happens tomorrow he is so in trouble.

Thanks Drew you can stop the vision.
- Thank you Vira. We have seen enough. Said Drew.

CHAPTER 13
TIME IN COURT

- The court session is now open. Said the Dragon Spirit. May the defender please present his position?

   Louisiam rose on the left side and started to present his case to the council.

- I accuse William of having interfered with the future that Eos and I were supposed to have together.
- Would the defender present his case?

   Eos rose on the right side but just when she was about to talk, the council asked:

- Are you the defender?
- Yes. Said Eos. Is there a problem?
- Do you accept your future with Louisiam?
- No.
- Then you may proceed.
- Everyone falls in love. I fell in love with William. But I guess royalty cannot choose who they love. Louisiam came in and grabbed William. He had already sentenced him before

this court. He had sentenced him for 100 years in "Hell". I then asked him for a court session, which he gave me, but he tortured William all night.

- Thank you Eos. Louisiam you may continue.

Louisiam presented his case to the council but while he was doing so Scott got up. He walked towards Louisiam with rage in his eyes. When he was a meter away from Louisiam, Scott said: "wall up". A shield that stopped anyone from coming inside the shielded area and that stopped anyone from going out went up around Louisiam and Scott. Scott wanted to kill Louisiam but when he got close to him a force pushed him away. The screen disappeared and Scott went flying on the wall behind him. Everyone looked at Louisiam. One of the council members said:

- Only a spell could do such a thing.

Eos ran to her brother to see if he was all right. He had blood running down his forehead. Eos turned to the council and said:

- No Elf could do such a thing.
- Who would cast a spell upon him and why? Said the Demon.
- I think it's his sister but I don't know why.
- Bring Eona right now.
- Are you sure it's her? Asked Scott to Eos.
- Prepare to run if it's not. Said Eos.

Eona was brought in a few minutes later. The council asked her a few questions. After five minutes, Eos said to Scott:

- If they keep asking her these unnecessary questions we'll never get our answer. Eos turned to the council and asked:

- May I ask her a question?
- Go ahead but I doubt you'll get anywhere.
- Eona are you jealous of your brother?
- No.
- Do you think he's weak?
- I use to.
- What made you change your mind?
- A Witch.
- What do you mean?
- She gave him a spell.
- And there you go. You now have your answer. All you had to do was ask the right questions.

The council looked at Eona and said:

- You are banished from the eleven kingdoms on Melda Cemmen. If you even enter any of the kingdoms, you shall be killed. As for you Eos, you may love whom your heart desires.
- Thank you for your time. Said Eos.

William grabbed Eos and kissed her. He was happy that he did not have to forget her.

CHAPTER 14
A POWER IS REVEALED

The night was cold for the month of May but the stars were still shining bright. Eos was watching the stars. At around eight, William entered the room. William closed the door behind him. He approached Eos and sat beside her. William, while approaching her, asked Eos:

- What are you looking at?
- The stars. Do you want to watch them with me?
- Why not? They are beautiful.
- Which one is your favourite?
- The North Star because wherever you are it always helps you find your way.

They watched the stars for twenty minutes before William said:

- I love you
- I love you too. Said Eos.
- Will you marry me?

William pulled out of his jacket a little blue box. In it there was a diamond ring. Eos looked at the ring and at William before saying that she did want to marry him. Eos and William approached each other to kiss. But just as their lips were touching Eos had a terrible headache. In her head, Eos saw terrible images. She saw a war between Demons and Elves with Vampires and Spirits. Her vision then followed an arrow into someone's heart. She did not see who received the arrow. Then the vision stopped. William then asked her:

- Are you O.K.?
- My powers are back.
- What did you see?
- I saw someone get shot in the heart and die.
- Who?
- I don't know

William helped Eos get on her feet. He then placed her on her bed so she could relax. William left the room to tell everyone about the vision Eos had. Back in the Eos' room, a figure was moving in the dark. The figure slowly came out of the shadow. It was Louisiam. He had entered just after William had left.

Meanwhile, in the living room, Scott noticed Louisiam had disappeared. Scott went to Louisiam's room to check if he was there but on his way he heard his voice in Eos' bedroom. Scott stopped and listened. Louisiam was talking to Eos who was sleeping:

- I am sorry I behaved like a jerk the other night. It wasn't my fault. William is a great guy. I am glad you found someone who doesn't only love you for your throne. I wish I could find someone like that. It would be nice if you gave me a word of encouragement but you're asleep so I will leave you alone now. Sleep well.

Louisiam left the room. He got out and closed the door behind him and when he turned around he was surprised to see Scott. Scott said:

- Did I scare you?
- You surprised me.
- Why were you surprised to see me?
- I thought you were still in the living room.
- I went looking for you when I realized that you weren't there.
- For how much time have you been standing there?
- I heard the whole thing. It was really good. I'm glad you moved on.

Scott pulled out his hand. Louisiam did the same to shake hands with him. But before there hands could touch, Scott removed his hand and said:

- I still don't like neither you nor the Wood-elves.

A few hours later, in the darkness of her room, Eos woke up. She got out of bed and walked to the living room. When she arrived in the living room, Scott said:

- I thought you were sleeping.
- I was. I just woke up.

Simon got up from the sofa he was sitting on and approached Eos. Simon asked Eos:

- Can I speak with you in the corner?
- Sure.

They went into the East corner of the room then Simon continued:

- Is that ring on your finger new?
- No. That's the ring that tells others that I am the queen of the Vampires.
- Not that one the other one.

Simon grabbed Eos hand and looked at the ring that William had given her. It was a ½-carrat-diamond white gold ring. Simon showed the ring to everyone else who was sitting in the living room. Simon then asked Eos:

- Why did he give you that ring?
- It was a gift.
- Just a gift. I have trouble believing that.
- That's your problem. Now let go.
- Why? Are you afraid I'll find out something you don't want me to know?
- No. You are hurting me.
- He asked you to marry him.
- Yes and I don't care if the Oracle did not want me to marry him. Now let go.

Silence overcame the room. You could now hear the inhaling and exhaling of everyone else and the crackle of the floor as someone was walking down the hall. It was too quiet and Eos did not like it.

CHAPTER 15
A BLACK FIGHT

From the hallway that led to the rooms, a figure appeared. Everyone turned to see who was arriving. William then emerged from the comforting shadow in which he should have stayed. When William entered the living room, he saw that everyone was looking at him. William got nervous. Scott got up and pulled William back in the shadow. Eos turned to Simon and said:

- I hate you.
- I'm trying to protect you.
- Next time protect me from danger and not from love.

Meanwhile, in the shadow, Scott was talking to William. William started:

- Don't you dare give me a speech.
- Why do you think I'm going to give you a speech?
- She's suppose to marry Louisiam. Our life will be in danger if we do not do what the Oracle told us to do. The Elves will not be happy.
- I don't care what the Elves think.

- Then why are we here?
- Are you willing to sacrifice your life for hers?
- I would die every day for the rest of eternity if it would give her an extra one to live.
- Wow! You really love her. When are you planning to do the wedding?
- We haven't decided yet.
- I could organize it for next week.
- If Eos doesn't mind and if you can do it by then, I don't mind.

William and Scott went back to the living room where they announced the date of the wedding. Eos jumped in her brother's arms because she was so happy. Scott then said:

- Wow! I got a hug.
- Thank you. Said Eos.
- Give me your hands. Said Scott to Eos and William.

William and Eos gave one of their hands to Scott who placed them together before saying to them:

- You both go have fun tonight.

William and Eos left the mansion to take a walk under the stars. The night was almost over and the day was ready to replace the night. After walking two blocks, they heard a voice in the shadow in front of them:

- Well, well, well, who have we here?

A guy came out of the shadow. He was dressed in a black coat and its hood was over his head. The man removed his hood and William and Eos recognized Neo. William looked at Neo and asked:

- Where are your friends?
- Who are you talking about?
- The other Blackhoods. Are they in the shadow too?
- Well, since you know where they are. Guys, you can come out.

Twenty other Blackhoods came out dressed like Neo. Two grabbed William by the arms and another grabbed Eos. A few seconds later, the one that was holding Eos got punched and pulled over Eos' body. But then two guys pushed Eos on the ground and placed their feet on her back. Eos tried to get up but she drained all her energy trying. William shouted:

- Let her go.
- Why? Asked Neo.
- Because I don't want to hurt you.
- That's too bad because I do. I have many weapons and I was wondering if you have a favourite.
- No I don't.
- Great! We'll use mine. Said Neo while taking a small knife. I like small but painful things.

One of the guys that were holding William held his face still. Neo approached William and started to cut a line from the top of William's eyebrow to his cheek on his right side. William let them do it because he felt he deserved it. After cutting the entire line on William's face, Neo said:

- What would you like next?
- Well, remember when I said I didn't want to hurt you and your friends? Asked William.
- Yeah.
- I changed my mind.

William kicked the guy who had held his face and when his hand was free, he punched the other. Then, he grabbed Neo by the collar and said:

- Get your guys out of here now.
- Hey! Calm down!
- I don't feel like it. But I am going to let you and your friends get out of here. So if you want me to let you go tell them to leave.
- Guys leave.

The twenty Blackhoods left. William let go of Neo and pushed him away. Neo disappeared in the shadow. William then went by Eos and took her in his arms. She had the same mark as William on her face. William brought her back to the mansion. When William arrived back at the house, Scott saw Eos in the arms of William and asked:

- What happened?
- We met Neo.
- Just Neo?
- No. Him and his twenty Blackhoods.
- What did they do to her?
- Well...

William told the story to Scott while they took care of Eos. Marty then fixed William's wound. William then went to practice his fighting skills while the rest of the "gang" went to prepare the wedding.

CHAPTER 16
PREPARING THE WEDDING

Eos woke up the next morning and went to see William in the practice room. William had been practicing for five straight hours. When Eos arrived at the door, William was talking to himself:

- I was weak. I could have freed myself and help Eos but I was weak.
- You were not weak. Said Eos while startling William. You did your best in that situation.

William stopped practicing and went to Eos, side because he thought that she had not rested enough. William said to Eos:

- You shouldn't be out of bed.
- I'm fine, I swear. You couldn't have beaten twenty-one guys on your own.
- I should have at least been able to protect you.
- It is not your job to protect me.

Just when William was about to ask something to Eos, Essie entered and said:

- We await you in the living room for a party.
- We'll be right there. Eos turned to William and asked: What did you want to tell me.
- Forget it. We have to go to a party.
- Are you sure?
- Yes. Lets go. 'Of course I wanted to tell you something but I was scared to tell you. Didn't you see that?' Thought William. 'Maybe you could ask me later.'
- Sure. Said Eos. I'll ask you later.
- What!?
- I'm your soul mate. I can hear you think when I want to.

Eos took William's hand and they went to the living room where everyone was waiting for them. When William and Eos had sat down, Essie said:

- Since you are getting married we have gotten you a few gifts to celebrate the occasion.
- We, the Spirits, will start. Said Gabriel.

Gabriel handed a box to William. The box was decorated with the Spirit's alphabet. It was made of Forca wood; Wood that had once existed in the Human kingdom but that was now extinct. William took the box and opened it with his left hand. He reached in with his right hand but he felt nothing in the box. William removed his hand but before it was out of the box, a Dragon Spirit came out of it. The Dragon went around William before entering his body by his heart. It then went trough all the veins of William and came out of his heart before becoming a tattoo on the middle finger of his right hand. Eos turned to Gabriel and asked:

- What happened?
- The Dragon Spirit mixed with his spirit and made him stronger of heart.
- Are you okay William?
- I feel great. What's the next gift?

Halir got up with a box in his hands. It was bigger than the first one but less beautiful. He gave the white cardboard box to Eos and she quickly opened it. Inside was a silver dress with a white under-dress. It had been made by the Ladies of the Wood-Elf kingdom. The dress was stitched with silver thread in which the light of the moon was captured. The Elves had given Eos the wedding dress she would have worn if she would had married Louisiam. It was a great honour to have that dress even if she was only half-Elf. Eos said to Halir:

- Thank you.
- Now you will look like a real queen. Said Halir.
- Hey! She's mine.
- Calm down Will. Said Eos.

Then Louisiam got up and gave to Eos another gift. He gave to her a cape that was as red as blood that she could wear while she was sitting on her throne watching over her kingdom. It was now time for the last gifts. Scott gave to William a new black coat; the kind he had always wanted. Then he approached Eos with a small box. She opened the box and saw a ring. It resembled a lot the one she already had but it was made of gold. Eos looked at Scott and said:

- But I... (She was interrupted by Scott.)
- I know you already have one but this one is different. It belonged to mom. Ashka gave it to me when I was twelve. Now I want you to have it.

Eos looked at the ring for a few minutes and then placed it on the table beside her. She did not want the ring. Eos then got up and went to her room. As she left Scott said to her:

- Eos, you forgot your ring.

Eos kept on walking away without looking back. She went to her room. Scott, seeing that Eos did not stop, said again:

- Eos!!!
- Shut up Scott. Said William. She doesn't want the ring.
- William, maybe you should go after her. Said Essie.
- No, she needs to be alone.
- Nobody wants to be alone when they are sad.
- Trust me. She wants to be alone.
- Do you want to have supper then?
- Okay but keep some for Eos.
- As you wish your highness.

Everyone went to the kitchen to eat dinner. After everyone was done eating, William made a plate for Eos and went to her room. When William arrived in front of her bedroom door, he knocked and asked:

- Can I come in?
- Who is it?
- Will.
- You can come in but close the door behind you.

William entered the room and closed the door. Eos was lying on her bed looking at the ceiling. William placed the plate he had brought for her on her desk. He then pulled up a chair close to the bed and sat down. William looked at Eos and said in a soft voice:

- I brought you something to eat and your ring.
- Thanks for the food but I don't want the ring.
- Why not?
- I never saw my mother. I don't know anything about her. Why would I want her ring? I have no use for it.
- Neither does your brother but he keeps it.
- I'm not like my brother.
- I know. You're better.
- What did you want to ask me before the party?
- Are you sure you're ready to go home? Your life there will be very different from this one.
- I am ready to see my home for the first time.

William kissed Eos on the forehead and then sat beside her on the bed. Eos placed her head on his stomach and William placed his arm around her. Meanwhile, in the living room, everyone was trying to decide where they would have the wedding. Scott said:

- Louisiam.
- Yes. Said Louisiam.
- Could we do the wedding in your kingdom?
- I'm afraid not?
- Why not?
- First of all it would change my people's future. Secondly, Eos and yourself could never enter the capital because of the curse you carry. No demon can see my city.
- What do you mean by demon?
- Your tattoos are demons which mean you have an evil spirit in you.
- So you're saying that Lyco, protector of the sunset, a Wood-elf, is an evil spirit.
- No. I am saying that the vampires made him become evil so he would ask to be killed. But the Oracle would never want to kill him so she destroyed him instead and that's how you

got your tattoos. You got them as a revenge for what your people had done.

- You're a liar.
- Go ask the Oracle if you don't believe me.
- Stop it. Screamed Essie. We will do the wedding here.
- Are you crazy? Asked Scott. This use to belong to a human Lord.
- What's wrong with that?
- It's not nice enough.
- Then we will do it outside. The backyard is at least ten acres. Is that alright with everyone?
- Fine.
- What about you Louisiam?
- It is a great idea.

Meanwhile, two blocks down the street, at the Blackhoods' mansion, Neo was preparing his next plan. He was being aided by Alex, a dark haired green eyed guy, who was the same age as Neo. Alex asked Neo:

- Do you have a plan?
- Yes. We are all going to go to the wedding of Eos and William.
- What do you want to do there?
- You'll see.
- Neo! Said Liv who had heard their conversation. I'm not going to hurt Eos again.
- Look who's talking. It's the one that was supposed to make sure Eos never learned who she was.
- Why? You never told me why.
- What?
- Why was I supposed to keep Eos from finding out who she was?
- Because we were paid one million dollars each by Jonathan

to keep her away and he would have given us more if we had succeeded.

- Is that the only reason?
- No. He's going to kill me if the new mission is not completed before he comes back.
- 'You're going to die either way.' Thought Liv. 'If he doesn't kill you, I will.

Liv went to her room on the third floor while Alex went to set the table for supper and Neo continued to enrich his plan. Meanwhile, back in Eos' room, William was still with Eos. After a while, Eos said:

- You shouldn't be here William.
- Why!?
- The groom can't see the bride before the wedding. It's bad luck.
- I'll be on the other side of the wall if you need me.

William left the room and went to his disappointed that he could not spend time with Eos. When William was gone, Eos heard a voice in her room:

- Now you've done it.
- Who's there. Asked Eos.

A figure slowly appeared on the chair in the corner of Eos' room. As the figure became clearer, Eos realized it was Karl. After he had completely appeared, Eos asked him:

- How did you do that?
- It's one of the reasons I was chosen. I can become invisible.
- Why were you using it now?
- I wanted to make sure you were okay.

- I'm fine.
- Do you want a hug?
- I'm fine. Insisted Eos.
- Okay. There was a pause before he continued. I think somehow you remember your mother.
- What? I saw her for a minute and that's all.
- You know you saw her.
- So?
- Well then you do remember her.
- Shut up and get out.
- I'm sorry.
- Get out! Screamed Eos.
- I said I was sorry.
- Get out! Leave me alone! Screamed Eos.

Eos' screams ran down the hall to the living room and to William's room. When Scott, Louisiam, Simon, Gabriel and William heard the screams, they ran to Eos' room. When Karl heard them coming, he turned invisible and ran out. Scott entered the room followed by the others and approached Eos before asking:

- Are you okay?
- Don't ever let Karl get close to me when no one else is around.
- Why?

Eos did not have time to answer before a vision entered her mind. Scott grabbed her before she fell to the floor. Eos saw a girl putting a drop of liquid from a vial in a plate filled with food, a guy eat the food and dying. When Eos came back, Scott asked:

- Are you okay now?
- I had a vision.

- What did you see?
- Someone will die…(she was interrupted by Simon.)
    -You already had that one. We already know it.
- It is not the same one. Someone poisoned a guy who died and then a girl was queen. But they were humans.
- A Blackhood will kill Neo. Said Scott. She has to be ranked high. Maybe his sister or cousin.
- If you had a vision of him then we have to help him. Said Gabriel.
- No, let him die. Said William.
- Will. Said Eos.
- What!? He almost killed you and he hurt me.
- Just because someone hurts you doesn't mean you have to let them die.
- Eos, we don't help humans. Ever not even a little.
- Why not?
- Because they will want to kill us when they will learn we exist not be our friends.
- The Blackhoods know we exist.
- And they want to kill us. I'm done talking about this.
- William get back here now.
- No.

Eos only said William when she was angry at him. William had just refused to do as Eos had asked him. Everyone knew this was going to get ugly. Eos went hyper speed and pushed William on the wall suspending him from the ground by the throat. Eos turned to the others and said:

- Leave us alone.

Everyone left the room and Scott closed the door behind him. Eos let go of William's throat while he coughed for air. They had been acting since Eos had a vision. William looked at Eos and said:

- I thought we were going to act out the anger.
- I'm sorry I got carried away.
- Did you really have the vision about Neo?
- I did.
- Are you really going to go tell him?
- I will tell him but only if I stumble upon him before he dies.

William smiled. They looked at each other getting closer to one another with each seconds that passed. When their lips finally touched, the passion was unleashed. That night Eos and William slept in the same bed. They were risking bad luck. At midnight, before going to bed, Scott checked on William and Eos. When he saw them sleeping in each others arms, he closed the door and went to his room. The next morning, everyone was getting ready for the wedding. The day had finally arrived. Meanwhile, the Blackhoods were getting ready for their surprise visit at the wedding. They each brought two guns; one with normal bullets and one with silver bullets. In the room of the two lovers, William was awake but didn't want to get up because he didn't want to wake Eos. William kissed Eos and the forehead and she opened her eyes. She lifted her head to look at William who said:

- Hi. Had a nice sleep?
- Yes and you?
- Better than usually. Do you want breakfast?
- Sure. What are you making?
- What do you want?
- Pancakes.
- I'll be right back.

William got up and went to the kitchen. When he arrived, everyone pretended they were not preparing the wedding. William paid no attention to them. After getting the pancakes ready and on two plates, he brought them back to the bedroom. After having breakfast in bed, William and Eos went their separate way. William left her room as the girls entered the room. The boys were talking in the living room where William joined them. After a few minutes they started to talk about how William's life would change. Drew asked William:

- How does it feel to have only seven hours left as a bachelor?
- It's okay.
- Are you sure? Asked Karl. You won't be able to exchange her if you don't like her anymore.
- I wouldn't exchange her for the world.

They kept on talking for another hour before William and Scott got tired of it and left. They went to William's room to grab his sword and then went to the fighting room to see who had the best techniques. Back in Eos' room, the girls were talking about the wedding and about how happy they were for Eos. Merrill asked Eos:

- Are you nervous?
- A little but I'm more excited.
- I'm so happy for you. Said Juliet. I wish I could find my perfect guy.
- I thought you had already found him in my brother.
- I don't know if he loves me.
- Would you like to dance with him?
- Thanks. I would love to dance with him.

A few hours later, everyone was preparing for the wedding that was only three hours away. The elves were preparing the feast for the occasion. The girls were dressing in a light blue strapless dress. Eos was putting on her dress. Essie then arrived with a white calla lily bouquet. There were six flowers in the bouquet and it was attached with a light blue ribbon. Eos thanked Essie. The girls were finishing their preparations when someone knocked at the door. Juliet answered the door. It was Scott. She said to him:

- Come in.
- Thanks. Can I talk to Eos.
- Eos, your brother wants to talk to you.

Juliet let Scott in the room. Scott entered and approached Eos. Scott asked his sister:

- How are you? Asked Scott.
- I'm fine.
- Are you sure?
- Yes.
- Then let's go. It's time.

Eos took the arm he had offered him and they started to walk towards the door that led outside. William and Halir were waiting for the bride to arrive outside with the elves. Everything was perfect. It was seven o'clock and Bora, protector of the north wind, was passing on this hot June 7th. Everyone was standing. Juliet, Merrill, Drew, Karl and Marty were standing at the front with Louisiam. Essie and Gabriel were the first to come down the aisle. When they reached the end, Essie placed herself on the right of William and Gabriel on his left. William was wearing is long black coat and his hair was spiked as usually. Eos then entered accompanied by Scott. Eos could not stop smiling. At the end of the row, Scott kissed her sister on the cheeks and gave her hand to William who thanked him. After half an hour, they arrived at the big question. Halir asked:

- Eos Anoura, do you take William Henulka as your husband, to love and to hold, through sickness and in health, 'till death do you part?
- I do. Answered Eos.
- William Henulka, do you take Eos Anoura as your wife, to love and to hold, through sickness and in health, 'till death do you part?
- I do. Answered William.
- I now pronounce you, husband and wife. You may kiss.

Eos and William kissed under the stars. It was now time for the coronation. Essie and Marty approached with the crowns. Louisiam got up and approached the newlyweds. He then said:

- Bring forth the crowns.

Essie brought Eos' delicate crown on a red cushion. The crown was made of glass veins that contained the blood of the past queens, of Selene, of Lyco, of William and of Eos. The veins held a crest of power in the middle that came down to her nose. Louisiam took the crown and placed it on Eos' head, who was kneeling before him. Eos then rose and her red cape was placed on her shoulders. Marty then brought William's crown on a blue cushion. It was a simple band out of which spikes came out and went towards the front of the crown where the emblem of the vampires was engraved. Eos took the crown, placed it on his head and then said to him:

- Rise, King William.

Everyone applauded the new vampire king. After a few minutes, everyone returned inside. The vampires went in first followed by the elves. When the vampires stepped in the living room, they stopped. Someone was waiting for them. Neo, Liv and Alex were sitting on the couch. Neo looked at them before getting on his feet and saying:

- Congratulations! Eos, you look so beautiful.
- But not as beautiful as when you were out of strength on the ground. Said Alex.
- Here hold this. Said William to Eos while giving her his crown.

Scott and William approached Alex and Neo. Scott grabbed Neo and William grabbed Alex by the collar and pushed them against the wall. After getting over the pain in his back, Alex looked at William and asked:

- Did I find your weakness?
- What do you think you've found?
- The biggest weakness you can ever have: unconditional love.

William bashed Alex head in the wall behind him. Alex was almost knocked out. After Eos thought that Alex had endured enough pain , Eos said:

- William, Scott, behave yourselves in front of our elfin guests.
- Sorry sis.
- But... Said William
- Let me handle it. Said Eos.

Scott let go of Neo and stepped behind his sister. William let go of Alex who almost fell forward and returned by his queen's side. Eos then slowly approached Alex. She looked at him for a few minutes before punching him in the nose. Alex grabbed his nose in pain. Eos then said to him:

- That's for putting your foot on my back.
- Not bad for a human girl. Said Alex. But for a vampire queen, it's a bit disappointing.

After that comment, Scott and William were ready to kill Alex. When Neo saw that they were going after Alex, he got in the way of Scott and the original fights started. After a while Liv approached Eos and said:

- Your boys are acting like kids.
- My boys are children. They are only two years old in my kingdom.
- Make them stop.
- My guys will only stop when yours stop.
- Fine. Neo, Alex stop it.

The boys stopped fighting. William and Scott returned beside Eos. Liv walked away from Eos and went beside Neo and Alex. Eos then looked at the humans and said:

- Leave now.
- You have no politeness. Said Neo. We should at least be able to eat and drink before we leave.
- If you think you can stay after...(William stopped Eos.)
- A snack then you leave.

The humans went to the dining room followed by the elves. The vampires, Halir and Louisiam stayed in the living room. Everyone wanted to know why William had let them stay. William answered:

- Do on to others as you'd have done to you.

Everyone was satisfied with that answer except for Eos. When Eos and William were alone, Eos asked William:

- Why did you really let them stay?
- You wanted to tell him he was going to die.
- Thank you. Here's your crown.

Eos gave him his crown and he placed it on his head. They both went into the dining where everyone was getting something to eat. After everyone had eaten, it was time for the traditional father/daughter dance. But since Eos' father was not present Scott would dance with her instead. While they were dancing together to the sound of the calm music, Eos asked her brother:

- What are you going to do when I go dance with William?
- I don't know. Why?
- Can I make a suggestion?
- Go ahead.
- You could go dance with Juliet.
- Doesn't she want to go dance with someone else?
- She said she wasn't going to dance unless it was with you.
- Then I'll dance with her.

After the song had ended, William and Juliet arrived and the boys changed partners. William danced with Eos while Scott danced with Juliet. While they were dancing, William whispered to Eos:

- You really look beautiful in that dress.
- Thanks.
- Are going to go tell Neo that he will die soon?
- Yes. I just have to find him.
- He's over there.
- Thanks.

- I'll come with you to make sure he doesn't kill you.

When the song had ended, William and Eos walked towards Neo, Liv and Alex who where standing in a corner of the room. When they arrived close to them, they didn't have time to say anything before Neo said:

- Yes we're done eating and we'll be going now.
- Wait. Neo, can I talk to you in private?

Neo and Eos went a few meters away from the others. Simon, Gabriel, Scott, William, Liv and Alex were watching them. Eos looked at Neo and said:

- I have visions of the future.
- So!?
- The last one I had showed me you being killed by a girl that is part of the Blackhoods.
- So, what am I supposed to do? Watch out for every girl? Neo paused. Did you really think I was going to believe you?
- No. But I had to try to save your life.
- When you get the vision that says you're going to die, call me. I'll throw a party with my friends.
- I'm being serious.
- So am I.

Neo walked away from Eos and left the building with Alex and Liv. After they were gone, William approached Eos and asked her:

- Did he listen to you?
- No. But I found out why someone wants to kill him.

William smiled because of what Eos had said. A few seconds later, applause were heard. They all turned towards it and saw Eona standing at the door. Eona came in and said:

- Congratulation to the newlyweds.
- Eona. Said Eos. Walk out that door right now and you get to keep your life.
- I can't.
- Why not?
- Because just like you, my brother is all I have left.
- Is that all.
- I know you won't kill me. Besides, I can only die in battle.

Eos pushed Eona on the wall with her body weight while she caught a knife that William had thrown her. Eos then look in the eyes of the princess. Eona looked back and tried to free herself. Louisiam and Halir approached Eos and pulled her away from Eona. While they were doing that William tried to free Eos. Soon, Eos, William, Scott and Simon had pulled out their swords while Louisiam and Halir had pulled out their bows. Eona was trying to slip out unnoticed. Then they heard someone scream:

- Meo! (Stop!)

Everyone turned around and looked at Essie. She had screamed for them to stop. She looked at everyone and said:

- Can't you see what you're doing? Please find a common ground. Do not let this end in the death of innocent people.
- I agree with Essie. Said Louisiam. We shouldn't kill Eona.
- That's not what I said Louisiam. Your sister must die she was banished from all kingdoms. By law, she must die tonight. It is your choice by the hands of who. Chose wisely.

Louisiam's hopes had just shattered. Since the day Eos had been found his whole world had crumbled to pieces and now Essie had just turned those pieces to dust. Silence fell over the room. Eona had just been seen by Marty and he was using his telekinesis to keep her from escaping. Louisiam reopened his eyes and said:

- She will die at the hands of the highest authority present.
- It's between Louisiam and Eos. Said Scott.
- No, Eos as more authority them me against her because I am her brother.

Eos took the small knife back in her hand and approached Eona who had just been freed from Marty. Eona was backing up into the wall trying to escape just like a scared animal about to be killed by a predator. Eos looked at Eona and said:

- I'm sorry. You brought this upon yourself.

Eos pushed the knife into Eona's main artery and let go of it. Eona fell to the ground while her blood left her body. Eos closed her eyes and turned around. She then reopened her eyes and walked to her room followed by William. When Eos arrived in her room she laid down on the bed on her stomach and started to cry. William entered and closed the door. He then sat beside her and started to rub her back. After a few minutes, William asked Eos:

- Can I do anything for you?

Eos turned towards William and wiped her eyes. Eos tried to speak but she didn't know what to say. She couldn't believe that she had killed Louisiam's sister. William helped Eos sit on the bed and gave her a hug until she wanted to let go. William then wiped her eyes and they kissed. A kiss lead to another more passionate then the next and soon they were in an embrace. Their bodies and souls were connecting like the sky and earth when lightning strikes. They had met their perfect match.

CHAPTER 17
SO IT ENDS

The next morning, in their mansion, the Blackhoods were getting ready to have breakfast. The cook arrived with the plates and placed them on the table. Everyone sat down and started to eat. After a couple of bites, Neo started to cough. He was chocking. Alex tried to help him but he was chocking on his tongue. There was no way to save him. Neo fell to the ground where he stopped moving. Alex took his pulse but there was none to take. Neo was gone forever and nothing would change that. When Alex told everyone, Liv ran in his arms to cry. Liv was now queen of the humans and leader of the Blackhoods. But Alex thought of something that made Liv hold her breath. Alex looked at Neo and said:

- Something is wrong.
- What is it? Asked Liv.
- At the party, Eos told Neo that he was going to die. How did she know?
- She did it. She killed him.
- Maybe. Guys, gather your weapons because we are going to pay a visit to the vampire queen.

Meanwhile, in the castle of the demon kingdom, in the city of Hrychib, the King, Deith, was preparing his strategies with his general, Leihat. They would enter the battlefield the same way as last time except this time they would target the leaders of the army.

Back at the vampire's home, William was having a weird dream. He saw a little girl running around. She had brown hair and hazelnut eyes. After a few seconds, the girl stopped running and took William's hand. She looked at him and promised him that she would never leave and that she would never hurt him. After the dream, William woke up. His movement woke Eos who then asked him:

- What's wrong?
- I had a weird dream. He paused and asked her: What time is it?
- Eight o'clock.

Eos and William got out of bed and made their way to the kitchen to have breakfast. When they were almost at the kitchen, someone knocked on the front door. Eos went to open the door. When she opened it, she saw Alex, Liv and eighteen other Blackhoods. Alex then took Eos by the neck and pushed her out of his way. William approached Eos to see if she was alright. By the time they both got up, the Blackhoods had surrounded them. William made is way towards Liv but before he was too close to her, Liv took out a gun and shot him in the stomach. William fell to the ground in pain. Then, Alex looked at Eos and noticed that she was bleeding where William had been shot so he said to Liv:

- Do it again.
- Do what again? Asked Liv.
- Shoot him.

Liv did as Alex had asked. She shot William again, and again Eos had the same wound as William. Alex then asked Eos:

- Why did you know he was going to die?
- Who? Asked Eos.
    -You know who. I'm talking about Neo.
- I have visions of the future. What I see, I can prevent.
- Are you lying in my face?
- Why would I lie if I have nothing to hide?
- Liv, shoot him.

Liv shot William again but this time she shot his heart. William screamed in pain. His screams were heard in the entire mansion. Everyone ran towards the kitchen to see what was going on. When Alex heard that the vampires where coming, he said to Eos:

- This isn't over.

Liv shot William one more time before running out with all the Blackhoods. William fell to the floor where he started to cough blood. Eos approached William and placed him against the wall. The others arrived in the room soon after. When Scott saw William, he asked:

- What happened?
- We had uninvited guests. Said Eos.

Marty kneeled beside William and tried to remove the bullets but William pushed him away. Eos helped William get up and they both returned to their room. Eos made William lie down in bed. She then removed his shirt. Blood was still running from his wounds especially the one in his heart. She then took William's hand and placed her other hand on his heart. Eos grabbed the bullet and looked at William's face. William nodded yes to Eos. Eos counted to three and pulled out the bullet. William's claws pierced Eos' hand. As William relaxed, the claws slowly came out of Eos' hand. William let go and apologized for hurting her. Eos removed all the other bullets. After finishing, Eos washed her hands and returned to William's side. She then laid down beside him.

A few hours later, Gabriel and Simon were still talking outside. They had been there since Neo had left. Simon was talking to Gabriel. He was saying:

- ... So I turn to her and then...(Simon stopped.)

Gabriel looked at him for a few seconds and then looked up to the sky to see what Simon had seen. In the sky, flying over there heads were dozens of crows also know as the birds of death. Before the demons, in times of war, the crows flew over their enemies. The crows also came after a battle of any kind to eat the flesh of the dead and drink their blood. Simon and Gabriel looked at each other and ran inside to the living room where mostly everyone was. When they saw them enter, they looked at them wondering what was going on. Essie turned to them and said:

- You look like you saw a monster.
- We saw the crows, dozens of them. Said Gabriel.
- Where?
- Outside, over our heads.
- The demons will soon arrive. We must get ready for the next part of the battle.
- We can't fight them on our own.
- We've got the elves. Said Karl.

- It's not going to be enough. Said Scott. When demons lose, they come back stronger.
- Who can we ask for help?
- We could find you some extra hands. Suggested Simon and Gabriel.
- How fast can you get them here? Asked Scott.
- Six hours maximum. Said Simon.
- Leave now. We will meet you at the battlefield.

Gabriel and Simon left the mansion and headed towards the spirits kingdoms; Lithe and Mearas. When they were gone, Scott headed towards William's room to tell him and Eos that the Demons were coming. Four hours later, Simon and Gabriel returned with some help. Simon had found his four friends: Cloe, ex-Wood-Elf, Mathieu, ex-Wizard, Crystale, ex- Vampire, and Nickolas, ex-Wizard. Gabriel had found his three friends: Kali, a cougar Spirit and old Sindarin-Elf, Narishka, a wolf and old Wizard, and Malishka, Narishka's brother, a Dragon. Everyone greeted them before they all sat down to eat something before the battle. After eating they prepared their armour and weapons and headed towards the battle field. When they arrived at the battlefield it was three o'clock. At seven there was still no sign of the Demons so Eos turned to Simon and asked:

- Are you sure they were coming?
- I am sure we saw the crows of death.
- Could you go see if they're coming?
- No problem.

Simon headed towards the demon kingdom with Cloe. After twenty minutes had passed, they were back. The demons were on their way. They would arrive tonight guaranteed. Since they still had time to wait everyone sat down on the ground and had something to eat. As everyone sat down,

Eos and William saw someone appear over the ridge. But it could not be the demons because they were coming from the human kingdom. After a few seconds Eos recognized them. It was the Blackhoods. Everyone went back to their supper while Eos and William approached them. When they were close to them, William asked them:

- What are you doing here?
- We are here to make sure this war doesn't reach the humans. Said Liv.
- Stay out of our way and our range. Said Eos.

The Blackhoods did as Eos had asked and backed a kilometre away from the vampires and the elves. But what they did not realize is that they were not out of the elves' range. A battle was not what William had wanted on this day. He wanted something joyous on his birthday. Only Eos and Scott had wished him a happy birthday because they were the only one who knew. All he could do now was hope that no one would die. A few seconds later, Eos and the elves heard a horn. It was a demon battle horn. You could recognized it by its very deep sound. Soon after, the tremble of the drums was heard. Everyone got on their feet and into position. Fifteen minutes later, demons showed themselves to the eyes of the vampires. Eos turned to the elves who were about to fire and said:

- Daros sa beos. (Hold your arrows.)

No shot was fired as Eos had instructed. The demons then started to run towards the elves and vampires but Eos made the elves wait until the last minute before saying:

- Fota as beos. (Fire the arrows.)

Hundreds of arrows flew towards the demons. The demons who had been hit in their weak spot fell to the ground. When the demons got too close for the bows everyone took out their swords. Everyone on both sides was determined to end this war as quickly as possible. A few minutes later, all that could be heard was the sound of swords hitting each other. The spirits entered the bodies of the demons that were weak minded and made them kill themselves. Behind the demons who were fighting with swords, Leihat shot a well aimed arrow at Eos. When Scott saw the arrow, he screamed at Eos:

- Eos! Move.

Eos moved to the side to dodge the arrow, but she could not move quickly enough to miss the arrow completely. One of the feathers scratched her. She did not notice and kept fighting. A few minutes later, Eos and William started to fight back to back because the demons had surrounded them. Half an hour later, William and Eos switched sides. But an arrow that was supposed to hit Eos entered William's right shoulder and made him drop his sword. The arrow had pierced his muscle and he could not hold his sword in his hand because of the pain it caused. Eos tried to protect him by herself but the demons were getting too close. Eos then called for help. The spirits arrived immediately and Marty arrived a few minutes later. After he had made his way through the wall of demons, Marty kneeled beside William to take care of his wound while Eos took Yar in her hand. Eos then started to walk towards Deith who was hiding behind his troops. She had Tari in her right hand and Yar in her left. The noise from the battle was so loud that Deith and Leihat did not realize that Eos was close to them until she placed Tari under Deith's throat. When Leihat and the guards standing beside him saw

Eos, they all pointed their swords towards her. Eos looked at Deith and said:

- My sword is placed on the main artery of your neck. If I pull the sword, all your blood will spill out and you will die immediately.
- Put your swords down. Said Deith to his guards.
- Now grab your sword and fight me until death.
- Are you sure?
- Don't ask questions. I am giving you a choice. Do it or you're dead.

Deith took out his sword. It was a 36" slim silver sword. On the blade it was engraved *Tris Tari* which meant first queen. After examining the sword Eos said to Deith:

- This isn't your sword, is it?
- It is now.
- Where did you get it?
- My grandfather killed the first queen of the witches and since then we bring it to war. It's supposedly cursed. It is said that if you take the queen's sword, it will lead you to your death.
- Let see if it's true then.

Meanwhile, William was now healed. He turned to grab his sword and saw that is wasn't there. He realized that Eos had taken it. William turned to Simon and said:

- Where is Eos?
- At the other end of the battlefield with Deith. Answered Simon.
- Give me your sword.
- What are you going to do with it?
- I'm going to help Eos.

- Here. But bring it back.

William took Simon's sword and started to make his way toward Eos. Deith and Eos were starting to fight. Eos had the advantage because of her two swords. She blocked every move he made. Deith quickly got tired of it and so instead of aiming for her heart aimed for her hand. Eos could not block the sword so her left hand got cut and she dropped Yar. Deith and Eos then charged at each other. Both swords entered the bodies of their enemy. They both looked in each others eyes which were filled with pain. Eos asked Deith:

- How does it feel?
- It hurts. You?
- Ouch.
- On the count of three we take the swords out.
- 1, 2, 3.

They both removed their swords and fell to the ground. William arrived immediately after and asked Eos:

- Are you okay?
- Is he dead? Asked Eos.
- I think so.
- William, the sword is made of silver.
- I know. I can feel it. Are you going to be alright?
- Go get Merrill.
- Why? I'm not leaving you alone.
- Don't worry we'll watch over her. Said Gabriel and Simon.
- I'll be right back.

William left and ran towards Merrill. While he was gone, the demons started to leave the battlefield. He came back five minutes later with Merrill. Eos looked at her and said:

- I think you'll recognize the sword Deith had in his hand.

Merrill approached Deith who was lying lifeless on the ground. She examined the sword and froze when she realize which one it was. Merrill turned to Eos and asked her:

- Did he say where he got the sword?
- He said his grandfather had killed its owner. He only said she was the queen of the Witches.
- He was telling the truth. It used to belong to the queen of the witches. She was called Anarore. This sword saved her life many times so before she died she cursed it. Whoever would steal it from the witches would die shortly after. It is said that the robber died a few days later after Anarore. For as long as the sword is not in the hands of the witches, it will continue to kill those who take it as their own.

Merrill looked at Eos and then at the three boys before saying to all of them:

- We have to get her back to the mansion as quickly as possible. I think I can remove the effects of the silver. Give me the cape of the dead elf beside you.

Simon handed her the cape. Merrill shrouded the sword with it and then picked it up in her hand. She was not sure if the sword would take her as a witch or a vampire. She then handed it to Simon and then said:

- Head back home. I'll join you after I have gathered a few things.
- Do it quick. Said William.

William picked up Eos in his arms. Gabriel brought Yar and Tari while Simon took the sword of Anarore. They all returned to Edain where they would await Merrill. Demons then approached the body of Deith and picked it up to bring it back to Hrychib. The rest of the vampires looked around the battlefield for anything that could be kept. The elves gathered the dead and had a funeral. Half an hour after Eos had been returned to Edain, Merrill arrived with what she needed. Eos was getting worse by the minute and William could feel it. Her veins were now turning from blue to silver and blood was accumulating in her mouth. After a few minutes Merrill was ready with a potion and a spell. At that moment, Louisiam and Halir entered the room followed by the vampires and the spirits. When Scott saw Eos, he asked:

- What happened to her?
- A silver sword punctured her skin. Said Simon.
- Is she going to be alright? Asked Marty.
- If you let me do this spell, she'll have a better chance of surviving. Said Merrill.
- Start it. Said William.

Merrill removed the cape from the silver sword. She then poured the potion on top of it and started to say:

- Merrill Hilroy is calling the spirit of Anarore Learc. I have found your sword. Come and claim it.

A wind went threw the room and a figure appeared. A tall women dressed in white wearing a silver crown was now standing in front of Merrill. It was Anarore. She spoke to Merrill in a mystic voice:

- Why have you asked me to come back to this planet?
- To reclaim your sword and save the life of our queen.
- Why would I save her life? She is after all a vampire.

- She found your sword and she is the first one of all those who had a chance to claim it who did not want it.
- Give me my sword.
- Will you save her life?
- Consider it done.

Merrill turned to Eos to see if Anarore was telling the truth. Eos' wound was slowly closing, her veins were returning to their blue colour and her strength seemed to come back. Merrill then took Anarore's sword in her hands and gave it back to the queen who then disappeared. William held Eos in her arms and kissed her. Scott then said:

- I guess now is a good time to show you what I found.

Scott took out a white gold necklace. The chain held a tree of which you saw the roots. Everyone was hypnotized by its beauty except the elves. Louisiam asked Scott:

- Where did you get that?
- It was under an elf's sword at the battlefield. Do you know what it is?
- It's the necklace of immortality. Made by the elves for the elves. But the humans have always tried to steal it from us.
- You are still protecting it!? Said Essie.
- Yes.
- But why? The humans have forgotten about their past since almost a thousand human years.
- One day, the Blackhoods may convince every human that we exist.
- I think it won't be anytime soon.
- It will happen when we least expect it. If we stop believing in bad things, it does not make them go away.
- Will. Said Eos.
- What is it? Said William.

- I want to go home.
- We need Jonathan and Ashka to return home. We cannot leave people of the future in the past.

Just when Eos was about to say something, a gas bomb entered threw the window. Everyone except the spirits fell to the ground. Then a spirit catcher entered and trapped all the spirits. The front door opened and Jonathan came in. He had acquired the "technology" from the Blackhoods. He grabbed Eos, took the necklace of immortality and, before leaving, waved goodbye to the spirits.

CHAPTER 18
RETURNING WHERE YOU BELONG

Two hours later, Eos woke up. She was in a place she did not recognize. It was dark, cold and damp. The wall behind her was spotted with moss. This room had not been used in a long time. Suddenly, she heard Jonathan say:

- It's about time you wake up.

Jonathan was sitting at a table about two meters away from her. When Eos looked at Jonathan, she noticed she had been locked up in a prison cell. Eos got up and headed towards the bars while saying:

- Let me out now.

When touched the bars, she was shocked by an amount of electricity that would have killed most humans. Eos fell to the ground barely conscious. Jonathan looked at Eos and said:

- Oh yeah, I forgot about that. He paused before saying: Do you know what day it is?
- The eight of June.

- And it's eleven o'clock.
- So what?
- On the eight of June, according to the human calendar, at the last minute of the day or midnight, whoever is wearing the necklace of immortality will lose his body and will give it to the nearest spirit who will be able to customize it as he wishes. The one who was wearing the necklace will be erased from the face of Melda Cemmen. I will then be able to rule over the vampire kingdom.
- You can't get the throne unless I give it to you.
- You missed one detail. I can make myself be seen as you.

Eos tried to remove the necklace from her neck but she could not break the chain. It was protected by a spell that the elves had asked to have place upon it to the witches and Jonathan had added a spell that didn't let you remove the necklace. Eos looked at Jonathan and asked him:

- Can I ask you something?
- Go ahead.
- Can we go back home?
- What!?
- If you kill me, you are stuck in the past forever. You can't go home unless everyone that came to the past goes back. Trust me. If we didn't need you, we would already be gone.

Jonathan sat down and thought about what Eos had said. Was she telling the truth or was she just trying to save her life. Meanwhile, at the vampire's home, they were waking from their sleep. When Scott saw the spirits trapped he freed them. William then noticed that Eos was gone so he asked the spirits:

- Where's Eos?
- After you fell asleep and we were trapped, Jonathan entered

took the necklace of immortality and Eos before leaving. Said Cloe.

- Are you sure he took the necklace? Asked Louisiam.
- He had it in his hands.
- Louisiam, I have a feeling you know something we don't. Said Drew.
- You'd be right. At midnight on the eight of June, whomever wears the necklace will give his body to the nearest spirit and that person will disappear from the planet's face.
- So if we don't remove the necklace from Eos' neck by midnight we'll never see her again. Said Marty.
- You put it so simply.
- We'll have to split up. Said Scott. Everyone pair up with a spirit. Halir, stay here just in case.

When they all went their separate ways to look for Eos in the neighbourhood, it was 11h15. Meanwhile, Jonathan was still thinking about Eos' proposition. Eos was still in the cell. At 11h30, the vampires had still not found Jonathan and Eos. Time was running out. At 11h45, Jonathan screamed:

- Ashka! Get in here.
- What do you want Jonathan? Asked Ashka.
- Cut the power to the cell.

Ashka did as Jonathan had requested. To Eos' eyes she looked a bit nervous around Jonathan. After the power was cut, Jonathan approached the cell and unlocked the door. Eos got out of the cell and then asked Jonathan:

- Could you remove the necklace?
- Sure.

Jonathan opened a book that was on the table and found the spell that would release the necklace's lock. After he had said the words, the necklace detached itself and fell from Eos' neck into her hand. Meanwhile, The vampires, the spirits and Louisiam had just found where Jonathan and Ashka were hiding. But midnight had just passed. In their heads it was too late. They would enter and kill Jonathan. The spirits burst through the door followed by everyone else. When they entered, they saw Jonathan closing the empty cell's door. Eos was no where in sight. Simon and Gabriel grabbed Jonathan by the arms and pushed him in the wall behind him while Karl and Drew caught Ashka who had came in the room to see what was going on. When Jonathan was pushed against the wall she heard a metal chain hit against his chest. Eos stepped out of the shadow and said:

- Enough! Let them go.

Everyone turned towards Eos. They could not believe she was still alive. In surprise, Scott said to Eos:

- Eos, you're alive.
- Thanks to Jonathan. The vampires would have had a replica of me as queen if it wasn't for him.
- Sorry we didn't get here in time.
- Jonathan, could I speak with you in private?
- Yeah, we can go in the bedroom.

Eos went through a door that led to a small bedroom and just before closing the door, Eos threw the necklace of immortality to Louisiam and said:

- I never want to see that necklace again.

Eos entered the room behind Jonathan and closed the door. Everyone was wondering what she was doing. Eos stood in front of Jonathan and said:

- When Simon and Gab pushed you to the wall, I heard a chain hit against your body.
- Do you mean this.

Jonathan pulled out a necklace from under his shirt. It was in the shape of a mouth holding between its teeth a drop of blood. The necklace was made from silver and the drop from a ruby. Eos looked at it for a moment. It was the necklace that told the world that he was the protector of the queen of the vampires. Eos then asked Jonathan:

- Why did you keep it?
- To remind me what made me lose everything I had.
- How could you lose everything because of a necklace?
- When you become a protector, you have to swear that you will forget your past, that you will destroy every emotion and that you will protect whomever you are chosen for at whatever cost.
- And you forgot your family to protect my mother but you failed. She was murdered.
- I'm going to tell you something nobody knows. But you must swear never to tell anyone unless I give you permission.
- I swear.
- I was in love with your mother. I had to watch her marry Lyco. I had to see her cry when she learned that Lyco had asked to be killed. Said Jonathan while his eyes filled with water. I had to see her suffer whenever she looked at you and your brother. I couldn't take it so... I ... killed her and I sent you away because I knew you would look like her. That's why I've been trying to kill you. To erase all the bad memories. I'm sorry. I'm really sorry.

Jonathan fell to his knees and started to cry. At first, Eos didn't know how to react. Eos soon dropped to her knees in front of Jonathan and looked at him while he cried. Eos then said:

- I promise I won't tell anyone.

Eos helped Jonathan get up and wiped his tears. Jonathan's heart broke when she touched his face. That's what he wanted and he wouldn't be able to keep it. Eos then said to him:

- You're not a protector anymore. You can have what you always wanted.
- The first thing I wanted, I murdered. The second thing I wanted slipped through my fingers a few days ago when she got married.
- Do you want to go home?
- That's the third thing I want.

Eos stepped out of the room followed closely by Jonathan. They all returned to the mansion. When they arrived at the mansion, William said to Essie:

- Open the portal. We're going home.
- No don't. Said Eos.
- Why?
- There's one more thing I have to do before we leave.

Eos took her sword and placed it in its scabbard that was attached to her belt. She then put on her coat and left the mansion. William turned to everyone and asked:

- Should we follow her?
- I think that if she would have wanted to be followed, she would have asked. Said Simon. But I can follow her if you want me to.
- Go. But come back if anything goes wrong to tell us about it.

The Blackhoods' mansion was about two miles away from the vampires' mansion. In the past, each mansion would have housed a family of the Blackhoods. They would have been the most important families of the human kingdom. The biggest one would have been housed by the royal family. Now it housed all the Blackhoods. A forged iron fence surrounded the building and its yard. There were cameras and a handprint identification system at the gate. Eos knew she couldn't enter by the front door so, she used her "vampire powers" to jump over the fence. In the yard there were a few Blackhoods with guns keeping watch. For a place that was only known by the Blackhoods, there was a lot of security. Eos looked for a place to enter unnoticed. She found an open balcony door on the second floor. She climbed up the drain pipe and went up to the balcony. There was no one in the room so Eos entered. She looked around to see if she could find out who's room it was. After a few minutes, she only knew that the room belonged to a guy so she left the room. When she left the room, she saw a name on the door: Alex. She then realized that it would be easy to find Liv's room. She listened to make sure no one was coming. Eos could hear nothing so she stepped out of the room and found Liv's room a few doors down. She placed her ear on the door. No one was inside. Eos entered and started to look for proof that Liv had killed Neo. She looked for a while without success. She was about to leave and when she saw a small box on the desk beside the bed. Eos sat on Liv's bed and opened the box. Inside, there was a small letter and a vial. Eos took the letter and read it. This was written:

1ˢᵗ day of May 2004

Dear Journal,

I have had enough of Neo. He keeps thinking he's king of the human kingdom. First of all, our family is not supposed to be ruling this race. It's supposed to be Guillaume's family. Secondly, the humans don't even know they have a king. I can't take much more of his "show off" side. If only he would have stopped when I asked him to. I've tried everything. Lately, I've been thinking of killing him. I know it might not be the perfect solution but it's the only one I haven't already tried. I hope everyone doesn't hate me for killing my brother.

Talk to you later, Liv.

Liv had been planning her brother's death for a long time. Eos took the vial in her hand. It was half way filled with a blue liquid. Eos opened the vial and smelled the liquid. It was poison. Only a keen sense of smell could have recognized it. Then, Eos heard footsteps coming her way in the hall. She placed the vial and paper in her inside coat pocket. She went on the balcony and made sure no guards were close. There were none. Eos jumped from the second floor and landed on her feet. As she made sure again that there was no one around, a knife was placed under her throat. A voice said:

- Where are we going?

Eos turned to the voice. A red headed guy with blue eyes showed himself. A dark headed guy with green eyes followed him. Eos knew both of them. They use to be in some of her classes. The first was called Guillaume and the other Philippe. Eos answered their question:

- I don't' know where you are going but I am going home.
- What were you doing in Liv's room? Asked Guillaume.
- What are you doing here?
- Answer mine and I will answer yours.
- All right. I was looking for clues to prove that it was Liv and not me who killed Neo.

- Did you find any?
- Answer my question first.
- We are Blackhoods. Did you find any?
- Yes and I also found something to solve a long mystery.
- What did you find?
- A vial of poison and a letter explaining that it was Liv who killed her brother and that her family was never suppose to be ruling.
- Give me the letter.

Eos took the letter out of her pocket and handed it to Guillaume. Guillaume removed the knife from Eos' throat and read the letter. After reading it, he handed it to Philippe who also read it. Guillaume had trouble believing what the letter said. He looked at Eos and said:

- Liv didn't write this. If her family weren't supposed to have the throne, it would have said so in the book about the history of the Blackhoods. You're lying.
- I'm not lying. Her great-grandfather, the one who stole the throne from your family, had the history rewritten. The real one is in Liv's room.
- You better have a great explanation to prove that she lied.
- I do. Tell Liv that I stole a piece of paper and vial from her room. Have her come to our mansion and I'll prove it to the Blackhoods. You can take your rightful place as king.

Guillaume handed the letter to Eos and let her run away. After Eos had jumped over the fence, Philippe sounded the alarm. All the Blackhoods came running over. Liv approached Guillaume and asked him:

- What's wrong?
- I saw Eos jump over the fence. Answered Guillaume.
- Did you see if she stole something?

- I saw a piece of paper and a vial.

Liv's face suddenly filled with fear. She ran inside to her room. When she got to her room, she saw that her box had been opened and that what was suppose to be inside had disappeared. She then went to her closet, opened a covert and punched in a code. The back panel of the covert turned around. Liv was relieved to see that all fifty eight books were there. At least the true history of the Blackhoods was still secret.

Meanwhile, Eos had returned to the mansion a few seconds after Simon who had not been needed. When William saw that she was back, he asked her:

- Is everything alright?
- There coming. Said Eos.
- Who?
- The Blackhoods.
- Everyone prepare your weapons.
- No! We will sit down and pretend that we are not expecting them.

Everyone sat down and pretended they were not awaiting the Blackhoods. Fifteen minutes later, someone knocked at the door. Eos got up and went to open the door. When she opened the door, she saw Liv holding up a gun to Eos' head. Liv looked at Eos and said:

- Give me my things.
- What things? Asked Eos.
- The ones you stole.
- What are they?
- You know what they are.
- I have no idea what your talking about.

- My patience is wearing thing. I will ask you one more time before I shoot a bullet threw your head. Could you give me my things back?
- I don't have them.
- Goodbye.

Liv pulled the trigger with a smile on her face. Eos closed her eyes expecting the bullet to hit her. But she didn't. Instead she felt Drew grab her and pull her to the floor at the last second. The bullet went straight on and hit the wall. The transparent glass front part broke in pieces and the liquid silver ran down the wall while the solid piece fell to the ground. Eos looked at Drew and asked him:

- How did you know it was silver?
- She had a smile on her face.

Drew helped Eos get back on her feet. Eos looked at the Blackhoods and asked them:

- Would you like to come in?

Eos and Drew moved out of the way. The Blackhoods entered one by one. Drew then closed the door and every vampire got on their feet. Liv turned to Eos and said:

- Would you now give me my letter?
- Oh. That's what you wanted. Sure. You can have your letter.

Eos took out the letter from her pocket and read it to everyone. Every Blackhood was shocked to hear it. Eos then gave the letter back to Liv and said to the Blackhoods:

- By the way, if you are all wondering why the history does

not mention that Guillaume's family is supposed to be ruling, it's because Liv as all fifty-eight books of the original version in her bedroom.

- How do you know about that? Asked Liv.
- Your code is so easy to know. You were always a simple girl. But come on, your birthday. Everybody knows your birthday.
- The throne is mine, accept it.
- It is. Said Guillaume. But there is a rule that says that the Stewart replaces the King because the King's heir is too young. The Stewart must give it back to the true heir to the throne when he is old enough. The throne was supposed to be handed to my family when my grandfather turned eighteen.
- Are you dethroning me?
- No. I'm giving you what is yours. Blackhoods, I am your King.
- All hail King Guillaume. Said Alex.

Everyone hailed their true king. Liv was then brought to the Blackhoods' mansion to be punished. Before leaving with the others, Guillaume approached Eos and said:

- Thank you.
- You're welcome. Don't you forget what I did for you.
- I won't. The Blackhoods will remember you in their true history.

Guillaume bowed to Eos and left the house. After Guillaume was gone, William approached Eos and asked her:

- What was that all about?
- We made a deal. I restored his throne and he let me escape from their home. Essie, we can go back home now.

Essie closed her eyes. She whispered words that no one understood. A wind then entered the room and circled everyone in the room to make sure all those that were needed were present. Essie told it that Simon, Gabriel and Eos were also coming with them. After the wind stopped, a portal opened. Gabriel and Simon said their final goodbye. Everyone went in one by one. Simon approached Cloe and kissed her. Everyone had passed through but him. As the portal closed, Simon slowly disappeared from the arms of Cloe. Marishka, Nalishka, Kali, Crystale, Mathieu, Nickolas and Cloe were left behind in the empty mansion. The portal reopened at the front gate of the capital of the vampire kingdom, Tindome. A ten foot wall surrounded Tindome. Two guards kept the gate while others walked on the platform at the top of the wall all around the city. When the guards at the gate saw Scott, they immediately opened the door and let Eos see her new home. Everyone in the village lived on a farm. Of course, not every farm grew the same thing. People exchanged a type of food against another. In this kingdom, there was no money. People didn't buy things, they shared. Fifteen hundred people shared and helped themselves. The city had survived on its own since -900. As they walked towards the castle, every villager greeted them respectfully. It took them an hour to get to the castle that was on top of a small hill. The castle was made of grey marble. It looked like a fortress on its own. There were many towers at the three different levels of the castle. On top of the door, the vampire's crest was graved in the wall. The crest showed a river in front of mountains with a bit of trees. Under the river was a banner on which it was written "Coadunatio abicio constituo incomitatus" or Together we stand alone. Under the banner was a star with pointy ends to represent the night and its evil meaning. At the front door of the castle, the two guards who were keeping it bowed to Eos and said to her:

- Welcome home your highness.

Eos stopped between the two guards while everyone else entered the castle. Eos looked at the guards and said to them:

- You can call me Eos and don't bow just nod.
- As you wish.

Eos entered the castle decorated with gold and peridot stones. In the hall or throne room, there were columns decorated with gold dragons with peridot eyes. The dragons represented the Anoura family. Eos was attracted by them and approached one of them. When she touched it, she felt a force run threw her. Eos removed her hand from the column. Now, each time she would look into the eyes of a family member she would see the dragon. A few moments later, the front door opened and a girl entered. She looked as old as the others. She approached Scott who was now beside Eos and said:

- You're back.
- Yes. How have you been?
- Nothing exciting happened.
- You haven't changed.
- Did you find your sister?
- She's right beside you
- Hi I'm Lecksha. Said Lecksha turning to Eos. And you're Eos.
- How are you related to me? Asked Eos.
- I'm your cousin. You're mother's sister is my mother.
- Mom had a sister!? Said Eos to Scott.
- Yeah. But we don't know who she is.

Lecksha turned towards everyone to see the new faces and the ones she already knew. When the eyes of Lecksha and Ashka met, Lecksha saw her life flash before her eyes from a bird's eye view. She backed up into Scott in fear. Scott caught her and asked:

- What's wrong?
- I...I... Said Lecksha.
- Breathe and then tell me what you saw.
- I saw my life flash before my eyes from a bird's eye view and saw Ashka somewhere else in my life.
- There are many people we have seen before but we can't remember.
- She's the first person I saw.
- You mean she's your mother, my aunt.

Everyone looked at Ashka and awaited the truth, an explanation or both. Ashka was thinking of a way to tell the truth without hurting anyone. She took a deep breath and started to explain the situation:

- I am your mother Lecksha. A few months after you were born your father disappeared.
- I guess that runs in the family. I hope I don't do that. Said William.
- Will, shut up. Said Eos.
- I tried to raise you, Lecksha, by myself. Said Ashka. After two years, I decided that I couldn't do it by myself. I decided it was best if another family took care of you. I'm sorry but I had no other choice.
- Yes you did. You had time to raise Scott but not me.

Lecksha pulled out her sword and charged at her mother. Marty ran and placed himself between the two. Lecksha's sword entered Marty's heart. When Lecksha realized what had happened, she asked Marty:

- Why did you do that?
- My parents thought me that no matter what your family does that upset you, it never means that they don't like you.

Marty fell to the ground. Eos ran to his side. He was fading but Eos slapped him in the face to keep him a bit longer. Marty looked up at Eos who told him:

- Heal yourself.
- I can't. I cannot save my life. For me, my powers only heal wounds that could not kill me.
- But you can't die.
- You don't need me to heal you.
- I know. But I need you to be my best friend.

Marty's mouth filled with blood and his eyes slowly closed. Eos shook Marty and tried to wake him up but he was gone. William and Scott tried to comfort Eos but she pushed them both away. A few seconds later, Simon approached her and tried to do the same. When he touched her, Eos turned around and punched him in the face. When she realized what she had done, Eos made sure he was alright. Simon could not feel physical pain. Simon helped Eos get on her feet and tried to comfort her while she cried in his arms. Everyone else stood around them saying nothing. Out of the silence, Lecksha said:

- I'm sorry but he was stupid to stop me.

Eos stopped crying and wiped her tears while rage filled her eyes. She turned towards Lecksha and said to her:

- He was stupid!?
- He'd still be alive if he wouldn't have jumped in front of me and…
- Shut up. Lecksha, I never want to see your face unless I ask to see it. Is that clear?
- As you wish, your highness.
- I give you and your mother ten seconds to leave this castle before I shoot an arrow threw your heads.

Lecksha left the castle followed by Ashka. After they were gone, Eos turned to her brother and asked him:

- Where is my room?
- Third floor, last door on your left.

Eos started to go up the stairs. Before she had reached the second level, Scott asked his sister:

- What do we do with Jonathan?
- As he killed anyone? Asked Eos even if she knew no one else knew the correct answer to that question.
- No.
- Then there's nothing to do with him.
- Can I throw him out?
- No. Give him a room on the second floor.
- What!? Are you crazy? He tried to kill us.
- Scott! I have no patience at the moment.
- Sorry my Lady. I will do what is requested of me.

Eos turned around and continued to make her way to her room. She burst threw the door and slammed it shut behind her. Eos went strait threw the gigantic bedroom and on to the balcony. She stared at the Domya river that she could see from her bedroom. It led to Yrch lake that was 200km from the capital. Downstairs Scott grabbed Juliet by the arm and brought her in a corner. He then turned to her and kissed her. After he stopped, she asked him:

- Since when have you loved me?
- I can't remember. But Marty's Death made me realize that if I don't tell you now that I love you, I may never be able to.

Juliet grabbed Scott and kissed him. Scott and Juliet had found who they were destined to be with for the rest of their lives. Two days later, everyone in the vampire kingdom showed up to greet the new queen. A servant would announce every family as they came in. Eos was not paying attention while William greeted everyone with a smile. After two hours had passed, Drew's family was announced. They introduced themselves to the king and queen:

- I am Ringa. Said Drew's mother.
- I am Nwalme. Said Drew's father.
- I am Vilya. Said Drew's older sister.
- I am Caleb. Said Drew's younger brother.

Drew approached his family that he had not seen for many years. Drew's mother was so happy to see him that she had tears coming down her face. After a few minutes, Drew turned to Eos while she said to him:

- You have the week with your family.
- Thank you, Eos. Said Drew.

Drew`s family bowed to Eos and they left towards their home in Porë. On their way out, they passed a family that was also related to someone in the group. When they had arrived in front of Eos and William, they presented themselves:

- I am Essie's father. My name is Lanco and I am a spirit.

- I am Inya, Essie's older sister.
- I am Naraka, Essie's mother.

Essie was also given the permission to leave with her family. Juliet and Karl also did the same thing when their family arrived later that same day. Merrill's parents would never come because they were a wizard and a witch and because they thought their daughter had been dead for nine years. William's family was now walking threw the front door. They presented themselves to Eos:

- I am Cleor, mother of William.
- I am Aruor, father of William.
- I am Peter, oldest brother of William.
- I am Lewa, older sister of William.
- I am Alexis, older brother of William. Alexis paused before he said: Since when are you king?
- It as been a week in human time. Answered William.
- You've married the queen that we've been searching for so long!?
- Yes.
- You know she's not pure. No vampire could have pointy ears, blond hair and blue eyes.
- She half wood-elf.
- How could you betray your kind so easily?
- Love conquers all. It makes no difference what you look like.
- We are pure. We are keeping the race alive. The mixed should be banished no matter what their status are.

William went hyper speed to get to his brother and then used superstrenght to punch his brother in the stomach. Alexis went flying into a column and fell to the ground. William then turned to the rest of his family and said:

- If you do not like her that's fine with me but don't come into my life to destroy it.
- The council destroyed your life when they took you away. Said Lewa.
- No. They saved who I truly was. With you I would have had to destroy myself.

Eos approached William and took his hand. William looked at her and she said:

- Iro ato tece te sawe ar mel. (Leave them with their thoughts of us.)
- Nal mi er an osse na were at etca. (But I want my family to approve of you.) Said William.
- Afo umkyar naur na were ar mi ra ar mel. (They do not need to approve of I or of us.)

Alexis heard William and Eos speak in an elfin tongue and got on his feet even if he was in pain. "Normal" vampires did not speak the language of the elves. He took out a small knife and started to approach Eos and William. When he was close enough, he tried to stab Eos but a green wall suddenly appeared between him and her. Eos turned around and saw her brother. She thanked him. Scott turned to the guards and said:

- Guards throw the Henulka family out. Said Scott.

Alexis was the only one who had to be brought outside by force. Before the door shut in his face, Alexis screamed to William:

- This conversation is not over.

A few minutes later, the door reopened and a girl looked around. She entered the castle and was followed by a man and a women. The women said to William and Eos:

- I am Ella.
- I am Colver. Said the man.
- I am Inya. Said the little girl. Where's my brother Marty?

On the last word, Eos closed her eyes and lowered her head. She was scared to tell the truth to the young girl. When Ella saw Eos' face, she asked her:

- What is wrong your highness?
- If you would have come two days ago, you could had seen him alive.
- He's dead!? Since When?
- Tell them Will. I do not have the heart to go on.
- Your son died two days ago. He stopped Lecksha from killing her real mother, Ashka. Said William.

Inya started to cry in the arms of her father. After a few minutes of silence, Inya moved away from her father and approached Eos. Inya took Eos' hand and dropped what she had taken out of her pocket. Eos looked at what Inya had given her. It was a necklace that had a stone at the end of it. On one side of the stone it was written best friend and on the other it was written Marty. Eos asked Inya:

- Why do you give me this?
- Because I know he would have been your best friend.
- But it's yours.
- You need it more then I do.
- There will be a ceremony at the blood river in eight hours to honour him and his life.

Ella, Colver and Inya left the castle in tears. Eos looked at them leave the castle. William took Eos in his arms and gave her a long kiss on the forehead. He then told her:

- You have a part of him now.
- It's a necklace.
- But it's something he made.
- I'll go get changed.

Eos kissed William on the cheek and left him to go to their room. William gave his crown to a servant and went to help Scott to bring the body of Marty. The body was placed on a portable bed. A white sheet was placed over him. His wound had been burnt so that the blood stopped running. Eos came down a few minutes later. She had a black dress with a blue under dress. Eos was also wearing the necklace Inya had given to her earlier. Merrill arrived a few seconds after. William, Scott, Merrill and Eos left for the blood river. It took six hours and a half to get there. A few minutes later, Marty's family arrived. Colver kneeled down beside his sun and reopened the wound to let his blood run into the river. His empty body was then burned. As the flames engulfed the body, Merrill, Scott, William and Eos returned to Tindome. The family stayed behind to watch Marty's body disappear into the flames.

CHAPTER 19
SAVING A TALENT

The darkness of space had covered the blueness of the day's sky. The stars and the first quarter of the moon were shinning in the sky. The wind was softy blowing threw the open balcony door of William's and Eos' room. William was sleeping deeply but Eos was having a dream. She was seeing Marty who told her:

- I give you my powers because as a spirit I have no need for them. Use my powers wisely because if you do not, they will be taken away from you.

Eos then woke up as she felt an energy pass threw her. She was not sure if Marty had really given her his powers or if it was only a dream. It was only two in the morning so Eos went back to sleep. The next morning, after breakfast, Drew stopped Eos in the corridor and asked her:

- Do you remember what you promised me?
- I said I would free you from your curse.
- I know it might not be a good time for this but when are we going to go?

117

- Go get ready. We will leave in an hour.
- Thank you.

Drew ran upstairs to go get ready. He could not believe that his curse would finally be removed. On his way downstairs, William saw Drew ran up. He approached Eos and asked her:

- Why is he so happy?
- I told him that I was going to keep my promise and bring him to the wizard's kingdom to have his curse removed.
- You just got home and you want to leave already!?
- No, I just want to keep my promise.
- Be careful.

They passionately kissed until William had a vision of the dream he had had on their wedding night. He stopped kissing Eos and backed a bit away from her. Being worried, Eos asked him:

- What's wrong?
- I saw a dream I once had.
- What was it about?
- It was a girl running around and I was trying to catch her. She told me that she would never leave me.
- It was only a dream.
- Maybe you're right but their might be something more about it.

William and Eos gave each other a hug when Drew came running down the stairs. When he stopped at the bottom of the stairs, Drew asked Eos:

- Are you ready?
- In a few minutes.

- I'll wait for you at the door.

Eos went upstairs to get her sword and bow. When Simon passed her, he grabbed her arm. Drew had told him that they were going to the wizard's kingdom, Finwe. Eos looked at Simon who said:

- I'm going with you.
- I promised this to Drew so I will do it alone. You should go looking for what your heart desires.
- And what's that?
- You should go see if Cloe waited for you.
- I couldn't do that.
- Are you afraid she found someone else?
- Yes.
- Don't live in fear. Go find out if she's still waiting for you.
- Can I really go?
- If you want to.
- Thank you so much.

Simon ran downstairs and left for the spirit kingdom, Mearas. After getting her weapons, Eos said goodbye to William and left the castle with Drew. Eos and Drew were out of the capital after half an hour of walking. Two hours later, they passed threw William's hometown, Kotya. It was a small town of about one hundred and fifty people. Most houses were made of wood. Most villagers saluted the queen. Eight hours after they had left the castle, Eos and Drew sat down to eat something. Eos had caught a deer which they cooked and hate some of it. The rest, they left for the animals. After eating, Drew leaned on a rock with a blanket and Eos leaned on him with hers. When the fire died, Bora, protector of the north wind, blew threw. Drew shivered and asked Eos:

- Are you cold?

119

- I don't feel the cold because of my elf side.
- I'm cold.
- We can share my blanket.

Drew pulled a part of Eos' blanket over him. After Eos had fallen asleep, he watched her sleep while playing with her pointy ear and her hair. He fell asleep a few minutes later.

Meanwhile Simon was arriving in the capital of the spirit kingdom, Feanor, where he used to live. He went looking for Cloe. He knew where she used to live but he wasn't sure if she was still there. When he found Cloe's house, he looked threw the window. She was sleeping in her room. He decided to wait until sunrise to go see her. That morning, at about six o'clock, Simon saw Cloe wake up. After she had left her room, Simon knocked at the door. Cloe was surprised to hear someone knock at the door this early but she went and opened the door. She opened the door and saw Simon. After a few seconds, she said to him:

- What are you doing here?
- I came to see you.
- It as been one hundred and sixty-three years since we saw each other. What took you so long to come back?
- You wouldn't understand if I told you.
- Do you have something to hide from me?
- No I don't. I'm sorry I disappeared during that kiss.
- You remembered!?
- Yes. And I would like to finish that kiss.

They kissed while the sun was rising from her sleep and while the moon went to sleep in her place. (The elves, the spirits and the vampires consider the sun to be feminine.) When they stopped kissing, Simon saw a guy approach them and he asked Cloe:

- Who's that?
- I'm Simon.
- Oh, you're the deserter.

Simon wanted to kill the guy but Cloe stopped him. She told the guy to go prepare breakfast while she talked with Simon. When he was gone, Simon asked Cloe:

- Why didn't you wait for me?
- I did wait but I got tired of waiting after one hundred and sixty years. We have been dating for three years. I'm sorry.

Cloe touched Simon's face with her hand. He was not looking at her. He then pushed her hand away from him and walked away. Before Simon was to far to hear her, she said to him:

- You will always be in my heart.

Meanwhile, the light of the sun was touching Eos' face which made her wake up. The two blankets were completely on Drew. Eos shook Drew and he woke up slowly. The sun reflected in his blue-green eyes and his light brown hair was blowing in the wind. Eos helped him get on his feet. Drew folded the blankets and placed them in a bag he carried. They continued their journey when the entire sun could be seen over the ridge. Later that day, they passed threw the city called Ennas nicknamed the black city because, in a legend of the vampire kingdom, the city was once filled with the greatest evil. Since that time, no one walked threw that city at night because its citizen believe that the evil returns at that time. When Drew and Eos arrived at the blood river, the sun had started to set. Drew and Eos went swimming in the blood river. They drank a bit of blood and Eos filled a small bottle for William. They dried up and continued their journey.

Meanwhile, Simon was returning from his journey. When he entered the castle, he was seen by Scott who asked him:

- How did it go?
- I don't want to talk about it. Said Simon.

Simon climbed up the stairs and went to his room. Jonathan saw him go in his room and slam the door behind him. Jonathan decided to go see what was wrong. He passed threw Simon's bedroom door. When Simon felt him enter, he said to him:

- Did you come to laugh at my problems?
- You may not believe this, but I came to see what was wrong.
- Since when do you care about my life?
- Since we left the human kingdom.
- If you have to know, I went to see Cloe. She stopped waiting for me three years ago when she met her new boyfriend. She said she was sorry.
- She really broke your heart.
- And you won't believe what her new boyfriend said to me.
- What did he say?
- Oh you're the deserter.
- You should have killed him.
- Yeah. I should have.

Jonathan left the room. Simon was left to think by himself in his room. When the sun disappeared and the moon showed herself, Eos and Drew entered the Pearlas forest, a forest on the northern border of the wizard's kingdom. The light of the moon was pearly passing threw the leaves who had turned silver for summer. After five minutes of walking in the forest, Eos heard footsteps coming their way. She turned to Drew and said:

- Hide quick!

Drew climbed up a tree and pulled Eos up beside him. Four dogs walked beside the tree in which Eos and Drew were. The dogs then ran to their masters who shortly arrived beside the tree. They looked around but did not see the two vampires. They walked away. Eos was relieved. But just when she thought she was safe, the branch she was sitting on broke and she fell. Drew caught her and helped her get back on the branch. One of the wizards had heard the branch break so he ran back to the tree followed by the others. The wizard started to shoot light beams with his staff. After many tries, the wizard finally hit the branch Drew and Eos were sitting on. They fell out of the tree. Drew fell on a root and Eos feel on top of him. One of the wizards said:

- Look! A vampire travelling with an elf.
- Get them on their feet. Said the leader.

Eos and Drew were grabbed by the arms and pulled up. Eos saw that they all had tattoos on their faces; one on each cheek. On one side, they had two staffs formed into an "X" and on the other they had two hands holding a tree. Eos asked them:

- What do your tattoos represent?
- The staffs say that we are wizards and tree that we are protectors of the Pearlas forest. What does your ring mean?
- That I am married.
- Not that one the other one.
- That I am the queen of the vampires.
- The vampires have chosen an elf as their queen!?

The wizards all started to laugh at Eos. After a few minutes, Eos showed them her fangs. The wizards all stopped laughing. Eos said to them:

- My father was Lyco, protector of the sunset, and my mother was Selene, queen of all Vampires.
- Alright. Said a Wizard. Who is he?
- I am Drew, sun of Nwalme. I am a guardian of the prince Scott.
- Now let us go. Said Eos.
- Sorry, we can't. Our orders are to bring whomever is not welcomed to the king.

The wizards pronounced words that Eos and Drew did not understand. At that moment, they wished Essie was with them. They disappeared and reappeared in the hall of the wizard's castle. The king was playing with his sun that was but a little baby. The king had a crown on one cheek and the two staffs on his other. The wizard that had accompanied Eos and Drew said to the king:

- Sorry to interrupt your time with your sun your highness but we found these two in the Pearlas forest.

The king gave his son to his wife who left the room. The king got out of his chair and approached Drew. He lifted Drew's shirt and said to him:

- You fell on one of the spikes under the trees and are loosing blood fast.

Eos turned to Drew to look at his wound. His shirt was stained with blood Eos could not believe that she had not noticed before. She approached Drew and placed her hand on his wound. She pushed lightly on it and removed her hand. Drew's wound was gone. Drew looked at Eos and asked her:

- Since when can you do that?
- Last night. He gave me his powers.

- But...
- Shut. Said Eos while placing her hand on his mouth.
- Who are you? Asked the king.
- I am Eos, daughter of Selene, queen of he second kingdom.
- You are the queen of all vampires!?
- Yes.
- The vampire with the gifts of the elves?
- Yes.
- Guards! Fetch a target.

Two guards stepped out of the room by a door on their left and came back a few minutes later with a target. They placed it on the other side of the room about fifteen meters from Eos. The king then said to Eos:

- Shoot an arrow on the target.
- If I hit a bulls-eye, you do me a favour.
- Deal.

Eos detached her bow from her back and took out an arrow made from a tree called the Villyasse. It was a tree that only grew in the Fuin forest. The bow and the arrows used to belong to Lyco. She aimed precisely at the middle of the target then released the arrow. The arrow went strait across the room and into the exact center of the target. Eos then turned to the king who could not believe is eyes and said:

- Now let's discuss the favour you owe me.
- What do you want? Asked the king.
- I want you to remove the curse my friend carries.
- What is his curse?
- Whenever he paints something, the life of the object his taken from it to be but on the canvas.
- That's a very big favour.
- I'm sure my bow can help you make up your mind.

- There's no need to get mad.

The king snapped his finger and a servant approached him. The king said something in his ear and he left the room. He came back a few minutes later with a big old book. The king took the book and opened it at about the middle. He then said aloud:

- Lythiot meriat luthos herich.

A beam of light left the book and turned around Drew. It passed threw him and went back into the book which slammed shut. The king then said to Eos and Drew:

- It as been removed. Now we will send you home. Luthas almatath homitas.

They disappeared and reappeared in front of the gate of Tindome. Eos thanked the wizard which had accompanied them. He disappeared after bowing to her. Drew and Eos walked the rest of the way to the castle. When they arrived home, Drew went upstairs and Eos went to the living room to see William. When she pushed opened the door, William was surprised to see her and said:

- Back already!?
- I can go and come back later.
- No. I was just surprised to see you.

William grabbed her hand and brought her close to him. Eos took out the little bottle of blood for William. He took it and placed it in his pocket. Eos got closer and placed her head on his shoulder while he held her. Jonathan then ran in and said:

- Eos! I'm so glad you're here.
- Why? Asked Eos.
- I think I made mistake.
- What is it?
- When Simon came back, he was mad because Cloe had found another guy. So I told him that if I had been at his place I would have killed the guy. Jonathan paused for a minute. And I think he took me seriously.
- Where is he?
- He's gone. He left on a horse when the moon appeared. He went west.
- Come with me.
- Where are we going?
- Were going to stop Simon from doing something wrong.
- That might be a problem.
- Why?
- Because he left an hour ago so theoretically, he will arrive an hour earlier. That leaves him plenty of time to kill the guy.
- We still have to hope.

Eos grabbed Jonathan and pulled him out of the room. William was left by himself again because of Jonathan. Eleven hours later, Simon arrived in Feanor. He knocked on Cloe's door and the guy answered the door. Simon asked him:

- Can I speak to Cloe?
- No. She's not yours, she's mine.
- I won't ask another time.
- And I won't change my mind.

The guy took out a sword that he had been hiding behind his back. He showed the sword to Simon and said:

- You'll never see her again.

Simon took out his sword to defend himself. They fought for about five minutes. Then Simon got angrier and angrier. He struck fast to the guy's stomach. The sword penetrated the body. Simon took his sword out of the body and it fell to the ground. The blood that was on the sword started to run down on his hand. When Simon realized what he had done, he threw the sword on the floor. Just then, Cloe came out of the house, and Jonathan and Eos arrived. Cloe said to Simon:

- I knew you were jealous but did you really have to kill him?
- I...I was defending myself.
- Then why his your hand full of blood?

Simon didn't had a word. He picked up his sword. He turned around and passed by Eos and Jonathan. A few seconds later, the council appeared in front of Simon. The spirit said to Simon:

- Simon, we arrest you for the crime you have committed. You have betrayed the first and the second rule of the protectors. Your trial will be held in two days. Bring the one you protect and the people you think will be able to help you. Have I made myself clear?
- Yes.

Simon disappeared. Jonathan held Eos and disappeared. They all reappeared in the castle's hall. Eos turned to Jonathan and asked him:

- Why didn't you do that to go stop Simon?
- Oops. I had forgotten I could do that?

Eos turned around and Simon had already disappeared. William then entered the room while Jonathan went upstairs. William then asked Eos:

- Are you here to stay or do you have to leave again?
- I'm afraid we have to leave.
- At least we leave together. Where are we going?
- To the council's castle.

William and Eos went to the living room where Scott and Juliet were enjoying themselves. Eos approached Scott and said to him:

- I have something to ask you.
- What is it?
- Could you take care of the kingdom for four days while we go see the council with Simon?
- Yeah. Sure. Why does the council want to see you?
- Simon did something he wasn't supposed to do.
- I'll see you in four days.

That night, Simon accompanied by Eos, William, Drew, Karl, Merrill and Jonathan went to the council's castle. When thy arrived, forty hours later, they were showed to a room that had seats on both side of it. On one side the council was already waiting for them. They sat in front of them. After they were seated, the spirit rose and asked:

- Who will represent Simon here tonight?
- I will. Said Eos.
- Sit down Eos! Screamed the wood-elf. You do not have the right to represent him.
- Why not?
- Because you were the person who allowed him to go when you left for the wizard's kingdom. Said the witch.

Eos sat down without adding a word. Then the hobbit rose and asked again:

- Who will represent Simon?
- I will. Said Drew.
- Why will it be you? Asked the demon.
- Because I owe a favour to Eos.
- Alright. We, the council, accuse Simon of killing another spirit for personal reasons instead of protecting Eos. Said the sindarin elf.

Drew stepped forward. He then turned around and look at Simon before looking at Eos. He then turned to the council and said:

- I think Simon killed the spirit to protect himself even if it seems that he as killed out of jealousy. But we all know that things are rarely what they seem.
- Why would he have to defend himself against a spirit which is a kind know for its peaceful character? Asked the wizard.
- If the spirits are the most peaceful kind of Melda Cemmen why would any of them try to kill another? I know why. Have you ever been jealous?
- Please keep in context. Said the spirit.
- Answer the question. There is a point.
- Yes. Said the hobbit, both elves and both spirits.
- Of course. Answered the witch and the wizard.
- A couples of time. Said the demon and the vampire.
- Maybe. Said the dwarf.
- As you can see, you have all been jealous at one point. So could he have killed by jealousy? Asked Drew.
- No.
- Why not?
- Because protectors have no feelings. Said the vampire.

Eos couldn't not take much more of this. She could not believe that the council actually believed that a person could actually remove all emotions from their soul. She then got up on her feet and said:

- What!?

Everyone turned to her and Drew sat down because he knew she had a lot to say to the council. The spirit said to Eos:

- Please sit down. This is not your time to talk.
- You will hear me now. Ordered Eos.

The members of the council started to speak to each other because they were surprised that a queen would speak that way to the council. Eos then said to them:

- I just want to tell you something.
- Then speak. Said the vampire.
- Have you ever wondered if the spirits who become protectors were happy with their restrictions?
- Nature chooses them and then they decide if they accept their paths. Said the animal spirit.
- But do they know they have to get rid of their souls to become protectors? Eos paused but she received no answer so she continued: Have you ever wondered why Jonathan and Simon did things they were not supposed to do?
- I do every day. Said the wood-elf. But I have a pretty good idea.
- It is not my fault. It is because they cannot have a life of their own. They are jealous of everyone else.

The council turned to each other again and discussed of what Eos had said to them. After a few minutes of talking, the witch turned to Eos and asked:

- Why is Jonathan still with you?
- Because I forgave him and I gave him the choice to leave or stay.
- We now know what will be the consequence for Simon. Simon, please rise.

Simon rose like the council had asked and looked deep into their eyes hoping to see what was coming. The spirit said to Simon:

- We have agreed to lower your consequence. You will be haunted by that day for the rest of you life. Now leave and please don't come back.

Everyone bowed to the council and they left to return home.

CHAPTER 20
A VOYAGE TO RAMAR

Simon woke up from his sleep. He looked outside by the big window in his room. It was still dark outside. Simon had woken up because he had seen in his dream what he had done earlier in the week. He turned around and went back to sleep. The next morning, after everyone had finished breakfast except for Simon who was still asleep, Halir arrived at the Vampires' castle. One of the guards at the front door showed him the way to the dinning room. When Eos saw him she shook his hand and said:

- What a nice surprise. Why are you here?
- Louisiam wanted me to come tell you that he is requesting your presence at his wedding next week.
- Louisiam is getting married!? Said Scott.
- Yes, I know, it his hard to believe but it's true.

Eos hit Halir and Scott who were beside her in the stomach because what they had said. Halir then continued:

- Of course she looks a bit like Eos so he might not be over her yet. Get ready and I will lead you to Ramar.

Everyone stepped out of the dinning room to go get ready. When everyone was out of the dinning room except for Halir, Simon entered. He was surprised to see Halir so he asked him:

- What are you doing here and where is everyone?
- I came to invite everyone to Louisiam's wedding so everyone went to get their bags.
- Oh.
- Are you alright?
- Yeah. I just had a dream that woke me up in the middle of the night.
- Do you want to talk about it?
- No. I'll be fine.

Simon went to the kitchen to get something to eat. Eos had just contacted Ashka. She would sit on the throne while everyone would be gone. But Eos had warned her that if she caused any trouble, she would get killed. Essie had just returned to the first floor when Gabriel came threw the front door. When she saw him, she asked:

- Where were you?
- I went back home to see Marishka, Nalishka and Kali. Did I miss anything? Asked Gabriel.
- Marty is dead. Scott and Juliet are dating. Drew doesn't have is curse anymore and Simon killed Cloe's new boyfriend.
- I leave for a few weeks and all that happens.
- Time goes by fast.
- Where are you going?
- At Louisiam's wedding.

After a few minutes of talking with Essie, Gabriel went to find Eos. When he found her, he asked her:

- Can I speak with you?

Eos turned around to see who wanted to speak with her. When she turned around, she saw Gabriel standing there with his arms open waiting for a hug. Eos gave him a hug. She then asked him:

- Where have you been?
- I went to see my friends. Is it true that we are going to the wood-elf kingdom?
- Yes and you are welcomed to come with us to go see your old species.

Gabriel thanked her many times. He could not believe that he was finally going back. Half an hour later, everyone joined outside of the castle. Everyone climbed on a horse. Halir had a pure white horse and Eos a white one with silver hair. William had a pitch-black horse and Scott a dark brown one. The rest of the horses were light brown and some had black hair. Eos climbed on her horse called Lesta while everyone climbed on theirs. Halir leaned forward close to the ear of his horse and said:

- Kabakevo nitev na Ramar, Golath. (Ride fast to Ramar, Golath.)
- Kabakevo nitev, Lesta. (Ride fast, Lesta.) Said Eos.

The two white horses took off at full speed followed by Gabriel's horse while the others were left behind. When the three noticed that no one was following them they went back and explained to the others how to make their horses move fast. Ten hours later, they entered the forest that surrounded the city called Coa. It was the last city of the vampire kingdom before entering the human, elfin or spirit kingdom. They stopped to take a break. They got off the horses to decide which way they would go next. Halir gave them their options:

- We can pass threw the Human kingdom by their forest which connects to the Fuin forest or we can pass over the mountains in the spirit kingdom.
- The horses cannot follow us in the mountains so it will take more time. Said Eos.
- Then we will pass threw the Human kingdom.

They got back on their horses and took the dangerous road into the Human kingdom. They could not meet any human or they would probably get killed by them. Halir and Eos were constantly listening for coming people. Finally after three hours an half that seemed like eternity, they entered the Fuin forest. They were now safe. They continued for another hour before being stopped by forest protectors. They carried bows decorated with silver and gold leaves. Their quivers, decorated with a silver and golden border, were brown and had silver stitches. The arrows in their quivers had green leaf shaped feathers attached with silver treads. One of the guard asked Halir:

- What are they doing here?
- They are here for the wedding. Answered Halir.
- You know the rules better than anyone, General. No demon may see the capital.
- Only one of them is half-Demon.
- We do not speak of that. There is an evil force upon two of them.
- Since when is Lyco evil?
- Lyco!? You may pass.
- Thank you.

They continued their road to the capital. When they arrived at the gate of the capital, it had been twenty-four hours since they had left Tindome. The gate was decorated with two elves facing each other that both had a hand on a rolled piece of paper. It was to represent the friendship between the two kinds of elves. When they arrived in front of the castle, servants unloaded their horses and brought their things to their rooms. Halir then brought them in and showed them to their rooms. The walls of the castle were made of carved wood. The carvings represented the richness of the King and of the kingdom. In their rooms, the beds were decorated with vines carving. The sheets and the pillows covers were decorated with golden treads. When Eos and William were settled in, Halir came in and said to Eos:

- Will you please follow me? Louisiam wishes to see you.
- Of course.

Halir and Eos stepped out of the room and went downstairs. They went into the throne room where Louisiam was waiting. When they entered the room, Louisiam said to Eos:

- I'm glad you came. I have something for you.

A servant brought a long wooden box and gave it to Eos. Louisiam had had the box taken out of storage when he had heard that Eos was coming. She opened the box and inside there were two 18" swords. One had a golden handle and a gold vine-like line on the blade. The other was exactly the same except it was silver. In each of the vines it was written: *Guardian of the Fuin forest.* Eos took both swords and tested them out. After a few minutes, she asked Louisiam:

- Why do you give me these?
- I thought you should have them. Answered Louisiam.
- Why?
- They were your father's.

- I don't want them. Said Eos while placing the swords back in their box.
- It is a gift, keep them.
- I don't want them. Said Eos while her tattoo turned red.

Scott was upstairs kissing Juliet when he felt his shoulder burn where his tattoo was. He left Juliet alone and ran downstairs to the throne room. Back in the throne room, a guard shot a sleep dart at Eos because he was afraid she would hurt Louisiam. When the dart hurt Eos, she became very sleepy immediately. She then fell on the ground fast asleep. Scott then entered the room and when he saw Eos on the floor, he asked Louisiam:

- What did you do to her?
- My guard shot her a tranquilizer. Answered Louisiam.
- Why?
- Because she wanted to hurt me.
- What did you do to her before?
- I only gave her a gift.
- What was it?

Louisiam took the box that Eos had dropped on the floor. Louisiam opened the box and showed the swords to Scott. Scott looked in Louisiam's eyes and asked:

- What are they?
- Your father's swords.
- Why do you have them?
- He was a guard of the Fuin forest before he became King of the vampires.
- Why do you have them?
- We took them when he died to remember him.

Scott grabbed Louisiam by the collar and pushed him against the wall. The guard was ready to shoot Scott but Louisiam told him not to. After he was sure that the tranquilizer had been put away, Scott said to Louisiam:

- He is our father.
- I know but...
- But what?

Louisiam did not say anything. Scott let go of Louisiam and kneeled beside Eos. Eos was lying on her stomach. Scott lifted her shirt and showed the tattoo to Louisiam. The demon was showing all of his body and the lines were flashing red. A force was coming out of it that Louisiam could no bare much longer. Scott looked at Louisiam and said:

- He's almost free.
- I'm sorry.
- You're sorry or was that your plan?
- At first, I wanted him to be free but when I saw what it was doing to Eos I changed my mind.

Scott looked at Louisiam and then left the room with Eos in his arms. He brought her back to her room and placed her on the bed. When William saw Eos, he asked Scott:

- What happened?
- You wouldn't understand.
- Why not?
- It's between me and Eos.

Scott left the room but just before he closed the door, he said to William:

- Don't touch her tattoo.

He slammed the door and went to his room to think. William approached Eos and saw, through her shirt, a red light. He was attracted by it so he approached his hand. Simon suddenly appeared and pushed William off the bed and on the floor. William looked at Simon in amazement and in fear. The light from the tattoo slowly dimmed and disappeared. Simon then said to William:

- Do not touch her tattoo when it's red.
- Why not?
- Because if you do all your anger will be taken from you and given to her which may free her father from his long sleep. And right now, we do not want to do that.

Eos slowly woke up. When Simon realized it, he disappeared. William stood on his feet and approached her. She didn't know where she was for a second but William told her how she had gone from the throne room to their bedroom. A few hours later, there was a knock on the door. William went to answer. Again, Halir was standing there. William asked him:

- What do you want now?
- I want to apologize for what happened earlier and I wanted to tell you that lunch is served.
- I'm not hungry so go away.
- Wait! I am. Said Eos while approaching the door.
- But you have to rest.
- No. I'm fine.
- She has the gifts of the elves. Said Halir. A few calm hours and she is back to normal.
- See you later William.

Eos kissed William on the cheek and left with Halir. She seemed to be more at home among the elves then among vampires. William returned inside the room and sat on a sofa. Downstairs, on a long table, dressed with a white cloth, was placed a feast. There were fruits of every kind. There was also deer and a clear drink which the elves made from nectar. None of the vampires had come to this feast but Eos did not care. She enjoyed her time with the elves. After eating, the elves recited the poem about Lyco.

When the end of the forest met the sunset,
He rode in on the east wind.
He came to our call; the call for a protector;
A protector for the Fuin forest.
His name was Lyco Andune (sunset).
Like all elves, he respected Nature
But he did more than the others.
He protected the forest for ten years (elfin years: 1= 100 human years)
Until he met Selene Anoura (sunrise).
The sunset met the sunrise and fell in love.
The sunrise was the queen of the vampires
And the sunset was the protector of the forest.
One day, the sunset left the kingdom.
Selene and Lyco got married.
They had twins the next year
And, on that day, that painful day,
Lyco asked to be destroyed.
He was destroyed and his spirit was locked up;
Locked up in his children's bodies;
In what he feared the most.
And since then, since that day,
There as never been a sunset.

Silence fell in the room. The elves had heavy hearts when they told that story. It reminded them to much that everyone was standing on the edge of a knife and if they made a small mistake, they would fall. After a few minutes, Eos said:

- It is a very nice poem, but a bit sad.
- That is the way life is. Said Louisiam.

Louisiam approached Eos and gave her the swords she had refused earlier. They were in a dark green case made to be placed on someone's back. Eos did not wish for her father to get angry again so she took the swords. Eos turned to Louisiam and said:

- Can we test them out?
- Why not?

Louisiam took out his twin swords. They had gold handle and white gold blades. Louisiam looked at Eos who was already in position and said:

- On guard.

They started to fight against each other. The four swords were clinging as the hit each other. The other elves watched with great attention. The two were very good at coordinating their feet movement with their swords movements. At the end of the room, a door opened and an elfin girl entered the room. When she saw Louisiam and Eos fighting, she said:

- What is going on here?

Both Louisiam and Eos stopped and turned around to see who had asked the question. The girl was Ilya, Louisiam's fiancé. She was the daughter of Lily, protector of flowers, and

Iire, the first wood-elf. Eos turned to look at Halir and said to him:

- She is like me.
- What do you mean by that? Asked Ilya.
- Never mind.
- Louisiam, why do you play games when you should be getting ready for tonight?
- It is to control my stress. Said Louisiam.
- May I interrupt you? Asked Eos.
- Who are you and what do you want? Asked Ilya to Eos.
- I'm Eos, daughter of Selene. I just wanted to tell you that even if you force someone to do something, they will only do it when they want to.
- It always makes me laugh that an elf rules the vampires.

Eos didn't mind when people made fun of her mixed heritage. But when they made fun of her people directly or indirectly, she got angry. While Ilya was too busy laughing, Eos took one of her sword and placed it under Ilya's throat. Eos then to said Ilya:

- You say one more bad thing about my people and I will cut your tongue so that you will have to keep your evil comments to yourself.
- If you hurt me Lily and Iire will hunt you down until you're dead.
- I can easily get rid of your parents.

Then, the same door form which Ilya had entered from opened again. This time, it was Gabriel who entered the room. When he saw Eos holding a sword under Ilya's throat, he asked:

- What's going on?

- Nothing. Said Eos while putting her sword away and heading towards the door.

Eos left the room and Halir followed her. Gabriel took some food and something to drink before sitting down with the elves. Outside, Halir grabbed Eos' hand and asked her:

- What happened with Ilya?
- I don't know. I feel as if my father did not like her but I don't know why.
- You have reached the red so he stays with you forever and each time you reach red again, there will be another part of him with you. If your brother reaches red, it will accumulate on what you have already achieved.
- What happens when he reaches maximum level?
- Lyco will be free but no one knows what will happen to you or your brother.
- Then we must keep him locked up for as long as we can.

Halir let go of Eos. She went to her room where William was still on the sofa. William looked up at her and asked:

- Had fun with the elves?
- For a while then I met Ilya.
- Good for you. I sat on a sofa waiting for my wife.

William's eyes filled with water but Eos did not notice. She closed the door and when she turned around, she saw a drop of water fall to the ground. She approached William and sat beside him. She placed her hand on his back and then asked him:

- Why do you cry?
- Ever since Halir arrived at our castle, you've pushed me aside. Maybe, you should have married Louisiam.

- Will, I'm sorry. No matter how it seems, I want you to know that I have always loved you and that I will love you until all the years of this land have faded away.

William put his hand on Eos' cheeks and pulled her in closer so that their lips met and touched for a few minutes. They then laid down on the sofa and fell asleep. William had his arm over her and his hand was on her stomach. Two hours later, someone knocked on the door. Eos woke up startled by the noise and William was woken by Eos' movements. Behind the door, a voice was heard:

- My Lady, my Lord, we bring you gifts from the elves.
- Come in. Said Eos.

Two girls came in. They were both dressed in green dresses. The first one to enter had silver-green eyes and hair as golden as the rays of the sun. The other one had eyes as blue as the ocean and dark blond hair. William and Eos stood up and approached them. The first girl spoke:

- My name is Rila. I bring gifts for William, son of Aruor.
- My name is Vanya. I bring gifts for Eos, daughter of Lyco.

Rila first took out a silver robe. It had leafed shaped buttons. Vanya took out the gift for Eos. It was a shoulder-less white dress that was decorated with pearls and diamonds. They then gave a crown to Eos. It was a simple gold band but in front there was a diamond shaped bright stone. Eos asked Vanya:

- What kind of stone is it?
- It is a star stone or a piece of star.
- A star!?
- Yes. We caught it and made it into a jewel. Louisiam insisted

that we give it to you. It is the first and last star in the night sky. She is called Faina.

- How did you catch it?
- We asked the protector of stars and he gave us a piece of it.
- Please pass on my thanks to Louisiam.
- And mine. Said William.
- We shall. The wedding is in an hour.

The two girls left the room. When they were gone, William turned to Eos and asked her:

- Am I really supposed to wear this dress?
- It's a robe and yes. Since we are in the elfin kingdom we shall follow their traditions.
- Fine. But this is the only time I will wear this.

William and Eos got dressed with their new clothes. It took them about fifteen minutes to get ready. They then walked hand in hand to the first level were Halir was waiting for them. He greeted them with a bow. He was dressed in a silver shirt with short sleeves that was made in the same design as William's robe. He guided them to the balcony of the castle. William thought: " *Why can he wear a shirt and I have to wear a robe?*" Eos heard it and answered: " *He is the general. He might need to protect Louisiam.*" The balcony was very big and, like the rest of the castle, was made of carved wood. The fences of the balcony were decorated with lilies of the valley that were small bell-like white flowers. The leaves of the trees were golden and the light of the fading sun was making them shine. Eos turned to Halir and said:

- It's beautiful.
- I shall pass it on to the ones who made it. Said Halir.

Then, Eos noticed something she had not before. On Halir's arm there was a tattoo. It surrounded his arm. Its two green borders were about 7mm thick. The center was blue and a bit more than 2cm. In the blue there were two silver and two gold lines that criss-crossed. The gold lines formed ovals and the silver formed diamond shapes. Eos then asked Halir:

- What is that on your arm?
- It is the same thing you have on your arm. Said Halir.
- I don't have that tattoo on my arm.
- I know. But this tattoo tells that I am a wood-elf as yours tells that you are a vampire.
- It is very nice.

Halir smiled and walked away. William and Eos grabbed some drinks before sitting down on the chairs decorated like the balcony. Many elves then greeted William and Eos to pay their respects to the daughter of the sunset. A few minutes later, Louisiam arrived. He was dressed like William except his robe was gold. His crown was made of white gold. There was a maple leaf at the front and the rest, a simple band, was decorated with trees. William and Eos rose and bowed to greet him. Louisiam then said:

- Thank you for being here and for wearing the gifts.
- Etkria kaloso. (You are welcome.)
- Eos, you will always surprise me. Just when we think you have chosen to push your elf side away, you bring it out again. You are definitely his daughter.
- Let's not talk about my father.
- As you wish.

Louisiam returned inside the castle while Gabriel came out. Gabriel seemed to never have become a spirit. He had his pointy ears and his hair, which went to his chin, seemed to have found its original golden colour. He was dressed in a silver-green robe. The elves greeted him as if he was royalty. Scott was the next one to arrive. He had a golden band around his head but was dressed as usual. He had not wished to wear the robe the elves had given him but he had worn the crown. Finally, the rest of "the gang" arrived. They came in dressed in their formal vampire clothes. When the hour of the wedding had arrived, the sun had faded and the moon was looking upon them with all her stars. Ilya and Louisiam arrived hand in hand and walked up to Halir who was waiting for them. Ilya was dressed in a white gown that was decorated with diamonds. It had no shoulders and they were golden elfin design on the arms. Halir then proceed. After the wedding, Ilya was named Queen of the wood-elves. A tiara decorated with leaves was placed on her head. Everyone then went inside for a meal. A few minutes later, Eos and William returned outside. To start a conversation, William said to Eos:

- It's a beautiful night.
- Yes. There are no clouds in the sky.
- But the sky is never as beautiful as you.

Eos turned to William quickly because she was surprised of what he had said. After a few seconds, she said to him:

- Thank you Will. That was very nice to hear.

William and Eos approached themselves from each other to kiss but were interrupted by Essie who said:

- Beautiful night, isn't it?

At the sound Essie's voice, William turned to see who it was. When he saw Essie, he turned to Eos and said:

- I'll see you upstairs.
- Will don't leave. Said Eos while grabbing his arm.
- Please do William. Said Essie. I want to talk to her alone.
- What do you want to talk about?
- Marty's death.
- It can wait.

Eos and William went to their room. William and Eos changed themselves, kissed and William went to bed. Eos stepped on the balcony for a few minutes. She could hear the sound of the party downstairs. When she came back inside, William was asleep. She went to bed and fell asleep listening to the music. The next morning, at first light, they started to pack for the journey home. Their horses were brought in front of the castle and loaded with their things. Scott, William and Eos said goodbye to Louisiam and Ilya. They then climbed on their horses and rode off in the direction of the sunrise. When they arrived home, William and Eos went to see Ashka. When Ashka saw them, she said:

- It's about time you got back.
- Sorry. Said Eos. I forgot to mention it was in elfin time.
- Well, now that your back, I have a message for you from the council.
- What do they want?
- They said they wanted to come visit you for a week.
- Visit me!?
- They didn't say why so I told them that you would be happy to have them in your home.
- When are they coming?
- Next week.
- Why did you tell them that?
- At first, I said that I couldn't give them an answer but then they said that it was very important so I told them they could come next week.

- Thank you for taking my place while I was gone.
- Anytime niece.

Eos did not respond to those last words. Ashka bowed to William and Eos and left the castle.

(HAPTER 21
A FLASHBACK OF A LOST PAST

A week had passed since "the gang" had returned from Ramar. Today, the council was coming to see them. Eos was stressed because she did not know why the council wanted to see her. William was by her side trying to calm her down. The council finally arrived at nine in the morning. When they had all entered the castle, they thanked Eos and William for their hospitality. After looking around the hall, the animal spirit said:

- Where is everyone else?
- They are upstairs. Said William. They thought you only wanted to talk to us.
- No, we want everyone to be there.

Eos called a guard to her and told him to go get everyone else. The guard bowed to Eos and went upstairs. When everyone had arrived, they went into the living room to sit down. When everyone was comfortable, the council presented themselves:

- I am Kano. Said the Animal Spirit.

- I am Poika. Said the Spirit.
- I am Oia. Said the Vampire.
- I am Mardesse. Said the Hauflin.
- I am Oron. Said the Dwarf.
- I am Leo. Said the Demon.
- I am Hui. Said the Sindarin- Elf.
- I am Iire. Said the Wood-Elf.
- I am Nessima. Said the Witch.
- I am Isilme. Said the Wizard.

Poika, Nessima and Oia were women while the others were men. Oia looked at everyone before saying:

- I suppose you are wondering why we are here.
- I am. Said Eos.
- We have come to explain to you your pass since your mother and father did not teach it to you.
- We don't need to know our past. Said Scott.
- Wouldn't you like to know why your father asked to be killed?
- I don't care why he did it. He did it.
- Calm down. I am sure there are some things you wish to know about your family.
- Yes there is.
- Then we shall begin telling you about them.

Hui and Iire began telling the story of the world because they were the oldest apart from Nature, Malerk, Lydia and Lumos. Iire's voice started like the wind softly blowing on the leaves:

- 12170 years ago, Nature discovered this planet.
- What about Malerk? Asked Eos.
- He was second to step on this planet and so did not discover it. As I was saying, Nature discovered this planet. Since,

Malerk and Nature were stuck on this planet, they made it their own. They created everything that you can find in the white and black kingdom of Aura. In -8527, Malerk and Nature married themselves. More then five hundred years later, They had twins; Lydia who would later be know as Oracle and Lumos who would vanish from Melda Cemmen shortly after the demons were created.

- In -6573, Nature created the Wood-elves. Said Hui. She created them from three of the four basic elements: water, air and earth. She created a being to the image of the people from the white kingdom. He had blue eyes, blond hair, pointy ears and a height of about 6'. She called him Wood-elf. She soon created more of his kind so he would not get lonely. The souls of the elves would be the souls of the trees. If a tree died so would an elf and vice-versa. After exploring the land, the first elf named the planet Melda Cemmen which means beloved land in the language of the trees. The sindarin-elves were created in -6505 the same way as the wood-elves but they were made to resemble more the people of the black kingdom. They would not be as conscious about not hurting anything that Nature created. Any questions?

- Why do you float? Asked Essie.

- We are part wind so we can float on the wind that moves close to the ground. Said Iire.

There were no more questions so Hui and Iire sat down. Mardesse and Oron then rose to talk about their species. Mardesse started with the story of the Hauflins:

- In -5987, Nature noticed that the Elves were only taking care of the trees and not of the smaller plants. So, she decided to make a smaller sized Elf. They were made exactly the same way but they were only around 3'5". Their souls were not connected with anything but they still took care of their gardens as if they were.

- You were made to be gardeners!? Said Karl.

- In a way, yes.

- Now, I will tell you the story of the Dwarves. Said Oron. In -5960, Nature was getting worried about Malerk's mountains that were sometime spitting fire or letting big pieces of ice and snow run down their sides. Nature created the Dwarves. She made them though enough to survive the chilling cold of the mountains. Thanks to our species no one as ever died because of a mountain outside the Human kingdom.

After Oron was done with his story, he sat down as did Mardesse. Oia soon got on her feet to tell the story of the Vampires. A story which went like so:

- A long time ago when Malerk and Nature formed the world, Malerk filled a river with blood. When she saw what he had done, Nature decided to show him that he had not won. In -5245, Nature found a use for the river. She took the blood and mixed it with earth. She gave the new being fangs and claws. It was almost as if they were neither animals, nor beings. They were simply creatures who needed to drink blood to survive and who feared the light of the sun. We, the Vampires, were only a proof that Nature was better than Malerk.

- They feared the light of the sun!? Said Drew. Vampires do not fear the sun.

- They did until they made a deal with the witches. It was a kind of peace treaty. If the Vampires were granted the opportunity to walk in daylight, they would stop trying to eliminate the witches. The witches agreed and since then we are no longer the night-walkers.

Oia sat down. The next species to be created were the humans but since no human at sat at the council since -698, Leo was going to explain their story. He started like so:

- The next species to be created were the Humans in -4923. Nature made them with water and earth and gave them a special power just like the other species. She gave him an inventive brain. It would help the Humans invent things to make their lives easier. Unfortunately, it would also lead them to their doom. Malerk knew that the Humans would lead to the destruction of Melda Cemmen so he created the Demons in -4912. Their only purpose would be to destroy the world of the humans. But when the shield or invisible wall went up between the human kingdom and the rest of the world, our purpose was put on hold. We were now free to live normal lives. But, of course, without forgetting that one day we would have to wipe them out.
- So your life revolves around your purpose? Asked Drew.
- Yes it does.
- That must be a nice life!? Said Karl.
- Do not mock our purpose for it is yours as well because you are half-Demon.

Karl did not add anything to the discussion. Leo was right. If Karl mocked the Demon's purpose, he mocked himself. Since there were no dragons around, Kano got on his feet to explain the creation of the dragons:

- In -4867, Nature realised that she had no one to take care of the sky. She made three different kinds of the same species that she called dragons. She made one with fire and ashes that would watch the sky and the volcanoes, another of ice and ashes that would watch over the mountains and one of water and ashes that would watch over the deeps of all water sources. The ice dragons resembled long snakes and often had horns and long whiskers. The water dragons also resembled long snakes but they have webbed paws. Their skin his covered with the same substance that makes fishes slimy. They have two pairs of eyelids; one transparent and one solid, and gills to breathe under water. The dragons made from fire walk on four feet. Their height is about fourteen feet and each wing measured almost the same. Their tail is about eight feet long. All Dragons can take the shape of a person.

Kano sat down after using up his breath. Nessima and Isilme would now explain the beginning of their species. Nessima started first:

- In - 4598, Nature thought of what would happen if she were to die. She was worried, that if it were to happen, that all her creations would die as well. For all her creations, she made protectors. Beings who were made from one of Nature creations and who were given the ability to appear physically as they wished. Their jobs were to protect the things they were made from. Nature made the following: she joined her son Lumos to a star to make him protector of stars, Lyco, protector of the sunset, Clorus, protector of the white clouds, Solano, protector of the sun, Luna, protector of the moon, Soara, protector of the birds, Niam, protector of mammals, Lez, protector of reptiles, Mythra, protector of water, Sout, protector of the south wind, Lut, protector of the west wind, Dido, protector of the east wind, Lily, protector of flowers, Planctus, protector of plants, Chinook, protector of warmth, Typhon, protector of the earth, Ceri, protector of the sky, Pois, protector of fishes, Ahuale, protector of the day, and Vira, protector of life.
- Malerk, of course, did the same with his evil thing. Said Isilme. He made the following protectors: Bora, protector of the north wind, Thor, protector of mountains, Chaos, protector of fire, Borealus, protector of cold, Nychta, protector of the night, Dedum, protector of death, Lorus, protector of dark clouds, and Frice, protector of ice. A few more protectors would be made by both Nature and Malerk for the things that kept the world balanced. They were: Fate, protector of the

future, Giorno, protector of the present, and Pera, protector of the past. They would also associate the royal family of the Vampires with the sunrise and the royal family of the Demons with lightning.

- In that year, Nature also decided to giver some of her powers to two new species: Witches, tamers of Nature's magic, and Wizards, keepers of Nature's magic. The Wizards were each given a staff in which the powers of Nature were placed. To the Witches, she gave a few of her powers and told them that they would have to learn and deserve the rest. Wizards and witches looked like humans except they were more powerful. Wizards were recognizable by their very dark hair and the Witches by their earth brown hair. We were created to make sure that the world of good does not collapse if Nature dies.

Nessima and Isilme were done and no one had any questions so they sat down. Kano rose to explain the story of the animal spirits:

- Our story is a sad one. In -1965, a fight erupted between the Dragons and the Wood-elves. They were fighting for a piece of land. The battle lasted a few months. It would have lasted longer but Nature made them stop because she feared the worst. After the Dragons and Elves had left the battlefield, the smoke cleared and revealed the dead. Nature looked to see if anyone she knew had died. She found her friend barely holding on to his life. He was badly burned; he had no more hair, his clothes were stuck to his skin and his face was badly burned. As his soul left his body, Nature made sure it would not disappear. A week later, when his soul should have left Melda Cemmen, it stayed in the body of a white tiger. Nature had chosen a tiger for his body because that was the animal that the Elves feared the most. He would now be able to take both shapes.

- Is he still alive? Asked William.

- Of course he is. He's right beside you.
- Gab!? Said Eos turning to him.
- Yes. I am the first Animal Spirit. Said Gabriel. I was a friend of Vanyar and of Nature. When I died that day, she saved me. Then I lived with the Wood-Elves and I was seen as royalty. I knew Lyco very well and when Louisiam wanted to give me to you, I could not refuse. You deserve to be surrounded by the mightiest of company.
- Thank you. But why aren't you part of the council?
- I didn't want to. Politics isn't my thing.

When Gabriel was done, Kano sat down and Poika explained the story of the spirits:

- We were simply created because there was no animals around when the first died. After that, if Nature chose to save someone they then had the choice of being an Animal or a normal Spirit. Most people who wish to become protectors chose to be normal Spirits.
- I was wondering. Said William. Why do you know so much about the first of every species?
- We, except for Kano and Poika, are the first of every species. Said Iire.
- But how could you have lived so long without aging or dying?
- Nature gave to the first of every species except for the human un-aging immortality.
- What happened to the first human?
- He died at the age of fifty of a disease.
- If he died so early who was the first human to sit at the council?
- The first and only human to sit at the council was Daniel, sun of Bruin, 1st Lord of the human kingdom. After he died in -698, he was not replaced. If you have no more questions, we will stop for the day.

No one had any questions, so the council retired to their rooms on the second floor. After they had walked upstairs, William turned to Eos and said:

- That was short for eleven-hundred years of history.
- I agree. Said Eos.
- Do you want to go do something while they rest?
- Sure but what?
- How about a walk?
- I'd love to.

William and Eos went outside, hand in hand, and walked to the lake called Yrch. Scott and Juliet were in his room enjoying their company. Drew was painting the view from his bedroom window. Merrill was trying to learn more about Nature's magic at the library. Karl was on his way to see Essie. Essie was in her room with Gabriel not expecting Karl to come see her. Essie and Gabriel had grown closer since his return from the animal spirit kingdom, Lithe. Karl arrived in front of Essie's bedroom a few minutes later. He entered without knocking and saw something that made him stop breathing for a few seconds; He saw Gabriel and Essie kissing. Karl took out Tuo, his sword, and without making any sound he approached Gabriel. When Karl was beside him, he grabbed him by the throat and lifted him in the air. Karl then said to him:

- She's not yours.
- Neither is she yours. Said Gabriel.
- Karl! Let him go. Screamed Essie.
- We are bound to each other. Said Karl to Essie. We are supposed to live together for eternity and it's not a spirit that's going to separate us.

After finishing his phrase, Karl pierced Gabriel's stomach and let go of his throat. When Gabriel was stabbed, he immediately changed into his tiger shape and ran out leaving a trail of blood. A few seconds later, Jonathan and Simon who had heard Essie scream entered the room. Jonathan immediately saw that blood was dripping from Tuo. Not knowing that Gabriel had been in the room, Jonathan asked Essie:

- Are you okay?
- He didn't hurt me.
- Then who was it.

No answer was needed from Essie because Simon had just noticed the blood on the floor and kneeled down to get a better look. Jonathan then asked Simon:

- Who's blood is it?
- Gab's blood.

Simon was afraid that he might be dead. If an animal spirit was wounded in his person shape, he could die for that body was technically already dead. While Jonathan and Simon were looking at the blood, Karl tried to sneak out. But he wasn't quick enough. Jonathan pushed him into the wall and asked him:

- Where's Gab?
- I don't know. Answered Karl. Why would I know?
- You should know because he is killable in Wood-elf shape.
- He ran out the door. I don't know where he went.
- Then come with me.
- Where are we going?
- Were going to find him and if I were you I'd hope he's still alive.

Jonathan and Karl left the room. Simon comforted Essie and said to her that he would return with news as soon as possible before leaving the room. Meanwhile, William and Eos had just arrived at the lake. There were trees all around it. The water was clear and you could see fishes swimming at the bottom. The sun was shinning as much as she could possibly do. William and Eos sat down on the soft green grass and enjoyed the view. Back at the castle, Simon had just found Gabriel and Jonathan had locked Karl in a prison cell for the rest of the day. Gabriel had turned back into his Wood-elf shape because he had lost too much blood to be able to keep his animal shape. He was lying on the balcony of his bedroom and there was blood around him. Simon ran to Gabriel and lifted his head from the cold cement. His eyes were barely opened. His strength was almost gone but he still managed to say:

- I've lost too much blood to take my animal shape. I will die soon.
- Don't give up. Said Jonathan who had just entered the room. Hope can still keep you alive.
- We must stop his blood from leaving his body. Said Simon to Jonathan.

Jonathan looked around for something to cover the wound. After a few seconds, he took a pillow cover and placed it on the wound. He then said to Simon:

- Hold it there. I'll go get Eos.
- Eos as gone to the lake. Said Simon. By the time she gets back, it will be too late.
- Then I must disturb the council.
- They will not like to be disturbed.
- I must at least try to save his life.

Jonathan ran down the hall to the council's bedroom and entered without knocking. When he opened the door, the council looked at him curiously and then Kano asked him:

- Why do you disturb our rest?
- Because a spirit is about to die.
- Which spirit?
- Gabriel.
- Lead the way.

Jonathan ran back to Gabriel's room followed by Nessima, Kano, Isilme and Iire. When they entered the room, Kano was terrified to see what Gabriel looked like. Nessima kneeled beside him and closed the wound. Then, they lifted him on his bed. Isilme then said to the others:

- We need to fill his veins with blood for him to recover.
- But how can we do that? Asked Simon.
- With a spell of course. I thought you use to be half witch.
- Will you need anything?
- Yes. We will need: the blood of an elf, the blood of the one who wounded him, something that represents why he was hurt, a bowl, something to mix, and unfortunately a bit of his blood.
- I'll go get them. Said Jonathan.

Jonathan left the room and went to the prison to see Karl. Jonathan could not let Gabriel die. He had to prove to himself that he was not evil. When he arrived face to face with Karl, Jonathan said:

- Karl!
- What do you want? Asked Karl.
- I want a bit of your blood to pay for the one you have spilled.

- I'm not giving you my blood.
- Then I'm taking it.

Jonathan passed threw the bars, hit Karl who fell to the ground and took out a knife. He cut Karl's arm with the knife and filled a vile with his blood. Jonathan then left Karl unconscious to go to Essie's room. When he entered he asked her:

- Could I have something to represent why Gab was hurt?

Essie gave her a few strands of her hair. He took them and kept them preciously. He then went to the kitchen to get a spoon and a bowl before returning to Gabriel's room. When he entered, Iire asked him:

- Did you get every thing?
- I didn't get the blood of an elf and, of course, his blood.
- I can give him my blood.
- Good. Let's get started. Said Nessima.

Nessima mixed all the ingredients that Jonathan had brought. Iire then added some of his blood and some of Gabriel's blood that was still liquid on the floor. Nessima mixed everything together and pronounced some words they could not understand. Magic rose from the bowl and went to Gabriel's heart. The potion made his heart pump faster which made more blood. When his veins were full, his heartbeat returned to normal. After they made sure he was fine, everyone left the room to let Gabriel relax. As promised, Simon went to see Essie to tell her that Gabriel was going to be okay.

At the lake, Eos and William were still relaxing. Eos opened her eyes to see that, by the sun's movements, six hours had passed since they had left the castle. She got up on her feet and William asked her:

- Why are you getting up?
- We've been gone for six hours. We should get back.

Eos took William's arm and helped him get on his feet. They made their way back to Tindome. When they arrived, Scott was waiting for them. As they opened the front door, Scott said:

- It's about time you got back. The council wants to speak to us again.

The three of them went into the living the room. Everyone was already there except for Simon, Jonathan and Gabriel. A few seconds later, The spirits entered the room. Jonathan and Simon were helping Gabriel walk. Gabriel's full strength had not returned yet. When Eos saw Gabriel, she went to his side. She then turned to Jonathan and asked him:

- What happened to him?
- I think Gab, Essie or Karl would be better placed to answer that question.
- Karl!? Said Eos turning to him. What did you do to him?
- I stabbed him in the stomach. Said Karl.
- Why?
- He kissed Essie.

Fire was burning in Eos' eyes but before she could do anything to Karl, Nessima said to her:

- Eos calm down and sit down. We have much to talk about.

Eos, Jonathan, Simon and Gabriel sat down. After they were seated, Oia got on her feet and told everyone that they were going to explain all the ages of the world. Hui started with the first age:

- The first age began in the year -900 when the species chose their leaders who would later be their Kings or Queens. The Wood-elves chose Vanyar, the father of Louisiam, the Sindarin-elves chose Alewan, the Hauflins chose Adem, The Dwarves chose Dore, grandson of Oron, the Vampires chose Klashka, granddaughter of Oia, the Humans chose Charles, descendant of Delgo, the Demons named Doomen as their king, the Witches chose Anarore, the Wizards chose Wendom, the Animal Spirits chose Daniel, the only Human to sit at the council, the Dragons chose Bonarco and the Spirits chose, Galadria. Those leaders lead their army against one another to have their perfect piece of land. After nine hundred years, we the council decided to make the wars stop. We asked all the species to tell us what they wanted in their kingdom. After a few months we gave every species their own piece of land. No species ever went to war for land again.
- Why did you wait that long to make them agree? Asked Essie.
- We do not like to intervene in the business that only concerns a few species.
- What happened to the Dragons?
- They were banished in the third age.

Hui sat down and Leo got up to tell the story of the second age. He started like so:

- The second age was very calm. The humans were starting to invent better weapons which made everyone else a bit nervous. These guns fired from a distance but made a lot more damage than an arrow. Their inventive brains were making them run towards their doom. Meanwhile, the dragons were also becoming a danger to the rest of Melda Cemmen. They were making deals with the other kingdoms. If they gave the dragons gold and treasures, they could get any information about any species.

- Why did no one stop them? Asked Merrill.
- The only way to stop them is to wipe them out. Nature would never agree to that. So in the third age, she finally found a way to separate them from the rest of Melda Cemmen. The Dragons were banished to an island about 200km off shore and the Humans were blocked away from the rest of the world and their memories of the other species were erased. The only problem was that the Blackhoods found out about the plan and found a way to preserve their memories. Now if you'll excuse us we will go rest before the sun rises.

The council went to their rooms. Everyone else went to get something to eat before going to bed. That night Essie slept with Gabriel. In the morning, everyone woke up a bit later than they usually did at about ten in the morning. The council were downstairs having breakfast. They had tried to wait for everyone but had given up at nine o'clock. Everyone that had not yet eaten went to the kitchen to get something to eat. After eating, everyone went to the living room to hear the story of the royal Vampire family. After everyone was comfortable, Oia started:

- Today we will explain the beginning of the Anoura family. It started with me. I married a Vampire called Seth. He was created a few days after me.
- So he's your brother!? Said Karl.
- We are creations and so have no father, mother, sisters or brothers. Seth and I had a daughter which we named Saoma in -1264. In -950, at the age of 31, our daughter got married to a Vampire called Lorix. Five years later, in

-900, they had a daughter called Klashka and, in -873, they had another daughter called Lera. Klashka would become the first queen of the Vampires and Lera the first General.

- What happened to Saoma and Lorix? Asked Essie.

- Saoma was killed by Witches in a battle and Lorix has been in exile ever since. He let grief take control of his life. I see him sometimes in the forest around the council's castle.

- Was he the only one to see her die.

- No. I saw her die too. She was hit by the spell of five witches. They had all done the same spell. Saoma's body filled with liquid silver in a matter of seconds. There was nothing else in her body. All her organs, her veins, her pores were full. After seeing his wife die, he left his species. Those images are engraved in his memory.

- I'm sorry I asked.

- It makes me feel better to share her death. Oia paused before continuing with Klashka's life. Klashka got married to a half-Elf and half-Dragon named Velliam in -720 and Lera married Kwame in -708. In -700, Klashka and Lera lead their army against the witches who were invading. That is when Saoma died. The battle favoured the Vampires. To save themselves, the Witches made a deal with the Vampires; the Vampires were given the ability to walk in the sunlight in exchange for stopping the war. In -598, Klashka gave birth to twins: Griffa and Oric. Lera latter gave birth to Sella. Lera and Kwame died poisoned in -450. Klashka and Velliam disappeared in -300.

- Who poisoned Lera and Kwame? Asked Essie.

- Their bodyguard did.

- Why?

- We never asked because the crime committed was high treason.

Oia was now done with her part so Poika rose to tell the story of Griffa. She started like so:

- Griffa was born in -598. Her life was not filled with much excitement. While almost all the other species were being attacked, the Vampires seemed to be spared from the war. In -227, Griffa got married to a Vampire called Larne. Together, they had a daughter named Salome in -207. Salome's life was calm as well. In -7, she was named queen. In the year zero, she signed the territorial agreement. She met her husband, Liam, while taking a political trip to Saeros, the Demon kingdom. After knowing him for four years, Liam and Salome got married in 33. Eighteen months later, Salome gave birth to Shawn and Nemil. Two years later, in 57, Salome and Liam had a daughter called Tillia. Shawn became head of the royal guards, Nemil became head of the city guards, and Tillia became queen in 257. In 285, Tillia married a Vampire named Deil. The following year, Tillia and her general, Clair, daughter of Oric, lead their army against the wizards. After fighting for four years, they finally signed a new agreement. The next year, Tillia and Deil had a daughter named Vistia.

Poika was out of breath so she sat down and Iire took her place to tell the story of Vistia:

- Vistia was born in 345 from Tillia and Deil. She had a brother called Logan who was born in 367. Vistia was one of the only queens to visit the hobbit kingdom after the signing of the treaty in the year zero. She was also one of the only queens to visit all the kingdoms in her life. She was very interested in history and geography. On her free time, she liked to read myths and legends. She met Nora, princess of the spirits, who became her best friend in 452 on a trip to the spirit kingdom. She married a wizard called Ore in 565. The following year, Tillia gave her throne to Vistia. A few months later, Vistia gave birth to Antelle; the year was 583. She was the only child of Ore and Vistia. Antelle married Rory, her best-friend, in 789. Antelle got the throne in 809 when her parents died of a disease. Antelle lead her army against the Dwarves from 790-795. Antelle and Rory had a son named Lee in 822. They also had a daughter called Cyntez in 849.

Iire stopped talking and was replaced by Kano. He started the story of Cyntez:

- Since Cyntez had met the elves when she was ten, she loved them. The ones she preferred were the Sindarin elves.

Kano suddenly got interrupted by Scott who said to him:

- How could someone love elves? They pretend to care for every living thing but they abandon them when they need them the most.
- We do not pretend. Said Hui. You should not blame an entire species for what one member of the race as done.
- He was afraid of his own children.
- Maybe he was. But he did what he thought was best for you.
- He should have been killed.
- Now, Scott, you crossed the line.
- There is no such thing as a line that must not be crossed when talking about Lyco.

As Scott finished his phrase, a thunder raged outside. Thunder raged louder after Scott said that he didn't feel scared by the warning and the lights went out. Then, a voice as loud as the thunder of the biggest storm was heard:

- I would stop if I were you, Scott.
- Well, you're not me. Answered Scott.

The lights came back on. A man with black hair, who was dressed in black and who carried a black sword was sitting on a chair in front of Scott. His head was lowered so you could not see his face. The council were bowing at him and looking at the floor. They seemed to know who it was. The man then lifted his head. His piercing blood red eyes looked at Scott. If you judged his age by his face, you would have guessed twenty-five years old. But you'd be wrong. He was 12350 years old. He said :

- I am Malerk, Lord of all Evil.

There was no word spoken by anyone. Everyone bowed to Malerk except for Scott and Eos. Scott was staring at Malerk in fear of what he might do next. Malerk then said to Scott:

- I know you do not like what your father did but it is not a reason to hate him and definitely not a reason to hate the Elves.
- It is a reason to hate your son.
- He is not my son. He is Nature's son.
- You're is father.
- He was a creation of Nature and so he is not my son.
- Why do you not take him as your son? Asked Eos.
- No son of mine would abandon his family and lead it to its doom.

No one said anything else for a period of time. Eventually Malerk sat down and so Kano decided to continue Cyntez's story. He said:

- Every spring, when the leaves changes from silver to green, she would go visit the elves. She spent her ninetieth birthday under the colour changing leaves where she met Haranyë. They became friends immediately and for five years their friendship grew stronger. In 1089, Haranyë and Cyntez got married. On that same day Cyntez inherited the throne. In

1107, Cyntez had her first daughter called Sera. In 1141, she had a second daughter named Leona. In 1178, she had a sun named Vedo. On a morning of the year 1387, Sera, Vedo and Ella, the general, along with a few guards took a trip to Nienna, the Sindarin-elf kingdom. They had two choices of roads; over the mountains of the spirit kingdom or through the dragon kingdom. They decided to go through the dragon kingdom. It was a choice that proved to be fatal. When they entered Domus, they were attacked by the dragons because their swords reflected the light of the sun. Only one guard returned severely wounded. Leona was the only heir to the throne left. After her mother died of grief in 1398, Leona took the throne. Cyntez lived long enough to see her daughter marry a Vampire named Kiril.

- You will hear the rest tomorrow. Said Oron.

The council and Malerk left the room. While everyone was leaving, William approached Eos. When he was beside her, he asked her:

- Are you afraid?
- Of what? Asked Eos.
- Of Malerk and the rest of the story.
- Both of them do not scare me.

William hugged Eos and they went upstairs. When William and Eos passed in front of Malerk's room they were stopped by him. Malerk asked Eos:

- Could I speak with you in private?
- Yes.

Eos kissed William before he went to wait for her in their room. Eos entered the room and Malerk closed the door.

They sat down in front of each other. Malerk started the conversation by saying:

- Do you love him?
- What!?
- Are you sure you love William. I don't want your father's mistake to be made again.
- I wouldn't change him for the world. He's the greatest person I have ever met. I hope that we die at the same time because I don't think that neither of us could live without the other.
- It's a better answer then your father gave me. The real question I wanted to ask you is: Would you agree to be my heir. If ever I would die, you would take my place as Lady of Evil.
- Why me?
- Because you're the daughter I always wanted.
- Don't die before I get an heir.
- I didn't.

Eos left Malerk's room and went to hers. William did not ask what had happened with Malerk. If she would have wanted to talk about it she would have brought up the subject. William and Eos went to bed. The following morning, everyone was up by eight. Everyone returned to the living room, where they would be told the stories of the remaining queens and possibly information about something else. When everyone was seated, Nessima continued:

- I will tell the story of Cleona. In 1409, Leona and Kiril had a daughter called Cleona. From the age of ten, Cleona was taught the art of sword fighting. From the age of twelve, she took part in many competitions of which she mostly won. In 1589, She met Nemesis, a half-Demon and half- Vampire, who became her best-friend. In 1685, Cleona took part in the council that decided the fate of the dragons who were putting many lives in danger. In 1740, Cleona took part of the council that decided to block the humans from the rest of the world. In 1798, Cleona and Nemesis got married. In 1816, they had daughter named Selene. Two years later, they had another daughter named Ashka.

Nessima stopped because Malerk wanted to tell the story of Selene and Lyco. He took a deep breath and started:

- Lyco was made in -4598 with all the other protectors. He chose to appear as a Wood-Elf. The Wood-Elves gladly accepted him as one of them and then named him protector of the Fuin forest. Selene was born in 1816 when Lyco was sixty-four years old. On Selene's eighteenth birthday, Cleona gave the throne to her daughter. The following day, Cleona and Nemesis left the castle and never came back. We know they are not dead but we do not know what happened to them. In 2016, Lyco and Selene met by chance. If Selene had not met Lyco she might have died. They fell in love. When Nature and I realized that he had fallen in love with Selene instead of Clorus like he was supposed to, we did everything to make him change his mind because we knew something was going to go wrong if he did not. But, in 2137, Selene and Lyco were married. What should never had happened came to reality. Everyone knew the future, they had spent so many years trying to prevent was going to pass. In 2150, Eos and Scott were born.

- Were you trying to prevent us from being born? Asked Eos.

- No. We had been trying to get you and your brother another father. It almost worked but Selene did not allow herself to fall for the other person. The night you were born, after finding out that you had powers, Lyco went to see the Oracle. He asked her to be killed because he realized the mistake he had made. But Nature and me decided to refuse his request to get killed. We decided it would be best for him to literally live with his mistake.

- Was he stupid!? He realized he had made a mistake when it was too late to fix it.
- He was not stupid. He must have had a part of the human brain in him. After learning that her husband was gone, Selene locked herself up in her room and Ashka took care of the twins. Two days later, Selene was found dead still holding her sword that had pierced her heart. The same day, Eos disappeared which made us think that maybe Selene had not killed herself. After a year of looking for Eos, we agreed that you were dead.

Jonathan could not take more of that story so he went upstairs. Malerk saw him leave but Malerk figured that he was leaving because he did not like to be reminded that he had failed. Oia then said:

- That is the story of your family. We are leaving tomorrow so if you have anything to ask or tell us do it tonight.

The council and Malerk left the room. Eos approached William who kissed her. Then, Eos said to William:

- I...
- I know. You have to go see Jonathan. Go! I'll see you later.

Eos kissed William and went to Jonathan's room. Eos entered his room without knocking and approached Jonathan who was looking outside. Eos said to him:

- The council is leaving tomorrow.
- Am I suppose to care?
- You should tell, at least Malerk, the truth.
- He will kill me.

- Not for love.
- I'm was a protector. To me love was like betrayal.
- You were able to tell me why wouldn't you be able to tell him.
- I'm afraid of what he might do to me.
- I'll go with you to protect you.
- I have no more excuses.

Jonathan followed Eos to Malerk's room where he knocked on the door. A few seconds later, Malerk opened the door and said:

- Can I help you?
- I have something important to tell you. Said Jonathan.
- Come in.

Jonathan and Eos entered the room and Malerk closed the door behind them. After they had sat down, Malerk asked Jonathan:

- What did you want to tell me?
- I am Jonathan, protector of Selene. Well, I was. I know the missing link to her death.
- Go on.
- I know who killed her and why.
- Who was it?
- It was a man who loved her and who couldn't contain his jealousy. He was mad because the one she had chosen had abandoned her. But because he couldn't stand to see her suffer, he killed her. The killer was her protector; the killer was me.
- You!? Her own protector.

Malerk grabbed Jonathan by the arm. A few seconds later, Jonathan felt his soul and his body connect. Malerk then pulled Jonathan who was trying free himself down the stairs to bring him to the living room. As they went down the hall Malerk called everyone to follow him. Jonathan was begging Malerk to stop while Eos was trying to convince Malerk not to hurt him. When everyone was in the hall, Malerk threw Jonathan on the ground and said:

- Tell them what you told me.
- I killed Selene.

Jonathan's eyes were to the floor. He did not want to see the look on everyone's face. Scott slowly approached Jonathan. Jonathan could only see the feet getting closer and he knew what was coming. Scott kicked Jonathan in the stomach who fell to the floor in pain. Eos stepped between Scott and Jonathan and said to her brother:

- Each time you hurt him, you hurt me.
- I'm going to kill him. Move out of my way or I will be forced to hurt you. Said Scott while taking out his sword.

Eos stared at her brother and did not move. Scott was about to push her out of the way when he got punched in the face by William. Scott fell to the ground and blood filled his mouth. William then said to him:

- No one touches my wife or my child.
- The truth about my mother's killer stays a secret. Said Eos. If anyone asks about it other than the ones who are here or in the presence of others, say nothing or tell them to come and see me if they want to know what happened to my mother. Is that clear?

Everyone agreed to what Eos said. They then all returned to their rooms where they had a good night sleep. Juliet took care of Scott before they went to bed.

CHAPTER 22
A GANG DIVIDED

The next morning, Malerk and the council left the Vampire kingdom and returned to their homes. Juliet spent the morning with Scott in his room while Eos and William spent the morning in their room. Scott was still mad at William for punching him in the face. Essie and Gabriel had gone to the lake. Merrill was practicing spells while Drew painted her. Jonathan and Simon were talking together. Karl was on his balcony. Everyone was calm. Around noon, Eos and William went downstairs to have a drink. They then sat together in the living room. A few minutes later, Scott and Juliet entered the room. When Scott saw William, he said to him:

- How could you?

Eos and William turned in surprise to Scott because they had not heard him enter the room. William then said to Scott:

- What have I done wrong?
- You took her side. Answered Scott.
- Yes, I took my wife's side. In what way is that wrong?

- We were best-friends. We always took the same side even if we did not agree.
- You were willing to kill my wife and my unborn child just to have revenge on Jonathan.
- Our friendship is over.
- That's fine with me.

Scott ran back upstairs to his room and slammed the door while William went outside and sat on the doorstep. Juliet went to see Scott and Eos went to William. When Eos arrived outside, she approached William and sat with him on the first step. For the first few minutes no one said anything. William broke the silence:

- I don't know why he's angry at me. Said William while turning to Eos. I only protected you.
- You did the right thing.
- But why did you protect Jonathan? If you hadn't protected him, none of this would have happened.
- I knew he had killed my mother since the night he captured me. He made my life the way it is. It's because of him that I met you.
- That's why you protected him!? Because by killing your mother and sending you to live with the humans, he gave you your dream life.

William left in fury to his room. On his way he passed Jonathan. Jonathan approached Eos and sat beside her. Jonathan then said to her:

- You told him why you protected me, didn't you?
- Yes. Said Eos.
- I want to tell you something about me and your mother. We kissed once when she and Lyco had just gotten engaged. She pushed me away and said that she couldn't kiss me because

I was a protector and I wasn't suppose to have emotions. She then reminded me that she was marrying Lyco and left. I can't get the thought out of my head that, if I would only have been a simple spirit, I would probably be your father.

- You would have been a great father Jonathan. But then again, Lyco isn't hard to beat.

Jonathan smiled and hugged Eos. Meanwhile in Scott's room, Juliet was trying to calm Scott down. Eventually, Juliet asked Scott:

- Why are you so angry at him?
- Because he didn't agree with me. Said Scott.
- And your going to let that destroy your friendship?
- That's not the only reason.
- What else then?
- You wouldn't understand.

Scott left his room and went to the basement where Merrill and Drew had been all morning. Scott approached Merrill and asked her:

- Can I ask you something?
- What can I do for you? Asked Merrill.
- I need a spell.
- For what?
- For disconnecting soul mates.
- who do you want to disconnect.
- That's none of your business. Find me the spell.

Merrill went to the wooden bookcase behind her and took out a black book called "Dangerous spells". She opened the book at about the quarter and gave it to Scott. All Scott had to do was to read the spell. Scott read the spell then said it out loud:

- Two souls you have connected; Two lives you have protected. They are no longer in need of your protection, so please separate William and Eos so that they may live and die without one another.

The spell worked. It destroyed William's and Eos' connection without them knowing. Scott then closed the book and gave it back to Merrill. He left the room while thanking her. William had just decided to go to the fighting room with his sword in hand. Eos was still outside with Jonathan. Scott went to his room to grab his sword before going to the fighting room. When Scott entered the fighting room, he said to William:

- William, I challenge you to a dual. The first one to beg for his life looses.
- Deal. Said William. Pick the weapon.
- Swords only.
- On guard.

They started to fight against each other. A few minutes later, Merrill entered the room. At that moment, a cut was made on William's arm. Merrill stepped out without being noticed. Merrill ran outside to see if the spell had worked. When Merrill opened the door to go outside she said to Eos:

- Are you hurt?

Eos and Jonathan turned to Merrill in surprise. Jonathan and Eos looked at he each other before Eos answered:

- We're fine.
- William is hurt. On his left arm. He's got a deep scratch.
- That's impossible. I'd be hurt too.

- It would if Scott wouldn't have done a separating spell.
- What!? Where is he?
- In the practice room with William.
- Jonathan, go get all the spirits and whomever you meet on the way and Merrill go get everyone else. Meet me in the practice room.

Jonathan disappeared and Merrill ran back inside. Eos followed her in but went to the fighting room. When she entered, Scott raised his shield around him and William. Jonathan and Simon arrived first. They were soon joined by Drew, Juliet, Karl, Essie, Merrill and Gabriel. Eos then said:

- Gab, Jonathan, Simon, go separate them.

All three guys went through the shield. Well, their spirit did. There bodies were left on the other side. There was no way to separate Scott and William without their bodies so they returned to their bodies. Eos decided to use plan B. She asked Juliet to divert Scott's attention with her power of controlling the elements just long enough for someone else to get in. Juliet made a thunderstorm but Scott did not even blink. Merrill tried a spell but it did not work. The only thing left to do was to wait and see. The fight went on for fifteen minutes. Scott then punched William in the face and pierced William's stomach with his sword. William fell to the ground and Scott's shield went down. The spirits grabbed Scott while Eos checked on William. Scott was then brought to a prison cell while Eos brought William to their room.

William woke up the next morning in his bed. His wound had been wrapped in bandages. Eos was sleeping beside him. Scott had been left in prison for the night. After looking at Eos sleep for a few minutes, William sat on the bed. He felt pain as he did and woke Eos. William turned to her and said:

- Good morning.

Eos sat beside William but said nothing. She looked at William and did not smile. After few seconds, she slapped him in the face and said:

- Don't ever do that again.
- Do what?
- Put your life on the line to prove you're right.
- I'm sorry.
- What happened Will?
- He challenged me.
     -That's not what I meant. What happened for you to be so mad at him and him at you?
- All my life, I have always taken his side even if I did not agree with him.
- Try to fix it please.
- I promise.

CHAPTER 23
AN INVITATION

A month had passed since Scott had tried to kill William. William had not done what Eos had requested of him. At the gate of Tindome, the guards had let a man riding a beige horse enter. The horse ran to the front door of the castle where his rider jumped off. He was carrying a letter for Eos. The man was asked to wait in the hall so there he waited. A servant went to get Eos. Eos arrived shortly after and asked someone to take the man's coat. The man removed his hood to show pointy ears, green eyes and silver hair. He removed his coat to show a normal body. But a few seconds later, he showed his dragon wings. Eos looked at him surprised. The man then said:

- Orek is my name. A messenger for Nature, I am. A message for you, I have.

Orek gave Eos the letter. It was an invitation to a party. Each royal family was invited. They could also bring some friends. Eos thanked Orek who would wait for them outside to show them the way. Eos called everyone and explained where they were going. Scott didn't want to go but was eventually convinced otherwise. Ashka would again watch over the kingdom. Their entire journey would take twenty-three hours if they did not stop. It took them six hours to get to Ennas where they stopped for a while. They then continued their road toward the Nishu mountains; The longest mountain chain stretching from the Hauflin kingdom to the end of the Dwarf kingdom along the blood river. They decided to take a detour through the Pearlas forest instead of going over the mountains. They were stopped by wizards who let them pass as soon as they saw Orek. Two hours and a half later, they arrived at Muerta. It was a small village located at the foot of the mountains. Orek got off his horse and knocked on the wooden gate. A hole in the door opened and showed two little eyes. A voice then asked them:

- Who are you and what do you want?
- Orek is my name. One of Nature's messenger, I am. To stay for the night, we wish. In the morning, get to nature's castle, we will.

The hole closed and he door opened. A little man showed himself. He was four feet at the most. He was a Hauflin. He looked at them and let them in. He showed them to an Inn where they could stay for the night. The beds were almost too small for them but it would have to do. They were woken by Orek at first light. Hauflins gave to them bread and water. They climbed back on their horses and continued their journey. In each village they passed, the elders hid in their homes while the children came to see who they were. Ten hours after leaving Muerta, they arrived at Nature's castle. The castle was made of white marble. The doors were made of wood. Orek approached the two guards at the door and they let them in. Orek led everyone to the throne room. A woman with hair as golden as the sun and eyes as blue as the ocean was sitting on the throne. She was dressed in a dress as green as the leaves of the trees. Orek bowed to her and said:

- Brought you the Vampires, I have.
- Thank you Orek.

Orek left the room. When he was gone, the women turned to them and said:

- I am Nature, Queen of Melda Cemmen. Thank you for coming.
- You're welcome. Said William. May we have a place to rest.
- Of course.

Nature called for Malerk. When he arrived a few minutes later, Nature said to him:

- I have not enough room in my castle for all of them because everyone else as already arrived. Could some of them stay in your castle.
- Why not? The Demons are already there. Said Malerk. I will take Eos, William, Simon, Gabriel, Essie and Jonathan.

Malerk left Nature's castle with the ones he had chosen while the rest were shown to a room in Nature's castle. Malerk's castle was made of black marble. It was as big as Nature's castle. When they entered, they saw the throne at the end of the room. His throne was decorated with Demon heads. Malerk approached it and sat down. He then asked Eos:

- Are you stressed about tomorrow?
- No. Said Eos. Should I be?

- You're meeting the Demon king, the son of the Demon you killed.
- I know. But I'm not afraid of him.
- He might want revenge.
- He can try.

The conversation ended there and everyone went to sleep. The next morning, Eos was the first to wake up. Without making any noise, she went downstairs where she sat on Malerk's throne. She closed her eyes and imagined what it would be like to rule all Evil. A voice then said:

- Is it fun to do my job?

Eos recognized Malerk's voice. She got off the throne immediately. Malerk approached Eos and said:

- You can have it as soon as you have an heir.
- I already have one.
- You'll have to wait until she can take the throne. Sit down.

Eos sat back on the black chair. Malerk explained to her everything concerning his purpose on Melda Cemmen. He then called his "evil" children to come and Meet Eos. Bora, Thor, Chaos, Borealus, Nychta, Dedum, Lorus and Frice appeared in front of them. Bora had chosen to appear as a Vampire. She liked that they could resemble almost every other species. Thor and Dedum had chosen to appear as Demons. Frice had decided to resemble a white oriental dragon but could also take the shape of a human. Chaos had also chosen to appear as a Vampire. Borealus, Nychta and Lorus appeared as dark-angels. They all talked together. Two hours after Malerk had arrived, Eos went back upstairs to get ready for the party. When she arrived back in her room, Eos found William still sleeping. She woke him up. Eos put on black pants with a dark blue shirt and her black coat. William was dressed all in black. When they were ready, Essie, Gabriel, Jonathan, Simon, Eos and William went to Nature's castle with Malerk. When they arrived, Nature was sitting on her throne and the party had already started. When Nature saw them enter, she said:

- Malerk, late as usually.
- How can I be late if I was never invited? Asked Malerk. I only lead them here.
- Then leave my castle.
- It will be my pleasure.

When Malerk had left the castle, the queens and kings of every kingdom introduced themselves. A woman in a white dress started:

- I am Galadria, Queen of all Spirits. I have been ruling the Spirit kingdom since -900. I am 3269 years old in human years. I am the first daughter of Poika.
- I am Louisiam, King of the Wood-Elves. I am the only son of Vanyar who died in 1769. I am 2089 human years old.
- I am Guenevieve, Queen of all witches. I am 584 human years old. I am the first daughter but second child of Sofy.
- I am Eos, Queen of the Vampires. I am 20 human years old. I am the daughter of Selene.
- I am Naurim, King of the Wizards. I am 325 human years old. I am the son of Kiro.
- I am Gallium, King of the Dwarves. I am 264 human years old. I am the son of Gama.
- I am Malta, King of the Hauflins. I am 386 human years old. I am the son of Malir.
- I am Alewan, King of the Sindarin-Elves. I am 3972 years old in human years. I am the first son of Hui.

- I am Daniel, King of the Animal Spirits. I am 2835 human years old. I am the only son of Bruin.
- I am Deimos, King of the Demons. I am the only son of Deith who died in 2004. I am 205 human years old.

As soon as Eos heard the name of Deimos' father, she knew he was going to ask her about his death. After presentations, everyone talked together. After a few hours, Deimos brought up the subject of his father's death. Deimos turned to Eos and said:

- I have heard that Malerk made you his heir. Is it true?
- It is. Said Eos.
- Does he really want a murderer as his heir?
- I wouldn't know if he thinks I'm a murderer like you do, but yes he does want me as his heir.
- You murdered my father.
- To save lives, we must sacrifice others. Beside, he lead himself to his death. He had the sword of Anarore.
- Where did he get that sword? Asked Guenevieve.
- My family has had it for as long as I can remember. Said Deimos.
- Can I have it back?
- We lost it when my father died.
- Anarore has it. Said Eos.
- Did you give it to her?
- No. Merrill, daughter of Isilme II, son of Isilme I, first wizard, gave it to her.
- Merrill died a few years ago.
- No she did not.

Eos went to the other side of the room to go get Merrill. She then brought her to Guenevieve. No one believed Eos that Merrill was the granddaughter of the first wizard. Isilme II had married a witch called Raaka and Merrill was their only child. After a few seconds, Guenevieve said:

- She is a Vampire not a witch.

Merrill moved her hands in front of her as if she was playing with a globe. A few seconds later, a black rose appeared in Guenevieve's hand. Guenevieve looked at the flower and then said:

- I better not catch any of your half blood Vampires with anything that belongs to my people again or...
- Or what? Asked Eos.
- Or they won't see another day.

Eos went hyper speed, grabbed Guenevieve by the throat and pushed her in the wall behind them. Everyone turned to see what was going on. Eos did not even noticed that she had the attention of everyone. Some one then asked Eos to let go of the witch but she did not listen. Eos then said to Guenevieve:

- If you set one foot in my kingdom, I will kill you.

Guenevieve could barely breathe because of Eos' strong hold. The elfin-dragons soon came to separate them. One guard grabbed Eos' hand and made her let go of her grip. They led Eos to the fighting room where Nature joined them. The doors were closed. William went to the doors that lead to the fighting room to help Eos, but the door locked when he touched it. The guards pushed Eos on her knees in front of Nature. Nature looked at Eos and said:

- How dare you strangle a member of the crown?
- She crossed the line. Said Eos.

- That is not a reason to strangle her. You were killing her.
- You can survive a minute when your being strangled. I would have stopped before that.
- You strangled her. Whether you were going to kill her or not doesn't matter.
- I have a feeling you don't like me.
- Let's just say you're not my favourite granddaughter.
- I'm not fond of you either.
- Do not talk back at me.
- Why?
- No one talks back at me.
- Yes, me.

Two guards grabbed Eos' shoulders and placed her face on the cold floor and held it there. Nature then approached Eos and said to her:

- Even when you become Lady of Evil, you will always have to listen to me.
- You wish. Said Eos.

Meanwhile in the hall, Malerk had just arrived. He knew Eos was in trouble. When he saw William still trying to force the door, he knew where she was. Malerk stopped William and murmured a few words which unlocked the door. Just when an elfin-dragon was about to hit Eos for saying what she had said, Malerk entered the room. When he saw Eos on the floor, he told the guards to get off her. Nature's guards listened to Malerk and got off Eos. Malerk then approached Nature so that their faces were an inch away and said to her:

- Stay away from my heir or I will kill yours.
- My heir is Lydia, our first daughter. Said Nature. You will kill your own daughter.
- If you hurt her again in any way, I will kill Lydia.

Malerk turned around and walked to Eos. He placed his hand on her back and lead her out of the room. Malerk and Eos returned to his castle by themselves because he had insisted. When they arrived at his castle, Malerk turned to Eos and asked her:

- How did you get on the floor in front of Nature?
- Deimos brought up the subject of his father's death and mentioned Anarore's sword. Guenevieve then asked where the sword was and I told her that Merrill had given it back to Anarore. She then said that she never wanted to see any of my half-bloods with anything that belongs to her species or she would kill them. I then told her that if she stepped one foot in my kingdom she would die. I was then brought in a room and was forced to bow to Nature and say that I would always do what she asked of me which I didn't do. Then you arrived.
- Why did Nature bring you to another room?
- I may have cut Guenevieve's supply of air for a while.
- I should be angry at you but I can't. You are like a daughter to me. You are the daughter I always wanted. Try not to snap again.
- I will dad.

Malerk hugged Eos and gave her a kiss on the forehead. Malerk then removed one of the two necklaces he had around his neck. It was a five sided long dark-blue crystal suspended by a white gold chain. After looking at it, Eos asked:

- What is it?
- It is a crystal from Mount Merelyn. It is a sign of power. It will replace your crest of power since you are no longer allowed to wear it because you are my heir.
- Thank you. Said Eos while exchanging her crest of power for the blue crystal.

Essie, Gabriel, Simon, Jonathan and William then entered the castle. Nature had thrown them out of her castle. They all bowed to Malerk except for Eos and they went to their rooms. Meanwhile in Nature's castle, everyone was getting some down time. Scott and Juliet were watching the sunset together. The light was reflecting on the clouds making them turn blue, red, purple and orange. Juliet said to Scott:

- Don't you just love the colors.
- Yes, they're nice.

While Juliet still had her eyes on the sunset, Scott got on one knee and took out a gold ¼ carat diamond ring. While Juliet turned toward him, Scott asked her:

- Will you marry me?
- Yes.

Juliet hugged Scott before they kissed under the fading sun and the darkening sky.

CHAPTER 24
TWO WEDDINGS AND A FIGHT

The next morning, everyone who was staying at Malerk's castle packed their bags and got ready to return home. When everyone was ready to leave, a knock was heard on the door. William opened the door and when he saw who it was, he said:

- What do you want, Scott?
- Is my sister there?
- Yes.

Scott tried to come in followed by Juliet. But when he tried to pass the front door a spell stopped him. Malerk protected his castle from his enemies with a spell that did not let anyone who wasn't wanted inside enter. Malerk looked at Scott trying to enter and said to him:

- You can't enter because no one wants you here.
- Malerk! Said Scott. I want to speak with my sister.
- I'll go see if she wants to speak to you. Said William.

William went upstairs where Eos was still making sure she had everything. He met her in the middle of the stairs to the third floor. William stopped her and told her that her brother was there. Eos continued her way down followed by William. She approached Scott who was still standing outside and asked him:

\- What do you want?
\- I wanted to tell you something?
\- Go ahead.
\- Juliet and me are fiancé.
\- Congratulation.
\- We would like to get married here. So we wanted to know if we could stay a few more days and if you wanted to be the maid of honour.
\- Is William you best man?
\- Is he my best-friend?
\- You can stay. But the rest of us are going back home. Have a nice wedding.
\- But Eos, you're my sister. You can't miss my wedding.
\- I can do what I want. I want to go home with or without you.

Eos walked away from the door and William closed it. But before the door was completely shut, Scott said to Eos:

\- Fine. Go home with your jerk.

William reopened the door just in time. Eos grabbed Scot by the collar and slammed him on the wall beside the door. Juliet was still stuck outside. William closed the door in Juliet's face while looking at her. He then stood beside Eos. William then asked Scott:

\- Who's the jerk now?

- If you kill me, Nature will kill you.
- First of all, why would Nature kill me for killing you? Said Eos. Secondly, why would I kill you? You're my brother.
- Then what do you want?
- I want you to apologize to William. After that I want you to forgive him for protecting me when you wanted to kill me and Jonathan. Finally, I want you two to become friends again.
- Our friendship is over. Deal with it. And I will not apologize.
- Are you sure?
- If I ever change my mind, I'll let you know.
- Get out and don't come home until you're ready to make peace with William.
- You can't be serious.
- If I ever change my mind, I'll let you know.

Eos let go of Scott and he left Malerk's castle.
Yesterday, Malerk had asked Valir to come to his room because he wanted to talk to him. Valir went to his king as he had requested. Malerk had then said to him:

- Valir, over the years you have served me well and not I must think of the future. I will soon no longer need you for my life will be complete.
- Will not leave you even if you do not need me.
- I want you to serve my heir from now on. I was planning to give your services to her. She will need help more than me.
- As you wish.

Malerk had thanked Valir and he had left the room.

A few minutes after Scoot had left, a Dark-Angel entered the room. He looked like a normal person except he had black wings and black horns coming out of his forehead. Malerk looked at Eos and said:

- This is Valir. He will lead you back to your home and will be eternally at your service.
- I do not need another protector. I have enough of William, Simon, Jonathan and Gabriel.
- Please take him.

Eos accepted Valir. Valir then went to get everyone who was at Nature's castle except for Scott and Juliet and brought them in front of Malerk's castle. As they left to return to Tindome, Juliet and Scott saw them leave. Juliet turned to Scott and asked him:

- Why did they leave without us?
- I wanted us to get married here but they had to return home.
- Will we see them soon?
- We will see them as soon as I can be friends with William again.

Scott went inside followed by Juliet who wanted to know more about the situation.

The next day, Eos and everyone who was with her arrived at the Vampire's castle. Scott and Juliet were getting ready to get married. Every king and queen had, except for Eos and William, extended their stay to see the wedding. Isilme would be the one who would marry them. When everyone was in place in the hall, Isilme said:

- We are gathered here today to join Scott Anoura and Juliet Hyunda in holy matrimony. I would like each of them to share their vows.
- Juliet. Said Scott. What a beautiful name. But a beautiful

name goes with a beautiful woman. Your eyes are like the sea. It is easy to get lost in them. Your smile is as radiant as the sun. Your personality is the perfect one. These and more are the reasons why I want you by my side for the rest of my life.

- I want to thank you for being my light when it was dark. Said Juliet. You make me feel like I'm the only one in the world. I hope our love grows until the end of time.

- Do you, Scott, take Juliet to be your lawful wedded wife, to have and to hold, from this day forward, for better, for worse, for richer, for poorer, in sickness and in health, to love and cherish 'till death to you part? Asked Isilme.

- I do. Said Scott while placing a gold band on Juliet's finger.

- Do you, Juliet, take Scott to be your lawful wedded husband, to have and to hold, from this day forward, for better, for worse, for richer, for poorer, in sickness and in health, to love and cherish 'till death to you part?

- I do. Said Juliet while placing a gold band on Scott's finger.

- I now pronounce you husband and wife. You may kiss.

Scott and Juliet kissed while everyone applauded. Champagne was distributed to everyone who made a toast to the newlyweds. After twelve hours of partying, it was now two o'clock in the morning so everyone went to bed. The following morning, a big breakfast was served to the guests. After breakfast, Orek approached Juliet and Scott and asked them:

- Follow me, could you?
- Lead the way. Said Scott.

Orek lead Scott and Juliet under the stairs. Orek pushed open a door that Juliet and Scott had not seen because it blended in with the wall. Orek entered and they followed. They went down a tight staircase until they reached a wooden door. When they entered, they saw a man sitting on a chair in front of empty prison cells. His skin was as dark as the blackest blue and he had pointy ears. He had his head lowered and his eyes closed. Orek said to the man:

- Stephen! Sleeping on the job, are you?
- I'm not sleeping. I was meditating.

Stephen opened his eyes and looked at Orek. His eyes were completely black. There was no white. Stephen got on his feet and showed something Scott and Juliet had not seen when they had entered. Stephen had a pair of angel wings and a pair of dragon wings that matched his body. Stephen then asked Orek:

- For you, what can I do?
- Do not mock me. Said Orek.
- I wasn't mocking you. I was just asking you a question. What can I do for you?
- To speak to your brother, I wish.

Stephen turned around and went to get his twin brother who was in another room. Stephen came back a few minutes later with Mickeal, his twin. The only difference between the twins was that Mickeal was white and had light blue eyes. Mickeal asked Orek:

- What can I do for you?
- Something for Nature, you can do.
- What is it?
- Take help from Juliet and Scott, you can.
- Never. Said Stephen.
- For what? Asked Mickeal.
- For capturing an offender of the law. Said Orek.
- Who is it? We will judge ourselves.

- To capture Eos, you need.
- What!? Said Juliet, Scott, Mickeal and Stephen together.
- You would convince her to surrender to Nature.
- You're right Orek. Said Stephen. Juliet and Scott are perfect for this.
- I'm not doing it. Said Scott. I'm not betraying my sister.
- It's a direct order from Nature, Scott. It's never a choice when it comes from her.
- I'll see what I can do.

Scott and Juliet left the room followed by Orek. Orek returned to Nature to tell her that they had accepted while Juliet and Scott went upstairs to their bedroom. When they had arrived upstairs, Juliet turned to Scott and said:

- Are you really going to do it?
- I don't know.

Back downstairs, in the jail, Mickeal turned to Stephen and asked him:

- Should we warn Eos?
- Nature would hate us but Malerk would like us. I say yes.
- You go, I'll cover for you.
- You would tell a lie to Nature!? I don't think you're capable of such a thing. If anyone stays, it has to be me. But I don't want to stay so we're both going.
- Fine.

The next morning, just after Juliet and Scott had left Nature's castle, Mickeal and Stephen flew off to go warn Eos. The twins arrived after fifteen hours of flight. Scott and Juliet were at least nine hours behind. When Mickeal and Stephen arrived at the Vampire castle's front door, they were stopped by the guards. The guard on their right asked them:

- Who are you?
- I am Mickeal and this is Stephen.
- Why do you wish to enter this castle?
- We have an urgent message for Eos.
- Wait here.

The guard went inside while the other watched over the twins. He found Eos and told her that Stephen and Mickeal were here to give her message. The guard returned a few minutes later and let the twins see Eos who was waiting for them in the hall. Stephen and Mickeal entered the castle and the door was closed behind them. The twins introduced themselves:

- We are Mickeal and Stephen, keepers of Nature's prison.
- If you are here who keeps the prison.
- Oh no, we left the prison empty. Said Mickeal.
- Don't worry someone is replacing us. Said Stephen
- Why are you here? Asked Eos.
- We came to warn you that your brother as agreed to do something for Nature. He will come here and pretend to ask for forgiveness. He will then convince you to give yourself up to Nature.
- Thank you for the message. Would you mind staying a bit longer.
- Why not?

Ten hours later, Scott arrived in Tindome. When they arrived at the castle's door, they were expecting to have to explain to the guards that they wanted to apologize to Eos, but the guards let them in. When Scott and Juliet entered the castle, they saw William and Eos sitting on their thrones with their crowns on their head. Mickeal and Stephen were standing beside them. When Scott saw the twins, he asked them:

- What are you doing here?
- I could ask you the same question. Said Eos.
- I came to apologize.
- You came to pretend to apologize.
- I didn't take the job.
- I find that hard to believe.
- Why?
- Because you were willing to kill me when I protected Jonathan.
- Get out. Said William.
- What!? Said Scott.
- Get out of this castle. You are banished from it.
- Eos, please.
- Go live with your beloved grandmother. I'm sure she will be happy to hear that you are willing to kill your sister for her.
- I'm sorry.

Scott and Juliet left the castle and returned to Nature's castle with every intention of making Nature punish the twins for what they had done. Stephen and Mickeal were given friendship rings which permitted them to enter the Vampire kingdom as they pleased. Mickeal and Stephen returned home and would again arrive earlier then Scott and Juliet.

(HAPTER 25
PLAN #2

Almost two days later, Scott and Juliet returned to Nature's castle. They were let in by the elfin-dragons at the front door. Orek was in the hall lighting the torches. When he saw the newlyweds, he asked them:

- What are you doing here? Be completed, the plan couldn't possibly.
- The plan failed. Said Scott.
- What went wrong?
- The twins got there before us and warned Eos.
- That's impossible. I spoke to them yesterday.
- We know what we saw.
- Please wait here.

Orek left them in the hall and went to the dining room where Nature was having breakfast. Orek bowed to Nature and said:

- News from Scott and Juliet, I have.
- Did Eos fall for it?

- To say that someone warned Eos before they arrived at the castle, I'm sorry.
- Who?
- It was the twins, they say.
- Bring Mickeal and Stephen to the throne room.
- As you wish.

Orek left and went to get the twins out of bed. Nature left the dining room and went to sit on her throne. When Orek entered the twins' room he was surprised to see that the twins were enjoying each others company. Something had changed. Orek interrupted them by saying:

- To see you, your queen demands.
- The way, lead. Said Stephen.
- Stop making fun of me and follow me.
- You forgot one important word.

Stephen had never liked Orek. Teasing Orek was one of his favourite pass-time. Orek was tired of it. He tried to jump on Stephen but he flew out of the way. Orek tried again but failed so gave up. Orek then said:

- Follow me please.
- You shouldn't do that. Said Mickeal to Stephen.
- I'm sorry. I didn't mean to hurt your feelings. Said Stephen with a sarcastic voice.

Orek paid no attention to Stephen and kept on leading the way to Nature. When they arrived in front of Nature's throne, they all bowed to her. Scott and Juliet were also there. Nature turned to the twins and asked:

- Did you leave your duty to warn Eos about Scott?

- Why would we betray you mother after serving you for more then three thousand years? Asked Stephen.
- If you did not betray me, why did Scott say that you were there when they arrived at the castle?
- I do not know. Maybe he is afraid to tell you why he truly failed.
- I wouldn't dare lie to Nature. Said Scott.
- Someone is lying and I want to know who. Said Nature.
- Why would I lie to you. Said Stephen. You are my maker, my mother. You gave me a purpose. I could not bare to betray you.
- Scott, are you lying to me?
- Never. Said Scott. Stephen is lying to you.
- Enough. Stephen and Mickeal, get to your job. Scott and Juliet, my castle is your home.

The twins went to the jail. Juliet and Scott went upstairs to their room. When they had left the room, Orek turned to Nature and asked her:

- What is your next plan?
- We wait four months. Said Nature.
- Wait for what?
- If we can't kill Malerk's heir, we will kill her child.
- Why?
- That way she will be forced to stay on the Vampire throne and will not be able to replace Malerk.
- Isn't that risky?
- Why would it be risky?
- Get Malerk angry, you might.
- He hadn't gotten angry in a very long time.
- Felt that way about someone before, he as not.
- Are you saying that if we fought each other that he would win?
- Of course not. You should be careful, I am saying.

- Don't worry. I will never show him my back.

Orek bowed to Nature and left her alone. Meanwhile, Mickeal turned to Stephen and asked him:

- How did you do that?
- Do what? Asked Stephen.
- Lie to nature without her knowing.
- I'm the evil one. It's in my blood.
- I was worried it wouldn't work.
- The trick is to be prepared and play on the opponent's weakness.
- My conscience couldn't have taken it.
- I don't have one.
- Of course. How could I forget.

Stephen and Mickeal continued their way down the stairs. When they entered the jail, they saw two people that looked exactly like them. Stephen knew about them because he had made the spell to create them. They were clones meant to disappear as soon as they saw the original. After a few seconds, Mickeal turned to Stephen and asked him:

- Is that who was replacing us while we were gone?
- Yes.
- How do we make them disappear?
- Stephen. Said Stephen to his clone.

The clone turned around and as soon as their eyes met the clone disappeared. Mickeal did the same with his. After the fakes were gone, Mickeal and Stephen did their job.

CHAPTER 26
FORGIVENESS

The following week, Eos and William decided to go read more on the royal Vampire family. Jonathan joined them. Eos mostly wanted to know more about her mother. Eos took the book on Selene while William sat down with the book on Klashka. When Eos opened the book, a piece of paper fell out and landed on the floor. Eos picked it up and read it. It was written:

Dear readers,

I writing to you this letter today, the 27th of January 2150, because I suspect that my protector is having feelings. Lately, he has seemed to be hating Lyco. My children will be born soon. I only hope they still have a father. I would like the council to proceed to a re-evaluation of Jonathan. If he does have feelings, I would like him removed from my side and replaced immediately.

Thank you in advance,

Selene Anoura

After reading the letter, Eos placed the book on the table beside her. But as she was about to go see William and Jonathan to show them the letter, she saw another piece of paper sticking out of the book. She read it and what was written on it explained why she had not sent the first letter. It was written:

Dear Queen Selene Anoura,

26ᵗʰ January 2150

I am writing to you on this day to tell you something that you were never suppose to know. The council and Nature don't know that I have sent you this letter so do not mention it. When you were born, like every heir to a throne, your future was predicted by the Oracle and Fate. We know what will happen to Lyco and your children but we cannot tell you. We tried for years to prevent the future by trying to convince Lyco to marry Clorus but he loves you too much. Jonathan was chosen as your protector because we thought that you would fall in love with him and marry him instead of Lyco. But it did not work. Jonathan loves you but you pushed him away because protectors are not suppose to have feelings. We have failed. On the 30ᵗʰ of January 2150, what we have been trying to prevent will happen. Hopefully some of it won't come to pass.

Hope we see each other again.

Malerk, Lord of all Evil

After reading the letter from Malerk, Eos went to see William and Jonathan. She showed them the letter from Selene first. After reading the letter, William said:

- She knew that Jonathan had feelings for her.
- Why didn't she send the letter? Asked Jonathan to Eos. This was three days before you were born and six before she died.

Eos handed the guys the second letter that she had found in the book. They read it and Jonathan read it again to make sure that he had read what was written. Eos then said:

- My father knew that he was suppose to be with Clorus and Jonathan knew that he was supposed to be with Selene. But Lyco met Selene when he wasn't suppose to and so she fell in love with him instead of Jonathan. She didn't send the letter because she no longer wanted to get rid of Jonathan.
- Jonathan, did you know you were destined to be with Selene? Asked William.
- I did. Said Jonathan. But Lyco destroyed the future that was supposed to come to the present.
- That's why Malerk said "we had been trying to get you and your brother another father" and Jonathan said "if I would have been a simple spirit, I would have been your father."

William, Eos and Jonathan continued to talk about it for the rest of the day. Three weeks passed before anything out of the ordinary happened. One day, Karl left the castle early in the morning and didn't come back until late at night. No one paid attention to it because Eos and William sometime did it as well. But Karl did the same thing for an entire month so everyone started to wonder what he was doing when he left the castle. The next day, Karl came back at eleven in the morning but he was not alone. He was accompanied by a person wearing a dark-red hooded cape. Karl and his friend made their way to his room. On the way, they were stopped by Valir who asked:

- Who is your hooded friend?
- It's none of you business. Said Karl.
- To protect Eos I must know the identity of everyone who enters this castle.
- Fine. Her name is Lecksha. She is an old friend.

Valir did not ask more questions and continued his walk through the castle. Valir did not know that Lecksha had been banished so he did not tell Eos that she was in the castle. Two weeks later, Lecksha returned to the castle. But this time, she was not so lucky. William saw them on the second floor corridor and stopped them. He then asked Karl:

- Who's your hooded friend?
- It's of no importance to you.

Karl walked beside William but William pulled out his arm and hit the wall beside Karl so that his arm stopped Karl. William turned to Karl and said to him:

- I am the king. If I ask something you answer me. Who's your friend?
- I'll tell him Karl. Said Lecksha while removing her hood. It's me, your cousin Lecksha.

William grabbed Lecksha by the arm and brought her to the hall. After stumbling down the stairs, Lecksha was thrown in front of Eos who was talking to the spirits. Eos and the spirits looked at Lecksha and at William. William then said to Eos:

- Look what I found with Karl.

Eos looked at Lecksha and at Karl. She was not happy that both of them had disobeyed her. Eos looked at Karl who was now standing between her and Lecksha and said to him:

- I had banished her for the murder of Marty.
- I know. I was the one who convinced her to come.
- Why?
- I love her.
- I thought you loved Essie. We all have the memories that prove you were in love with Essie especially Gab.
- I realised lately that I forced myself to love Essie and that I loved someone else.

After Karl was done talking, Eos passed him and approached Lecksha. She helped her get on her feet before saying to both of them:

- If you can keep weapons away from each other at all time except in times of war, I will let you two be together in this castle.
- We promise.
- Lecksha, It might not be your fault if Marty is dead. I may just have to accept your apologies for killing him.
- Thank you Eos. Said Lecksha. You won't regret this.
- I hope not.

Lecksha jumped in Karl's arms because she was so happy. For the next few weeks they were always seen together. A month after, Lecksha had been pardoned, Scott and Juliet returned hoping for the same thing. They sneaked in by a window in the ballroom but that failed. They were seen by Valir who unfortunately for them, unlike Lecksha, knew what had happened. Valir asked them:

- Where are you going?
- I'm going to see my sister.
- No you're not. You're going to a prison cell until your sister and her husband return from the lake.

Valir grabbed Juliet and Scott and brought them downstairs to the prison where he locked them up. A few hours later, William and Eos returned at the castle. When he saw them, Valir told them that Scott was back and lead them to him. When Scott saw Eos and William, he said to them:

- Is that how you threat all your guests?
- No. It's how I threat the unwanted one. Why are you here?
- I came to ask for forgiveness.
- Are you serious this time?
- Yes.
- I will forgive you on one condition.
- Name it.
- Never talk or see Nature or any of her elfin-dragon unless it is a matter of life and death.
- Cross my heart, hope to die.

William let Juliet and Scott out of prison. William and Scott became friends again but could never be best-friends. William could not forget that Scott had wanted to kill him.

EPILOGUE
THE NEXT GENERATION

Outside the snow was being blown in all directions by the wind. The cold made the air dry. The sun was rising. It was trying to warm the February air. As the sun came over the ridge, on the 27th of February 2178, a princess called Clarwena was born of Queen Eos and King William. She had hazelnut coloured eyes and brown hair. She looked a lot like her father. Her mother seemed to only have given her far sight. Clarwena was gifted with the following powers: super physical prowess and strength, telekinesis, future seeing, healing, control over the elements and mind travel. She was the most powerful Vampire in 12178 years or since the beginning of Melda Cemmen. The following day, Malerk came to visit his granddaughter and her new great- granddaughter. Clarwena was given a crest of power. Nature did not come because she believed that Clarwena would be exactly like Eos. While Clarwena was sleeping, everyone sat down together and they had a big meal to celebrate the end of a generation and the beginning of another.

PART 2: AMBASSADOR ALEXANDRE

CHAPTER 1
A NEW YET OLD FACE

A week after Clarwena's birth, as was the tradition, the council sent a protector for the heir to the Vampire throne. The spirit arrived that morning and was greeted by Jonathan and Simon. After finding out who he was, Simon went to see Eos in Clarwena's room to tell her that her daughter's protector was here. After putting Clarwena to sleep, Eos came downstairs. When she arrived, she saw the spirit dressed in a black hooded cape. Eos approached him carefully with the memories of the Blackhoods in her head. When Simon saw Eos approaching, he said to the spirit:

- This is Queen Eos.

The spirit turned around to look at Eos while saying:

- I am Marty.

Eos froze. Her best-friend had been saved by Nature and had chosen to become a protector. After nine months or 7 ½ human years of training, he had been sent to protect Clarwena. Eos jumped in Marty's arms and said:

- I missed you.
- Me too. Said Marty. That's why I'm your daughter's protector.
- Thank you for your powers.

Meanwhile, at Nature's castle, Nature hit the arm of her throne on which she was sitting with her fist. Orek who was standing beside her asked:

- What is the matter my Lady?
- I cannot complete plan B.
- Why not?
- My daughter told me what would happen in the future. A Vampire queen born in the 22nd century after the agreement will save Melda Cemmen from the Humans. She did not tell me which one it was so I cannot kill Eos or Clarwena.
- What shall you do now?
- I will make Eos suffer. I will raise Clarwena as my own daughter. Bring me Mickeal and Stephen.

Orek left the room and came back a few minutes later with the twins; the keepers of Nature's prison. When they had arrived with Orek, Nature asked them a question:

- Would you do something for me?
- Of course. Said Mickeal.
- I want you to kidnap Eos' daughter.
- What!?
- Do you have a problem with the mission?
- No my Lady. Said Stephen.
- Then leave now.
- As you wish.

Stephen and Mickeal left Nature's castle and started their journey to Tindome. They decided to walk because they were not in a hurry. After walking for half an hour, Mickeal asked Stephen:

- Why didn't you try to get out of this mission?
- I'm the evil one. Making people suffer is suppose to be my speciality. I couldn't disagree with her.
- Are we really going to kidnap Clarwena?
- Unless you think of a plan before we get there, we have no other choice.

The next morning, Stephen and Mickeal arrived at the Vampire's castle and were greeted by William. They bowed to the king. William then said to them:

- Welcome back friends.
- Thank you your majesty. Said Stephen.
- What brings you here?
- We came to see the new princess.
- She is sleeping for now but you may go as you please until you may see her.
- Thank you very much.

After William had left the room, Mickeal pulled his brother in a corner. After making sure that no one was near, Mickeal said:

- I can't do this. I can't betray them.
- Leave it to me. I'll take care of the job while you act normally.

Mickeal agreed with his brother and went to the living room where he found Jonathan, Valir and Simon talking together. It did not take long for Mickeal to join the conversation. Meanwhile, Stephen was making his way to Clarwena's room. When he arrived in the corridor something complicated his mission. Marty was keeping the way. Stephen approached Marty with his wings hidden. When he had arrived beside him, he asked:

- Can I see her?
- No, I'm sorry.
- I'm sorry too.
- For what?
- For knocking you out.
- You never hit me before and you can't hurt me because I'm a spirit.
- That's where you're wrong.

Stephen punched Marty in the face while showing his wings to him. Before Marty went unconscious, he saw Stephen's two pairs of wings and said to him:

- You're one of Nature's soldiers.
- Yes.

Marty was out of it. Nature's soldiers were the only non-spirit beings who could kill spirits. Stephen stepped over Marty and entered Clarwena's room. He gently took the princess in his arms to not wake her and left the room. He then sent a mind message to his brother to tell him that the mission had been accomplished. Mickeal and Stephen joined outside and left the Vampire's castle.

CHAPTER 2
A FIGHT OF POWERS

William was going to the library when he spotted Marty on the floor. He went to him and woke him up. When Marty was on his feet, William asked him:

- What happened?
- I was knocked out by Stephen.
- Why?
- Well... hum...
- Never mind.

William had just noticed that there was something different bout Clarwena's room. He entered slowly and saw what he was hoping not to see. William ran out of Clarwena's room and went to his where Eos was sleeping. William woke up Eos and told her:

- Something terrible has happened.
- What is it?
- Stephen has stolen our daughter.
- What!? Get the gang ready. Grandma will pay.

When they heard the news, no one took the time to pack. They only took their weapons and left. Drew, Essie, Merrill, Gabriel, Karl, Lecksha, Scott, Juliet, Valir, Simon, Jonathan, Marty and Ashka gladly joined William and Eos. The trip that usually took twenty hours took eighteen hours instead. When they arrived at Nature's castle, William entered by himself to make sure it wasn't a trap. William returned a few seconds later because he had been told by a guard that Nature was at the council's castle. They continued their road a few more kilometres to the council's castle. They entered the castle and went to the meeting room where the council discussed important subjects. As they entered the room they placed themselves around the room. They entered in the following order: Valir and Jonathan who went at the end of the room, Lecksha and Karl, Drew and Merrill, Scott and Juliet, Essie and Gabriel, William and Eos, and Simon and Marty who closed the door behind them. Nature was sitting at the end of the council's table and the council was in its normal order. Kano was at Nature's right, Poika was beside him followed by, Isilme, Nessima, Leo, Oia, Oron, Mardess, Hui and Iire on the left of Nature. Nature asked the intruders:

- How may I help you?
- I want my daughter back. Said Eos.
- I never touched her.
- Stephen kidnapped her.
- Did he really do such a terrible thing?
- Yes.
- I thought it was bizarre for him to have a baby in his arms.
- Give her back to me.
- I busy right now. I don't have time to go get your daughter.
- I'll make you time.
- I would stop talking back at me if I were you because that's what made you lose your daughter in the first place.
- Go get my daughter.

- I'm busy.

Eos approached the table and hit it with her fist. The earth trembled beneath them. Malerk had lent Eos her powers for a short period of time so that she may retrieve her daughter. The council looked at Eos in fear while Nature tried to hide hers. Eos knew she was afraid. She could sense it. Nature said to Eos:

- Anger never solves anything.
- Neither does ignorance. Said Eos. You can ignore me but I won't leave until I have my daughter. Call Stephen in here.
- Kano go get Mickeal and Stephen and tell them to bring the princess.

Kano bowed to Nature and left the room. Fifteen minutes later, Kano returned with the twins. Stephen had Clarwena in his arms. When Eos saw Stephen, she said to him:

- Give me back my daughter.
- You'll have to fight me to get her back. Said Nature.
- Name your terms.
- The first to be out of strength looses.
- Let's do it.
- Eos, you can't be serious. Said Simon. You're fighting Nature.
- I know. Don't worry I'll be fine.

Everyone made their way down the hall to the fighting room. Nature and Eos placed themselves fifteen feet away from each other. Stephen, Mickeal and the council placed themselves on the left of Nature and everyone else on her right. Kano explained the rules of the dual and gave them permission to start. Nature started by trying to drown Eos with a huge wave but Eos removed all the humidity from the air which made it evaporate. Nature then sent the powers of the East, West and South wind towards Eos. Eos opened her hand, palm facing upwards, and blew air towards Nature. All the gasses in the winds that were coming towards Eos froze and fell as ice on the ground where it shattered. Eos then sent a wave of lava towards Nature. Nature sent water towards the lava which made it cool down and solidify. Vines then came out of the ground around Eos and tightened around her. To not get strangled, Eos killed the plant. Eos then shot fire at Nature while she shot water at Eos. Eos used all her energy in the fire. Eventually the fire made the water evaporate and burned Nature. Nature collapsed but was still conscious. Eos approached Nature and said:

- Malerk has the power to destroy whatever you can create. You were doomed to loose against me.

Stephen gave Eos her daughter back and also gave her the ring she had given to him to permit him to enter the Vampire castle. Eos took Clarwena in her arms a few minutes then gave her to Marty before she collapsed. Malerk had taken back his powers. To return home, Eos and William rode on the same horse because she was too weak to ride by herself. When they arrived at the blood river, they stopped to give blood to Clarwena and Eos. William gave a glass of blood to Eos and said to her:

- You have to drink to get your energy back.
- How can I get some energy that I never possessed?
- What do you mean?
- I had Malerk's powers to defeat Nature. I spent more energy that my body possessed.
- I know. Please drink the blood.

Eos drank the blood for William. After being at the blood river for half an hour, they continued their trip to get back to Tindome. When they arrived at the castle, William brought Eos to their room and Marty brought Clarwena to hers. After Eos was asleep, William went downstairs and told the guards they were to never let Mickeal or Stephen enter the Vampire castle again. William then went back to his bedroom where he fell asleep beside Eos. The next morning, William woke up before Eos and went in the hall. He was going to do something he had not done for a long time. Eos woke up an hour later because she heard the sound of a cello. Eos went to the hall and found William playing the instrument. When William had finished the song, Eos applauded. William turned around and said to Eos:

- I'll put it away.
- You don't have to.
- That's not what my father would have said. I've been playing the cello since I was ten. Of course, my father didn't allow me to play. But I use to go to my aunt's house to play. She taught me how to play.
- Could you teach me?
- Why not?

William taught Eos how to play the cello. Every morning, they would practice together.

CHAPTER 3
UNCONTROLLED

A year had passed since the birth of Clarwena. For her birthday, her parents had given her a ball and a doll. She preferred the ball and it wasn't long before William and Eos were throwing the ball between them and Clarwena. Clarwena could still not control her powers. Eos would eventually have to help her with that problem. Meanwhile, upstairs, Essie and Gabriel were dancing together. As they were dancing, Gabriel said to Essie:

- I love you.
- I love you too. Said Essie.
- Would you be my wife?
- Yes!

Gabriel kissed Essie passionately and then placed a three diamond gold ring on her finger. They continued to dance for the rest of the day. Essie had a big smile on her face that she could not wipe off. Downstairs, in the basement, Drew was putting the finishing touches on an eagle he had painted. Merrill who was standing beside him was trying to make the eagle fly out of the canvas. For some reason, Merrill could not make the eagle move. She was concentrating more on Drew then on the eagle. When Drew was done he put his painting brush away and placed his arm around Merrill. Drew then said:

- Maybe this will help you.

Drew pulled out an engagement ring and gave it to Merrill. She jumped in his arms and they kissed. At supper, Gabriel, Essie, Merrill and Drew announced their engagement. Eventually, everyone went to bed. Because of what had happened to Clarwena a few months ago, Marty stayed in front of her bedroom door. A few hours after the sun had set, Marty heard a glass break in Clarwena's room. He opened the door to see what was going on inside and froze. Everything in Clarwena's room was turning in a tornado surrounded by thunder and lightning. Marty ran down the hall to Eos and William's room to tell them what was going on. When they were awake, William asked Marty:

- What's wrong?
- Your daughter is using all her powers at once.

Eos and William got out of bed and followed Marty to Clarwena's room. Gabriel, Simon and Jonathan joined them a few seconds later because they had felt the enormous energy coming from Clarwena's room. As they glanced at what was happening in the princess' room, they could not believe it. If they wanted to speak to each other, they had to almost scream. Eos turned to the others and asked them:

- Does anyone have any ideas?
- We could wake her up. Said Jonathan.
- How? Asked William.

- I was hoping someone would have an idea for that part of the plan.
- I could try to stop her telekinesis with mine. Said Eos.
- Be careful. Said William.

Eos closed her eyes and relaxed for a few minutes. She was evaluating how much energy it would take to stop Clarwena's powers. Eos opened her eyes that had turned red and seemed to have fire in them. Balls of fire then appeared in Eos' hands which spread to her arms and eventually covered her completely in fire. The boys started to get worried. They didn't know Eos was now able to do that. They were worried that Clarwena was burning Eos alive. A few minutes later, the tornado stopped and the storm around it disappeared. The fire around Eos disappeared and her eyes returned to their blue color. Eos did not collapse this time. For some reason, her body had evolved and was now capable of powering such forces. Clarwena would never have a problem with her powers again.

Two months later, Gabriel and Essie as well as Lecksha and Karl who had gotten engaged three weeks earlier got married on the same day. It was a way of saying that Karl was over Essie and that he was not jealous of Gabriel. Two weeks later, Merrill and Drew got married.

CHAPTER 4
THE NEXT GENERATION

Three years had passed since Eos had returned to the Vampire kingdom. Today, on the 13th of August 2209, a new life begun. Prince Alexandre was born from Queen Eos and King William. He had blue eyes and dark blond hair. He was born with the ability to read auras, telekinesis, super-strength, mind travel and extended hearing. He would eventually become one of the most respected princes of time. As with Clarwena, Malerk came to see Eos and William's new son. A month later, Drew and Merrill had a daughter named Arabella. She had sea-green eyes and brown hair. She would be capable of learning magic just like her mother. On the 27th of February 2210, Scott and Juliet had two boys: David and Nathan. They were almost exact copies of their father except for the pointy ears. On the 8th of March 2211, Lecksha gave birth to a boy that she and Karl named Jak. Is hair was almost black and his eyes were grey. Two months and almost a half later, on the 17th of May 2211, Gabriel and Essie had a daughter named Aura. She had the ability to transform herself into an eagle. Her eyes were exactly like her fathers; two different shades of blue, and her hair was dark blond. Five years later, in 2263, those who had powers had accepted them and had started to enjoy them. Alexandre was no longer scared of seeing everyone's auras. Clarwena could now create storms that could compete with Malerk's whenever she wanted. Arabella had learned a bit of magic from her mother. Aura had learned to fly. The others who had no special powers had learned other things. Nathan and David had learned how to play tricks on people. Jak had learned something a bit more useful. He had learned how to defend himself with almost no weapons. Today was Sunday. It was on that day that everyone in the castle practiced something they needed to perfect. Eos was in the hall with Clarwena. Clarwena was practicing her violin while Eos was practicing her cello beside her daughter. William was in the fighting room with Alexandre. Alexandre was being thought how to fight his enemies more with his mind them with his sword. William said to his son:

- I imagine this. You are surrounded by humans with silver bullet guns. There is a wood staff on the other side of the circle of humans. What do you do?
- I go hyper speed just after they pulled the trigger causing them to shoot each other. And now they're all dead.
- Alex, that only works if they all shoot at the same time. What do you do if they don't all shoot at the same time?

Alex thought about the answer to the question for a while. Eventually, he looked at his father and gave him an answer:

- You jump over the humans and grab the staff. You then do your best to stop or dodge the bullets. Eventually they'll run out of bullets and I can knock them out before running away from them.
- Very good. You've learned today's lesson.
- Can I go to the lake now?
- Did you practice your viola?
- Not yet.

- Practice one hour and then I will bring you to the lake.
- Alright.

Alexandre left the fighting room and went to get his viola.
He then sat in the hall beside his sister and started to practice.
When Alexandre had arrived in the hall, Eos left her cello
on the floor and went to see William. When Eos had arrived
beside William she asked him:

- How did it go with Alexandre?
- He as to much of you and me in him. He doesn't think before
he charges in.
- He is our son.
- He will be a great fighter. He will fight for the right
reasons.
- What did you promise Alexandre?
- I told him we would go to the lake, him and I, after he had
practised his viola for an hour.
- Do you mind if Clarwena and me join you?
- It would be an honour to have you at my side.

Eos smiled at William's comment. They hugged and then
kissed. An hour later, everyone stopped practicing and they
all went out for a picnic at the lake. That day was the best
anyone had had in a long while and it would be the best they
would have for a long time.

CHAPTER 5
THE MOST RESPECTED

Today was Alexandre's tenth birthday. For his birthday his mother and father had gotten him his first bow. The bow was made of ebony wood. Where he would place his hand, it was written in elfin: Alexandre, prince of the Vampires. Scott and Juliet had gotten him his first sword. The blade was made of platinum and the handle of white gold. Where the blade and the handle met was engraved the symbol of the Vampires. That afternoon, a messenger, ridding a beige horse, arrived at the Vampire castle. He was dressed in a black cape. Under one of his brown eyes was two staffs in the shape of an "X" and under the other was a rolled piece of paper. He was shown inside where he met Eos and William. After being greeted by the queen and king, the messenger said:

- I bring word from Naurim, King of the wizards. He cordially invites you to join his family at his table tomorrow night.
- Does he only invite William and I? Asked Eos.
- No. He wishes to meet all of your family; You, William, Alexandre, Clarwena, Lecksha, Karl, Jak, Scott, Juliet, Nathan, David and Ashka.
- Tell him I will do my best to bring everyone.

- As you wish.

The wizard bowed to Eos and William before leaving the Vampire castle. Eos gathered everyone who was invited at the wizard's castle. Before they left, Eos entrusted the throne to Gabriel and Essie for the time they were gone. The family left at around noon with Marty and Simon. The journey seemed to take more time than usual because after eight hours of travelling it started to rain and did not stop before they arrived at the castle of King Naurim. For the kids the journey seemed to take an eternity. When they arrived, the next day, they were greeted by the king's sister, Nova. She showed them inside and gave them some towels to dry up. Shortly after, King Naurim, Queen Sali and Prince Hobbes, who was now fourteen years old arrived to greet them. On the prince's shoulder was a peregrine falcon who was his protector. Beside the king was a jaguar who was his protector. Both animals only changed into their person shape when it was necessary. Naurim then said to the Vampire family:

- Welcome to my home. Thank you for coming.
- Thank you for inviting all of us. Said Eos. It was very kind of you.
- This is my sun Hobbes. He was only a baby when you last saw him.
- Nice to see you Hobbes. These are my children, Clarwena and Alexandre.
- Your hospitality is much appreciated. Said Alexandre.
- You are most welcomed young man. Said Naurim.

Naurim, Sali and Hobbes met and greeted the rest of the Vampire family. After meeting everyone, the kids went outside to enjoy themselves while the parents sat down to talk together. The rain had finally stopped. The adults mostly talked about politics. At seven o'clock the kids were called to supper. After washing their hands and faces, everyone went to the dining room where they all sat down. They enjoyed a four course meal composed of lobster bisque, a goat cheese and caramelized onion salad, a roasted pig served with mashed potatoes and vegetables, and a chocolate mousse with a raspberry sauce for dessert. After eating everyone was showed to a room where they could relax or go to sleep. The next morning, the sun was shinning and there were no clouds in the sky. Before leaving, the Vampires thanked King Naurim for his hospitality.

A week after they had returned home, they were invited to visit the Demon kingdom. This time, Eos, William, Clarwena and Alexandre were the only ones to go. When they arrived at the Demon castle, in Hrychib, they were greeted by Deimos, his wife Era and their son Peter. Deimos and William went hunting together while Eos and Era enjoyed each others company. Peter and Alexandre were enjoying bothering Clarwena while she relaxed under a tree. At supper, they ate the deer the Kings had killed that afternoon. The next day, they returned home. Later that year, they would go visit Louisiam and Ilya. When they retuned from the Wood-elf kingdom, Eos turned to Alexandre and said to him:

- Thank you for being so polite with everyone. I really appreciate it.
- You're welcome mother. Said Alexandre.
- As for you Clarwena, why didn't you thank them for inviting us?
- I didn't because Alexandre did it before me.
- That's because you're too slow. Said William.
- Dad.
- That's enough on that subject. Said Eos. Go rest in your rooms.

Clarwena and Alexandre went to their rooms. William and Eos had a glass of blood before going to bed. The night was darker then usually. There were clouds covering the stars and the moon. In the middle of the night, a black horse and his rider arrived at the Vampire castle. The man was let inside the castle by the guards at the front door. He then climbed the stairs up to the third floor. He stopped in front of Clarwena's and Alexandre's bedroom door but did not enter. He was looking for someone else. He continued down the hall to William's and Eos' bedroom. When he had arrived at the door, he entered the room. He sat on the bed beside Eos. He then placed his hand on her chest. As Eos felt the hand on her chest, thunder raged outside and she woke up. The man had already disappeared. William, who had also woken up, helped Eos calm down. They then both went back to sleep. The next morning, when Eos woke up, William was already out of bed and downstairs. She stretched herself and noticed that a black hand was imprinted on her chest where she had felt something the night before. She went to the bathroom to get a better look. When she looked in the mirror, she noticed that there was something more then just the hand. Eos now had a pair of black angel wings. Eos ran out of her room and downstairs. On her way down, she met Merrill. Eos stopped Merrill and showed her the wings before asking her:

- Do you know of any spell that does this?
- There are no spells that can give you wings.
- Then why do I have wings?
- I don't know.

Eos continued her way down the stairs and went to see William in the hall. He was talking with the spirits and Essie. Eos said to William as she entered the room:

- I need help.

235

- With what? Asked William as he turned around.

When William, Essie and the spirits saw the black wings they froze. No one knew what to say. Eos broke the silence by saying:

- Merrill said that there's no spell that is capable of giving someone wings. So I'm going to ask Malerk unless any of you know what did this.
- I will go with you. Said Valir who was coming down the stairs.
- I don't want anyone to come with me.
- How are you going to get there?
- I will take my horse.
- You can't take your horse.
- Why not?
- Because you have the black hand on your chest.
- I will walk then.
- The Hauflins won't let you past threw their kingdom for the same reason your horse will not let you ride him.
- How am I suppose to get there then?
- You will have to fly.
- I don't know how to fly.
- You do but you must find that knowledge in you and that's why I'm coming.

Eos left the castle with Valir. Outside, he showed her that she did know how to fly. Together, they made their way to Malerk's castle. After flying for fifteen hours, Valir and Eos arrived at Malerk's castle. When they entered, they saw Malerk sitting on his black throne. When he saw Eos walk threw the front door, he said to her:

- I knew you would come.

- When I agreed to be your heir, you said you would transfer a bit of your powers at the time.
- I did. What is the problem.
- If you told the truth why do I have black angel wings and why do I have a black hand on my chest?

Malerk got off of his chair and stood in front of Eos. He closed his eyes and wings slowly appeared out of his back. He had been born with those wings just like everyone from the black kingdom. Malerk then opened his eyes to look at Eos who was stunned and said to her:

- You have wings because I have wings.

Malerk placed his hand on the black hand Eos had on her chest. When he removed it the black hand had disappeared. Eos looked at Malerk and said:

- What did it mean?
- Nothing important.
- Malerk, what did it mean?
- Nothing. Do you mind if I return to Tindome with you? I want to go see what Clarwena and Alexandre look like now.

Valir, Malerk and Eos flew back together to Tindome. When they arrived, everyone from the old generation greeted Malerk. They were glad to see him again. Eos then asked Alexandre and Clarwena to come meet Malerk. They had seen him before but did not remember because back then they were only babies. When they had arrived, Eos said to them:

- I'd like you to meet your great grandfather.
- Hi. Said Malerk.
- You're the Lord of Evil. Said Alexandre.

- I am.
- Cool. I love your ability to create lightning and thunder.
- Maybe some day you'll be able to do that as well.
- He doesn't have the power to control the elements, I do. Said Clarwena.
- How are you doing Clarwena?
- I was doing better before you arrived.
- Clarwena, say you're sorry. Said Eos.
- I can't or I'd be telling a lie. You don't want me to lie.
- Go to your room to think about what you've said.
- And don't come out until we come and get you. Said William.
- As you wish your highness. Said Clarwena.

Clarwena ran up the stairs to her room. When she was gone, Eos turned to Malerk and said:

- I'm sorry. Sometimes I think Nature had an effect on her when she was captured.
- Don't be sorry. It's part of her rebellious character. She rebels against you just like you did against Nature, the closest thing you have to a mother.
- I hope you're right.

Malerk, Valir, Eos, William and Alexandre sat in the living room and talked together like families do. Meanwhile, upstairs in her bedroom, Clarwena was escaping from the castle through her window. After landing on the ground under her bedroom window, she went to the stables to get her horse. A few hours had now passed and it was time to have supper. As the others were sitting down at the dinning table, William went upstairs to go get Clarwena. When he arrived, Marty who was guarding the door, let him enter. William went in and came back a few seconds later. He looked at Marty and said to him:

- You're an idiot. It's the second time you let my daughter disappear.
- What do you mean? Asked Marty.
- She disappeared. She ran away. If ever something happens to her or if she runs away again, I'll have you killed.

William ran downstairs and told Eos and everyone who was with her. They immediately went looking for her. William went to the Nishu Mountains where Clarwena loved to go spend her day. Marty went to Cuile, the wizard kingdom's capital, to see if Hobbes had seen her. Alexandre went to Feanor and then to Ramar to see if the spirits or the Wood-elves had seen her. Eos and Malerk went in the direction of his kingdom to see if she was at Nature's or the council's castle. Thirteen hours later, Clarwena arrived at Nature's castle. She entered the hall that was dark because no torch was lit. After a few minutes, Clarwena said:

- Nature! Show yourself. I want to talk to you.

A torch appeared in the left corner of the room. The flame lit up the entire room. Nature followed by Orek was then seen by Clarwena. Nature gave the flame to Orek who lit up all the torches in the hall while she sat down on her white marble throne. Nature then said to Clarwena:

- I knew you would come one day.
- How did you know? Asked Clarwena.
- There are things I know.
- You can see the future like my mother and me.
- You never use your sight to see the future.
- I can only see what I can prevent.
- And what have you seen so far?
- Nothing.
- Then how do you know you can see the future?

- Can you see the future?
- No. My daughter can predict the future based on the past and the present. Why are you here?
- I met Malerk yesterday. I wanted to meet the good person who married the evil man.
- You have such a nice way of saying it.
- I learned that from my mother.
- Is it the only reason you came here?
- No. There is another. But I don't know if you can help me.
- What is it?
- I want the throne of the Vampire kingdom. I want you to find a reason to dethrone her.
- Any reason!?
- Any reason at all.
- I'll see what I can do.

Clarwena thanked Nature and left her castle. When Clarwena closed the front door, Orek turned to Nature and said to her:

- A passage to your dream, she as offered.
- Indeed she as. Death will soon catch Eos.
- But what of Malerk's warning?
- I will not touch her. No one will ever know it was my fault.
- What are you going to do?
- I will give her a vision.
- Of what? What could be powerful enough to kill her?
- Every face she could save when the last battle comes.
- You mean the one against the humans.
- Exactly.
- But there's over 590 million people she could save. A vision of each of them will have her having visions for 13415 days or nine and a half years if she as two visions per second.
- I know.

- That will make her brain overload and then shut down. It will kill her.
- It's the only thing that can kill her. I will then have solved Clarwena's problem and mine.
- But what if she's the queen that will save us all.
- I'm sure will be fine without her.

Orek did not had anything but he was starting to think that Nature was going too far this time. She was going crazy. Outside, Malerk and Eos were arriving. When they saw Clarwena climbing on her horse, Eos said to her:

- Why did you run away?
- I wanted to see Nature to find out why you didn't like her.
- Did you get an answer?
- No. But I found out that I like her. We have a common interest.
- Get yourself back home.
- No problem.

Clarwena left towards Tindome. Malerk and Eos looked at each other worried of what might happen next.

CHAPTER 6
AN UNEXPECTED LIFE SAVER

One year had passed since Clarwena had made a deal with Nature and Nature's part had not yet been fulfilled. Clarwena was getting impatient. On that morning, she got up and went to the stables to get her horse. Marty followed her closely. Clarwena rode off to the Nishu Mountains. The Nishu mountains were the mountains that separated the Vampire kingdom from the Hauflin's, the Witch's and the Dwarf's kingdom. At times those mountains became very foggy and so it was very dangerous to travel on them. When Clarwena arrived at the blood river, she got off her horse and walked the rest of the way. She walked for hours on the mountains before it was too foggy to see a few meters in front of her. Marty, who was still following Clarwena, said to her:

- Maybe we should stop until the fog clears.
- You can stop. I'm going on. Said Clarwena.
- Clarwena!

Clarwena did not answer and continued walking. After five minutes, the fog had gotten so bad that Clarwena could barely see in front of her. She took another step and fell into a crevasse. She managed to hold on to the ledge but her hand was slipping. She screamed for help to Marty. But Marty only heard her scream as a whisper. Clarwena's hand slipped off the ledge and she fell to her death. Clarwena closed her eyes because she didn't want to see how far she was falling. But just before she was out of reach, someone grabbed her and pulled her back up. Clarwena gave her rescuer a hug and said:

- Thank you Marty. I should have listen to you.
- Who's Marty? Said the man.

The fog dimmed and Clarwena saw a black haired and grey eyes young man who seemed familiar. Clarwena looked at his face and saw that he had two tattoos under his eyes. Under his left eye was two staffs in the shape of an "X" and under his right eye was a crown. Clarwena knew now who he was. She said:

- Hobbes!?
- Nice to see you again Clarwena. We should go back to my place to heal your wounds.
- Thank you but I think going back to my home would be best.
- As you wish.

Marty arrived just in time to see Hobbes and Clarwena disappear. Marty knew William would not be happy about that. Clarwena and Hobbes reappeared in front of the front door of the Vampire castle. The guards were surprised to see them appear but let them him. When Eos and William saw them enter, William asked:

- What happened?
- She fell in a crevasse she did not see because of the fog. But I saved her just in time. Said Hobbes.

- Thank you. Now go home. Said Eos.
- But, mom, he saved my life. You could at least let him stay for dinner. Said Clarwena.
- Hobbes, get out.
- As you wish your highness. Said Hobbes.

Hobbes left the castle as he had been told. When he was gone, Clarwena turned to her parents and said:

- Why do you hate him?
- I do not hate him, Said Eos. But I know he loves you.
- What's the matter with that?
- I think he wants two thrones at the same time.
- Is it so hard to believe that maybe he loves me for who I am and not for what I am?
- Yes.

Eos walked towards the door to go outside. As the guards opened the door, a more painful than usually vision appeared. It was followed by another and another. Eos fell on the floor with pain. Both guards approached Eos and William ran to her. The hours of visions had begun. For each second that passed Eos had two visions. Her visions showed her the faces of every living person on Melda Cemmen. Clarwena looked at her mother and whispered:

- Thank you Nature.

Clarwena went to her room. After ten minutes of trying to pull Eos back to reality, William brought Eos to her room. A day passed and Eos still had visions. William stayed by her side watching her and holding her hand that sometime turned blue because she squeezed it so hard. Another day passed and William hadn't closed his eyes for three days. He was too worried to fall asleep. At two in the afternoon, on the third day, something happened. Eos got enough control to scream something that could have been heard anywhere on Melda Cemmen. Eos screamed:

- Malerk, Help me!

The scream was so loud that everyone in Tindome had to block his or her ears not to become deft. Back at Malerk's castle, Malerk woke up in sweat. He got out of bed and washed himself before getting dressed. He then went to the fourth floor of his castle to the library. He got a giant black book on which it was written in gold "Ways to kill the immortal and to prevent the mortal from dying." Malerk sat at a desk in the middle of the room and started to look through the book. Malerk had seen in his dream Eos in pain and he had heard her scream for help. Finally, Malerk found the spell Nature had used. Under the spell itself was the counter spell. There were ingredients that would be hard to get. It was written:

You need:

→ The scale of a dragon.
→ The blood of the person who did the spell.
→ Something representing the visions the person is having.
→ The will to stop it.

You must mix all the ingredients together and then placed your hands on both side of the person's forehead and then pronounce the spell: "Visions you have sent to her/him so that she/he dies. I ask you to remove them. She/he no longer needs to die but to live."

Malerk closed the book and went to Nature's castle as fast as he could. He entered the castle calmly and bowed to Nature who was talking to Orek. Nature looked at Malerk and asked him:

- What do you want?
- Can I speak to you in private?

Nature rose from her throne and approached Malerk. She showed him the way to a darken corner of the room. Nature then said to Malerk:

- What is it?
- I've been thinking about the way we were ten thousand years ago. I've realized that I missed those days.
- Are you serious?
- Well... Malerk paused and looked directly at Nature's eyes before adding: No.

Malerk punched Nature in the face. He held her so she couldn't move and took a vile from his pocket. He captured the drop of blood that fell from Nature's mouth and then let her go. Malerk then approached Orek and said:

- Could you give me something?
- What would you like?
- A few dragon scales.

Malerk tore off two of Orek's dragon scales that he placed carefully in his pocket where he had placed the vial. Before heading out the door, Malerk said:

- Thank you for your hospitality and for your gifts.

He then left Nature's castle and then teleported himself to the Vampire's castle. When he appeared in the hall, he saw Alexandre sitting on his father's throne with his face in his hands. Malerk approached him and said:

- Do not worry about your mother. I have come to save her.

Alexandre lifted his head to look at Malerk. His blue eyes were covered with water. Alexandre said to Malerk:

- I know who did this. It is not normal for my mother to be having so many visions at once.
- Who do you think did this to her?
- Who could it be other then them? They always hated my mother. They always wanted to kill her. So they made a deal and now because of them she will die.
- Come here.

Alexandre got on his feet and went closer to Malerk who held him in his arms. Malerk then whispered in his ear:

- I will not let your mother die. I will save her. She will not die. I promise.
- She's upstairs in her room with my father.

Malerk released Alexandre from his grip and ran upstairs to Eos' room. When Malerk entered, he closed the door behind him. The noise woke William who had fallen asleep. William looked up at Malerk and asked him:

- Do you know how to stop this?
- I do. I have the counter-spell.
- Then let's do it.
- It's not that simple. I am missing one thing.
- What is it? I'll get it for you.

- I need to know what she is seeing and then I need something representing what she is seeing.
- How are we going to find out what she is seeing? When she has a vision her brain can't concentrate on anything else.
- She managed to scream for help didn't she?
- Yes, loudly as well.
- Then we can get her to tell us what she sees.

Malerk approached Eos and placed his hands on each side of her head. Malerk leaned forward, looked at her face and said:

- Eos, listen to me.

Eos tried to release herself from Malerk's grip by moving her head left to right but it did not work. Malerk then repeated:

- Eos, listen to me. What are you seeing?
- Faces.

William looked at Eos in surprise because she had answered the question. Malerk then asked her:

- Faces of whom, or of what?
- Mel... Melda... Cemmen.

Malerk released Eos who then screamed in pain. William looked away because he knew he could do nothing. Malerk then turned to William and asked:

- Have you got paper, ink and quills?
- Yes, in the library. Why?
- Go get them. I'll explain when you return.

William left the room and came back five minutes later with twenty sheets of paper, two quills and two bottle of ink. Malerk gave half the sheet to William, an ink bottle and a quill, and then said:

- Start drawing.
- Drawing what?
- The flags of every kingdom including my flag, Nature's and the Oracle's flag.
- I don't know all of them.
- Which one do you know?
- The Vampire's, the Wood-Elf's, the Demon's, yours, Nature's and the Wizard's.
- Then draw those, I'll draw the others.

Malerk and William started to draw the flags of Melda Cemmen. The flag of the Wood-elves was a tree separated in the middle. On one side, the tree was full of leaves and you could see the light of the sun behind it. On the other side, there was a dead tree and you could see the light of the moon behind its branches. The flag of the Demons was a black hand in front of a flame in front of which there were two red eyes that represented Malerk. The Dwarves' flag was three mountains in the middle and in their language it was written: "*We will stand and fight our enemy for as long as the mountains stand.*" The flag of the animal spirits was separated in the middle. On the left side was the face of Gabriel, the first animal spirit, and on the right side was his tiger shape. The spirits' flag had the Chinese symbol for eternity on the top and the symbol for life at the bottom. There were white and black shapes surrounding the symbols. Where the white and black met it was silver. The flag of the Sindarin-elves was separated in three parts. On the bottom part was the stars. On the upper left was the sun on a blue sky and on the upper right was the moon on a black sky. The flag of the wizards was the top part of a staff. It held a blue diamond-shaped crystal. The flag of the witches was two hands. In between the hands was a magic energy ball that looked like a sun. The Hauflins' flag was one medium circle surrounded by thirty-four interlocking circle. The ovals that the circles formed were dark green and the lines were blue. The Vampires' flag was a Vampire mouth which you could see the inside. Around the mouth it was pitch black. The flag of the humans resembled the necklace of the Blackhoods except it only had one level. The three triangles' sidelines formed bigger triangles on their opposites. Nature's flag was the planet Aura surrounded by its four moons and the four suns of that solar system. Malerk's flag was his red eyes on a black background. There were also other smaller red eyes around the big ones to represent the dark-angels and the evil protectors. Finally, the Oracle's flag was a crystal ball out of which came smoke under eyes that watched the crystal ball. After finishing the drawings, Malerk placed them all in a pile. He added the two dragon scales. He poured on Nature's blood and gave the pile to William. Malerk then placed his hands on both side of Eos' face and said the magic words. The blood and the scales sank in the paper and disappeared. A blue light then came out of the paper surrounded William and Malerk before going in Eos' brain. A few seconds later, a red light came out and divided itself in two. One went into the papers that burst into flames and the other in Malerk. William dropped the papers and Malerk let go of Eos. William looked at Malerk who seemed to have lost his strength. William asked him:

- Are you all right?

Malerk collapsed and fell on the floor. He had used all his energy to stop the spell. William told him to hold on a few more minutes and ran out of the room to go see the only person who could help him. William went to the basement where Merrill and Drew were teaching a spell to their daughter, Arabella. William entered and startled them. He turned to Merrill and said:

- I need your help.
- What is it?
- Malerk tried to save Eos. I think he saved her but when he finished the spell he collapsed. I think he's dying.
- What!?

William, Merrill, Drew and Arabella ran upstairs followed by Alexandre who wanted to know what was going on. When they entered the room, Merrill kneeled down beside Malerk. His eyes were open but he had difficulty breathing. Something was definitely wrong with him. Merrill said:

- He did like Scott he forgot to read the fine print.
- It's not funny Merrill. Said William.
- Now I know why it said you needed the will to stop it. Said Malerk. Because if the one who cast the spell doesn't want anyone to stop it, the one who tries to stop it will die.
- You can't die Malerk. Said Alexandre. The balance of the world will be destroyed.
- He's right. Said Eos. You can't die.

Everyone turned to Eos who was getting out of bed and approaching Malerk. Eos knelt down beside Merrill and said to Malerk:

- I will save you. You have saved my life so I will save yours.
- There is nothing you can do for me now. Said Malerk. Well, there is one way. But it would take a few hours. I don't know if I can last that long.
- What is it?
- The person or persons who have decided to do that to you

must agree that it as gone too far. But you must find out who was trying to kill you.

- I don't know who did this.
- Someone here knows.
- Who?
- Your son.
- Alexandre!?
- Yes mother, I know. Said Alexandre.
- Who was it?
- Your two rivals, Nature and Clarwena. I read it in their auras.
- My own daughter!? Said Eos in rage.

Eos got on her feet and grabbed her sword, bow and arrows before leaving the room. Eos went down the corridor and opened the last door on the left. When she opened the door, Clarwena said:

- Marty, how many times must I ask you to knock before you enter my room.

When Eos had completely opened the door, she saw Clarwena in the arms of Hobbes. Rage overwhelmed Eos. She took out her bow and fired an arrow at Hobbes. But just before the arrow left the bow, William pushed the bow to change the course of the arrow. The arrow passed right beside Hobbes' head. Eos looked at William then at Hobbes and said:

- What are you doing here?
- I came to see my girlfriend.
- If you do not leave now I will shoot an arrow threw your head and this time no one will stop me.
- See you later Clarwena.

Hobbes disappeared and Eos turned to Clarwena who was angry that her mother had interfered in her life. Eos said to Clarwena:

- You have betrayed me.
- I would never betray you, mother.
- I do not speak as your mother; I speak as your queen.
- What have I done to betray you?
- You've tried to kill me.
- I've never tried to kill you.
- Don't lie to me.
- Why not?

Eos was so mad that lightning came down and struck Clarwena who fell on the ground. Clarwena looked up at the sky and made lightning come down and strike her mother. But the lightning went around Eos and disappeared. Eos approached Clarwena and said:

- Nice try. But I now hold the power of the elements. Now come with me.

Eos lifted Clarwena with her telekinesis and led her to her room. Eos then lifted Malerk with her powers and went outside. Eos flew off to Nature's castle followed by Malerk and Clarwena who were floating behind her. When Eos entered Nature's castle, eighteen hours later, she dropped Malerk and Clarwena at the door. Clarwena had found her strength but Malerk was getting worse. Nature was sitting on her throne as if she had been waiting for them. Eos approached her and said:

- You will pay.
- I haven't bought anything so I have nothing to pay.

Eos used telekinesis on Nature, who didn't fight it, and brought her close to herself. Eos then continued:

- You tried to kill me with my own powers. I admit that it was an intelligent way to kill me. But now I'm afraid I will have to kill your daughter Lydia.
- You will not lay a hand on her. Said Nature.
- I will kill her unless you keep Malerk from dying.
- You have more love for Malerk then you do for your own daughter. How sad is that?
- You are no better. You have more fear for me then you do for anyone who has ever lived. I can feel your fear. One day you will beg me for your life.
- I will never beg to you.
- Release Malerk from this spell.
- Release him yourself.

Nature turned around and walked towards her throne. Eos pulled out her bow and shot an arrow at Nature. Nature leaned on the right side and the arrow passed right beside her. The arrow hit Nature's throne and fell on the ground. Eos put her bow away and took out her twin swords. When Nature heard the swords she whistled. Clorus, Solano, Luna, Sout, Lut and Dido appeared beside Nature. Eos looked at the six protectors and said:

- What's the matter Nature? Afraid you will loose against me one more time?
- I do not fight when it is unnecessary. If you wish to fight, you can fight them.
- I do not fight the bodyguards of my enemies; I fight my enemies.
- If you wish to fight me get rid of the bodyguards.
- With pleasure.

Eos closed her eyes. When she reopened them, Bora, Chaos, Thor, Borealus, Nychta, Dedum, Lorus and Frice were standing beside her. The "evil" protectors charged at the "good" ones while Eos walked towards Nature. Nature was standing in front of her throne and was worried about what Eos was going to do. When Eos was in front of Nature, she placed her hand on Nature's throat. Eos felt the veins and the bones before saying:

- You would be easy to kill. Sit down.

Eos pushed Nature down on her throne. Eos walked around the throne letting her left hand feel the chair. When Eos was on the other side of Nature, she bent forward so that her head was beside Nature's. Eos then whispered:

- Look at Malerk.

Nature turned her gaze to her husband. Eos was silent for a few minutes before continuing:

- In about five minutes, he will be dead. You will have killed him because you hate me. You can stay on your throne, if you wish, and have a front row seat to his death or you can save his life. It's your choice. Do you kill him because you hate me or do you save his life because you love him? Do you want him to rule evil or do you want me to rule evil?
- Stop! Screamed Nature while standing.

Every protector stopped fighting and looked at Nature. Nature did not wish to save Malerk but did not wish Eos to rule "evil". She approached Malerk and stopped the spell. Malerk was not going to die on that day. Nature then turned to Clarwena and said:

- I'm sorry if our plan failed.

Nature returned to her throne while Eos went to Malerk to help him get up. When Clarwena realized what had happened, she ran to Nature. Clarwena said to Nature:

- You're just going to give up.
- You will one day understand that some problems take a long time to solve. Said Nature.
- This problem could have ended now.
- Since Malerk knew the counter spell, I would have killed him and not Eos.
- So what!? One of your problems would have been solved.
- I never wanted to kill Malerk.
- Why not?
- Because I...

Nature was afraid of saying the rest. She was playing with her wedding ring that she still wore. Malerk, Eos and Clarwena knew exactly what she did not dare say. Clarwena said to Nature:

- You still love him. Fine. I'm going home.

Clarwena turned around and headed towards the door. When she was beside Malerk and Eos, Eos said to her:

- Where is your home Clarwena?
- What!?
- Where are you going?
- To the castle in Tindome. Where else?
- Do you think you're still wanted there?
- Are you banishing me? Are you banishing your own daughter?
- No, because my daughter died a few years ago.

- Then I'm going to live with my boyfriend, Hobbes.

Clarwena left the castle, stole a horse and rode off for Cuile, the Wizard's kingdom capital. Eos helped Malerk get up and brought him to his castle followed by the "evil" protectors. When they entered the castle, Eos brought Malerk to his bedroom where she placed him on his bed. Malerk looked at Eos and said:

- Thank you.
- You stay on that bed until you have all your strength back. If Nature or any of her soldiers walk through your door, my mind will be empty so you may send me a message.

Eos walked out of the room and left the castle to return to Tindome.

CHAPTER 7
THE ESCAPE

A year had passed since Clarwena had been banished. Alexandre and Arabella had fallen in love. Nathan was dating Aura. David had fallen in love with a half-Demon and half-Vampire named Coiva. Jak had fallen in love with a Vampire named Ilmen. It was now exactly 200 human years after Eos had met Malerk. Eos and William were dancing in the hall. Everything was perfect. But at eleven o'clock an alarm went off. Eos had no idea what was going on so she turned to William. William's face was full of fear. Everyone else came running in the hall. Eos looked at her brother and asked:

- What's going on?
- Something terrible has happened. We never thought it would happen. The Wizards had made the alarm when the shield was made between Earth and the rest of Melda Cemmen to warn everyone when the shield would come down.
- It's down!?
- In two weeks or 140 human days, the shield is coming down because all the humans believe that the rest of Melda Cemmen exist. As was agreed, all the species will meet in our kingdom dressed for war. But there's a problem.

- What?
- The elves and the Hauflins did not want an alarm so they
don't know the shield is coming down.
- We have to warn them. Scott, you go warn the Hauflins, I'll
go warn the Elves.

The alarm finally stopped. Scott ran upstairs and went to
get his weapons. Eos did the same. Ten minutes later, Scott
left with Juliet for the Hauflin's kingdom. Five minutes later,
Eos came down and said to everyone:

- I'll see you later.
- I'm coming with you. Said Alexandre.
- No you're staying here.
- Why? I want to help you.
- I will be flying to get there. You won't be able to keep up.
And you have to help your father prepare the troops.
- As you wish mother.

Eos kissed Alexandre on the forehead and William on the
mouth before flying off to Ramar. Scott took 23 hours to get
to Malina, the Hauflins' kingdom capital but Eos only took
twelve to get to Ramar. When Scott and Juliet arrived at the
Hauflin's castle, they were greeted with great hospitality. Soon
they were sitting with the king and his family for dinner.

When Eos had arrived in the Fuin forest, she had been
spotted by the elves. Elves did not like Malerk or anyone who
worked for him. From the ground, Eos looked like a dark-
angel. One of the elves took out his bow and shot an arrow
that had a tail that resembled a white flame and a head that
looked like a white drop right beside Eos' head. Eos did not get
bothered by it and kept on going. The elves did not like that.
They wanted her to land. Three arrows were shot this time.
One missed her but the others didn't. The second one went

in her left wing and the other very close to her heart. The two arrows made her loose her concentration. Eos fell from the sky. On her way down, Eos' head hit a tree trunk before she fell unconscious on the ground in front of the elves.

After dinner with the Hauflins, Scott and Juliet talked with the king. Scott said:

- We have come to warn you as was are agreement. The shield will come down in less than two weeks. You must get ready to fight.
- We do not fight. Said the king. Only our ancestors fought to have a place to call home.
- You must come to protect your homes.
- Humans will not wish to fight us. They will want to live in peace with us.

Eos woke in the hall of the Wood-elves' castle. Louisiam was standing beside her and Ilya was cleaning the wound Eos had on her head. They had not yet removed the arrows from her body and Eos could feel the one close to her heart each time she took a breath. Eos lifted her hand and placed it on the arrow's body. She turned towards Ilya and said:

- Move away for one minute or you'll get killed

Ilya got on her feet and moved away from Eos in fear. Eos took at big breath and pulled on the arrow at the same time. Her fangs and claws appeared. But as the pain dimmed, they disappeared. Ilya returned to Eos' side and placed pressure on her wound before covering it with a bandage. After both wounds on her body were taken care of, Eos got up and removed the arrow from her left wing. Eos looked at Louisiam and said:

- I have an urgent message for you. The shield is coming down in two weeks.
- Are you serious? Asked Louisiam.
- Why would I lie about something like that?

Louisiam turned around and looked back at Eos and Ilya. He then turned to a servant and said:

- Bring me Halir.

The servant bowed to Louisiam and left the room. Ten minutes later, Halir entered and said to Louisiam:

- You wanted to see me.

Halir's gaze turned to Ilya who was behind Eos. Halir could only see the black wings but not the face. He thought it was a dark-angel. He took out his bow and fired an arrow that had leafs has its tail and head before Louisiam could say that it was Eos. Eos heard the arrow coming towards her. She turned around and caught the arrow in her hand before it hit her. Eos dropped the arrow on the floor. Louisiam then said to Halir:

- Do you remember Eos?
- Not like that.
- She came to warn us that the humans all know the rest of Melda Cemmen exists. Prepare the army.
- As you wish. Said Halir while bowing to Louisiam and Eos before leaving.

Eos then headed towards the front door of the castle. When Louisiam saw that she was leaving, he said to her:

- Where are you going?

- I'm going to warn the Sindarin-elves.
- They will never let you in. I'm coming with you.

Eos and Louisiam took eleven hours to get to Forya, the capital of the Sindarin-elves' kingdom. If Louisiam would not had been with her, Eos would never had made it across the Past king river. When they arrived at the castle that resembled the Wood-elves' castle, King Alewan asked Eos:

- What are you doing here?
- I have come to warn you.
- Warn me about what?
- The alarm has sounded.
- Why should I believe you?
- Why shouldn't you believe me?
- Because you are the heir of Malerk, Lord of all evil.
- Why would I have come if it weren't the truth? Asked Louisiam.
- There are many spells in this world.
- Fine. Said Eos. Don't believe me. It was nice seeing you again. Hope you survive. But if you die know that it was your fault. I'll be at my castle if you decide to join us.

Eos turned around and headed towards the door. Louisiam stayed beside Alewan. When Alewan saw that Eos was leaving without his permission, he said:

- I did not give you leave to depart.
- I don't care. I have other things to do.
- Guards stop her.

All the guards in the hall stopped Eos from leaving the castle. Eos asked them many times to let her go and let her leave but none listened. Eos got angry and turned into fire. The guards let her go out of fear. A red light came out of Eos' back where she had her tattoo. In the Hauflin's kingdom, Scott's tattoo had also turned red. A white beam of light escaped from the twins' bodies before they collapsed. The lights met beside Eos and turned into a Wood-elf. Lyco had been freed. A few seconds later, Eos was helped back on her feet by her father. After Eos was on her feet, she said while pulling her arm away:

- Let me go.

When Eos saw that it was her father who had helped her up, she paused and felt her back. Eos noticed that her tattoo was gone. She looked at her father and said:

- Lyco!?
- Yes. Thank you for freeing me. The Sindarin-elves have just agreed to get ready for battle.
- That's great. I'll see you later elves.

Eos turned around and headed towards the door but her father stopped her by holding her arm. Lyco said to Eos:

- I'm coming with you.
- No. Said Eos. You're no longer welcomed in the Vampire kingdom.
- You are not the queen. Only your mother can banish me. She would never banish me.
- Wrong. First of all I am the queen and have been for the forty years of my life minus three days. Secondly, if Selene were still alive and ruling, she would banish you because you were scared of your own children and because you abandoned her.
- Selene is dead.
- Yes, therefore I can banish you. The only way you can enter

my kingdom is if you join the Wood-elves' army. Otherwise, I never want to see your face again. Now let me go.

Lyco let go of Eos' arm. Eos returned to her castle in Tindome. When Eos returned, William asked her:

- How did it go?
- Badly. But they will meet us here.
- What happened?
- The Forest protectors shot me down when I arrived and before I left, I got so mad that Lyco escaped.
- Your father is free!?
- Yes and I told him what had happened since he had been gone and then banished him. If I keep on going, I will banish you and Alexandre.
- Oh Eos.

William took Eos in his arm and gave her a hug. Suddenly, out of the silence, the sound of a horn was heard. William and Eos walked outside to see who was there. Five millions Dwarves were standing in front of the castle dressed for war. The Dwarfs' armour was thick. It had a chain mail layer and a leather layer. They then wore a helmet decorated with silver in which were engraved mountains. They carried axes made from Wood with an iron blade. Eos stepped down the stairs and said:

- Welcome.
- We have come to help if the worst should happen. Said Gallium, king of the Dwarves.
- Knowing humans, the worst will happen. Said Eos.
- If you are right, we will fight for Melda Cemmen.
- Thank you. Could I ask that your army settle outside the city walls? Because I fear we might not have enough place for every army.

- Of course.

The king told his troops to stay outside Tindome and there they went. William showed Gallium inside the castle and served him something to drink. An hour later, Galadria, queen of the spirits, and Daniel, king of the animal spirits, arrived. They had left their armies of 8 millions and 5 millions outside the city walls. Eos greeted them and showed them in where they spoke with Gallium. Forty-five minutes later, Deimos arrived with his seventeen millions soldiers. Twenty minutes later, Scott and Juliet returned with the Hauflins who were twenty millions. Eos greeted the king, Malar, son of Malta. After the king had went inside, Scott approached Eos and asked her:

- What happened?
- What do you mean?
- How did he escape?
- I was trying to explain to Alewan that the humans all knew that we existed but he did not believe me so I decided to leave but he didn't want me to leave and asked his guards to stop me. I asked them many times to let me go but they didn't listen so I turned into fire and he escaped.
- Where is he now?
- He's in the wood-elf's kingdom because I told him he couldn't enter my kingdom unless he was part of the wood-elves' army.
- You banished him!?
- I did.
- Nice job.

Scott and Juliet entered the castle while Eos stayed outside. Fifteen minutes later, Louisiam and Alewan arrived at the castle. They had brought twelve millions Sindarin elves and six and a quarter millions wood-elves. Alewan entered the castle while Louisiam stopped beside Eos. He whispered to her:

- Your father is part of my army. He wants to save Melda Cemmen.
- You may enter my castle and join the others.

Louisiam entered the castle where he talked with the others. Half an hour later, Sara, queen of the witches, daughter of Guenevieve, arrived in Tindome. After walking to Eos, Sara said:

- I come with my army to help you. I have brought thirteen millions.
- Thank you for coming. Said Eos.
- I also wish to apologize for what my mother said long ago.
- I accept your apology but I would have preferred to hear it from your mother.
- She preferred to stay at home and watch over her grandchildren.
- Come in please.

Sara entered the castle as Eos had asked her. Eos served her something to drink and then left her with the other queen and the kings before returning outside with William. Thirty-five minutes later, someone Eos did not recognized arrived. It was someone who looked like an elf except he had scaly skin and horns. He bowed to Eos and William before saying:

- I am Octet. I am the leader of the banished. I know we are not accepted by the people of Melda Cemmen but we do live on this land. Five hundred thousand of us wish to help you protect it.
- We will gladly accept your help. Said William. Please enter our castle so you may rest.

- Thank you.

Octet entered the castle and joined the kings and queens. Three hours later, King Naurim arrived at the Vampire castle. But he was not alone. Naurim had brought his son, Hobbes. After Eos had welcomed the king, Hobbes said to Eos and William:

- I would like you to meet my wife.

The girl that accompanied them showed herself. When Eos and William saw her, they couldn't believe their eyes. Hobbes' wife was Clarwena. Eos looked at Clarwena then turned to Naurim and said:

- Would you like to come inside?
- Of course.

Naurim entered the castle followed by Eos and William. Fourteen million wizards were waiting at the gates of the city ready to help Eos. Hobbes and Clarwena followed their parents in the castle but the doors were shut before their faces. Clarwena then said:

- I'm the princess. Let me in.
- You are no longer permitted to enter this castle. Said the guard on her left side.
- Why not?
- We do not know why but those were the orders that your mother gave to us.
- I will enter if I want to.

Clarwena tried many time to open the door with her telekinesis but it did not work. After a few time the guards started to laugh at her. Clarwena turned to them and asked:

- Why are you laughing?
- You will never be able to open that door. It is under a spell.
- Hobbes, open this door.

Hobbes tried to open the door with his staff but it did not even move. Hobbes turned to Clarwena and said:

- Whoever did this spell is too powerful. I can't do anything.
- Who could be more powerful than a wizard?
- The one who did this spell for Eos. Said the guard.
- Who was it?
- Malerk.
- Lets get out of here.

Hobbes and Clarwena teleported themselves outside the city walls beside the Wizards' army. After the kings and queens had supper, they all went to bed. Morning seemed to have arrived faster that day. Everyone got out of bed at first light and got dressed for war. The spirits were dressed as usual for they did not need armour. The Demons' armour was their tick skin. The Vampires wore black coats that had their tattoo on the shoulders. They also wore brown leather gauntlets that had a red border, the motto of their species and a sharpen tip star. The Elves' armour was striped gold and silver. The stripes were in a "V" shape. On the chest plate of the Wood-elves was the tree of death and life, and on the one of the Sindarin-elves was the moon, the sun and the stars. The Hauflins' armour was only a leather shirt because they had not gone to war in a long time. The Witches' armour was a chain mail shirt covered by leather armour and they wore gauntlets decorated with a protection spell. The Wizards were dressed as they were usually but they wore a black cape. Finally, some of the banished had armour and some didn't depending on which species they were. After getting ready, the kings and queens all joined in the hall. When everyone had arrived, Eos said:

- I want to thank you for coming once again. There is only one week left before the shield between Earth and the rest of Melda Cemmen comes down. I must first warn you that the humans will be hard to defeat.
- Hard to defeat! Said Deimos. Humans are not hard to kill. Spread fear in them and they will fall easily.
- You may want to take that risk but I will not. Their technology is a lot better then what it was when they were part of our world. We are better to be on the defensive then on the offensive.
- Do you have a plan other then protecting our side? Asked Galadria.
- I think that the Spirits, the Elves and the Hauflins should protect Nienna and Anoriel. The Demons and the Dwarves should protect Saeros. My people and the banished will protect my kingdom and the Wizards and Witches will spread on all borders.

Eos had just finished talking when Lecksha came running inside by the front door. She turned to Eos and said:

- You should come see this.

Every king and queen went outside to see what was going on. What they saw, they did not believe. The Dragons had flown over to help. Four Dragons landed in front of the castle's front steps. Their wings together were twice as long as their body. There were two reds, one green and one black. Dragons could not speak with words but could speak by thoughts. The green Dragon said:

- "I am Femur king of the Dragons. I would like to offer my help to protect Melda Cemmen."
- I gladly accept your help. Said Eos.
- We have also come to help. Said a voice.

One person got off each dragon: two women and two men. Eos looked at them. By the way they looked, Eos guessed that both women were Vampires. One of the men was a half-elf, half-dragon and the other was a half-Demon and half-Vampire. The first Vampire started to speak:

- I am Klashka, first queen of the Vampires.
- I am Velliam, first king of the Vampires. Said the half-Elf, half-Dragon.
- I am Cleona, ninth queen of the Vampires.
- I am Nemesis, ninth king of the Vampires. Said the half-Vampire, half-Demon.
- I am Eos, daughter of Selene.
- Yes, I know. You are the princess. Said Cleona. Where is your mother?
- She as been dead since 2150.
- What happened?
- Lyco asked to be killed the day my twin and me were born. The oracle destroyed him and cursed my brother and me. Tree days later, Selene was... killed herself.

Eos lied to Cleona about what truly happened to Selene because she knew Cleona would not spare Jonathan's life. Klashka looked a Eos and said:

- Rumours have come to our ears. You are Malerk's heir.
- I am. Said Eos.
- Do you have an heir?
- If you are referring to my daughter, I will not allow her to rule at my place.

- Since your daughter cannot replace you, I will.
- What!? You cannot dethrone me.
- I am the first queen and so I can dethrone any queen if she is not worthy.
- How dare you?
- You cannot rule this kingdom.
- Why not?
- We cannot trust you. You lived with Humans for too long and you are Malerk's heir.
- Are you sure you want to rule at my place?
- I will be better for the Vampires.

Eos turned around for a minute and faced William. Eos' eyes turned red like Malerk's. Eos then went hyper speed, pulled out her sword, pushed Klashka on the ground and placed Tari under her throat. Eos then said to Klashka:

- I appreciate you traveling many miles to help us, but you will follow my orders.
- I never followed orders and I never will.
- You will follow mine or will go back to the island you've lived on all these years.
- I want to stay and I will do as I please.

Eos was about to hurt Klashka when Malerk and a girl arrived. When they saw Eos and Klashka, they went to separate them. Malerk grabbed Eos by the coat and the girl helped Klashka get up. Eos then turned around towards Malerk. When Malerk saw her red eyes, he said:

- Calm down right now.

Eos relaxed and her eyes returned to the blue colour they usually had. Eos then asked Malerk:

- Why did you bring Nature?
- He did not bring Nature. Said the girl.

She removed her white hood and showed her face. It was Lydia also known as Oracle, the first daughter of Nature and Malerk. Lydia said:

- I have decided to come and help you even if my mother did not approve.
- I appreciate the help. Said Eos.
- Why were you fighting? Asked Malerk.
- She just arrived and she already wants the throne back because I am supposedly not worthy to rule this kingdom.
- Don't listen to her. She has left this world long ago, she no longer knows it.
- You know something we do not. Said Nemesis.
- I know many things you do not.
- I am referring to Eos.
- I know of a prophecy. A Vampire queen born in the 22nd century after the treaty will save the world from the humans. I believe that queen is Eos.
- Does it say how?
- No prophecy is that specific.
- We should get moving. Said Eos. It takes two days to get to some part of the border.

The four dragons flew off and every king and queen went to their army to get ready to move out. With the fifteen millions one hundred and fifty thousand dragons, the total of the army was brought to one hundred and thirty-three millions and nine hundred thousand.

CHAPTER 8
LET THEM COME

Three days were left before the shield would come down. For two days, everyone talked about their tactics and what they thought the humans' technology would be like. On the last day, everyone was quiet because they knew the end was coming. Meanwhile, in the human kingdom, the Blackhoods were getting ready. Peter, king of the humans, Mary, sister of Peter, and Ben, steward, were talking about how they would place their army. They had a force of 1 823 575 324 of which 100 000 were in planes,

1 200 000 in tanks, 120 000 in ships, 1 455 750 080 were on foot and

366 405 244 had been called to arms but had not been used yet. After talking for a human day, they decided that they were going to separate the forces in four except for the boats, which was in two, and place them on each borders. Three human days before the shield came down, the humans made their way to the borders of Earth. Each of the twenty-four Blackhoods except for Peter, Mary and Ben were in charge of a division. There was Max, 1st lord of the humans who acted as general, Alexei, lieutenant general of the 1st division, Kim, lieutenant general of the 2nd division, Paul, lieutenant

general of the 3rd division, Janele, lieutenant general of the 4th division, Patricia, major general in charge of the troops of the 1st division, Anne, major general of the marines of the 1st division, John, major general in charge of the pilots of the 1st division, Melany, tank coordinator of the 1st division, Danny, major general in charge of the troops of the 2nd division, Amy, major general of the marines of the 2nd division, David, major general in charge of the pilots of the 2nd division, Carlos, tank coordinator of the 2nd division, Ty, major general in charge of the troops of the 3rd division, Sarah, major general of the marines of the 3rd division, Luc, major general in charge of the pilots of the 3rd division, Ed, tank coordinator of the 3rd division, Dimitry, major general in charge of the troops of the 4th division, Maude, major general of the marines of the 4th division, Laura, major general in charge of the pilots of the 4th division, and Mitch, tank coordinator of the 4th division. On the last day, at 8 pm, the shield that had been up for 638 human years came down. It took two hours for it to completely disappear. When the shield was down, Malerk said:

- Let them come.

Malerk took out his black sword and Lydia took out her white composite bow. Lydia pulled out an arrow and fired a shot across the Maratulde River that was fifty kilometres wide. The arrow went across the river easily and into the throat of a human. As the human fell to the ground, the others around him looked to see what had killed him. When they saw that an arrow had killed him, they started to laugh. One of them said to the others:

- They think they can kill us all with arrows and sword. Look out! Here come the ancient people.
- What's going on here? Asked Danny who had came when he heard them laugh.

- They shot an arrow at us.
- What's so funny about that?
- They are using bows and swords.
- A bow and a sword can be deadly in the right hands as you can see by the body that lays lifeless at your feet. Now stop joking around and concentrate on the mission.
- Yes sir.

Danny returned to his post while the soldier returned to theirs. At the border between the elves' kingdom and the humans', Alexei was talking to his major generals. Alexei said:

- When we enter the Elves' kingdoms, I want everyone to be quiet because the elves can here everything even if it is kilometres away.
- It's no problem for the troops. They were trained to be as quiet as possible. Said Patricia.
- That's why I am sending your troops in the forest.

Patricia went to her troops and explained what they were going to do. They were going in and killing all they could find except for the leaders because Peter had requested that they be brought to him. At the border between Saeros and Earth, the Demons were ready to fulfil their purpose. The Demons did not worry about dying because each Demon had a different way by which they could die. If they found the weakness of one of the Demons, they could only apply it to about five more Demons in that kingdom. At the northern border of Earth, Janele had set up her troops. But there would be no need for them because no one was coming by that way.

CHAPTER 9
THE FIRST FRONT

Half the soldiers of the first front geared up and got ready to enter the elves' kingdoms. 90 984 380 soldiers went in the Fuin forest and the same amount in the Ytic forest. They entered the forest very carefully and quietly. The humans listened carefully for any noise. The only noise they heard were their steps and the noise the animal spirits made in their animal shapes. The wood-elves were hiding in the trees while the Sindarin-elves were waiting for the humans just outside their forest. The Hauflins were hiding at the roots of the trees while the spirits were invisible. The elves, the Hauflins and both kinds of spirit were observing their enemies. They needed the humans to believe they were alone before attacking them. They knew that they were all going to get killed if the humans saw them. After a few hours, the humans started to think that no one was going to stop them. In Nienna, the humans were almost at the end of the forest while in Anoriel, they were deep into the forest. When they had become confident that no one was around them they started to talk and to make more noise. The humans placed their guns on their backs. Some sat on the floor to take a break and others examined the giant trees. One of the humans approached one of the trees that had been standing since the beginning of the elves with his friends. He looked at the tree in every angle before turning to the others and saying:

- This tree could warm us in the winter for years. We should cut it down and bring it home.

After the soldier had finished his phrase, he fell face first on the ground. The others looked at him and saw that is back had been pierce by five arrows. The arrows had gained so much force that they had pierced his bullet-proof vest and killed him instantly. The others that were with him looked at each other in panic. Everyone got on their feet and took their guns back in their hands. They looked around but saw no one so they started to shoot in every direction. They were hoping to hit something. But everyone hid behind the tree trunks. Now everyone in the Fuin forest knew where the humans were. Meanwhile, in the Ytic forest the spirits approached the humans slowly. When they were close to them, they entered their body and made them kill their allies. When the humans were almost through the Ytic forest and halfway through the Fuin forest, they had lost more then half the troops they had sent. After Patricia was told the situation by one of the brigadier generals, she ordered a retreat. The humans returned to the border. Patricia then reported to Alexei and told him:

- We need another plan. They hide and kill us. They make so little noise that no one can hear them. The animals turn into people and kill us before returning to their animal forms and some of our troops turn against us.
- Where do they hide? Asked Alexei.
- Some in the trees and some on the ground.
- Then we will burn the forests.

Back in the wood-elves' kingdom, Halir and Louisiam called a meeting with Stephen, Galadria, Malar, Alewan and Haladin, the Sindarin-elf general. They met close to Aranelenna Lake. Louisiam started by saying:

- The humans have left our kingdoms but I fear that they will come back for revenge.
- I think they will use the elves' weakness. Said Malar.
- What do you know? Asked Haladin
- The Blackhoods know that your souls our connected with the trees. They will tell the others and they will come burn the forest.
- If you let the forest burn, you will be the one lying on the ground with arrows in his back.
- Calm down Haladin. Said Galadria. We will do all we can to protect the forests. But if we should fail, know that it is not our fault. You can only do so much to defend something. Then it is up to Fate to decide what happens next.

Haladin agreed with Galadria. They continued talking. When the meeting was over, everyone returned to their places to wait for the humans to come back. But the ones who went to Nienna would never make it across the past king river. Back in the human kingdom, they had just finished modifying the tanks for them to spit fire. They had arranged them just like a gas stove except when you turned it on it shot gas in to the flame. But before they left, Alexei stopped them and went to see John who was in charge of the pilots because he had a better plan. Alexei approached John and said:

- John!
- Yes sir. Said John while saluting Alexei.
- Send in the planes. Destroy everything that moves.
- Yes sir.

John went to see his team and explained what Alexei wanted them to do. Fifteen minutes later, every plane of the first front took flight in the direction of the Ytic and Fuin forests. When the planes were heard by the elfin kings, they turned to their troops and said:

- Everyone stop moving, planes are coming.

Every elf in Melda Cemmen passed on the message to the others who were with them. Everyone stopped moving. The only movement was their stomach going up and down as they were breathing. The planes moved over everyone's head a few time. John looked on his radar to find a target but he found none. It was the same for every other pilot. There were no signs of life in the forests. After a few runs, the planes returned to the base. When the planes landed, Alexei approached John and asked him:

- Are they dead?
- Nothing showed up on the radar. There is no living thing in that kingdom except for the vegetation. Answered John.
- That's impossible. They killed many of the soldiers with arrows.
- Sorry sir, we found nothing.
- Melany! Send in the flaming tanks.
- Yes sir.

The tanks entered the forests of Nienna and Anoriel. The spirits entered the tanks and killed the humans inside. As soon as humans were killed the tanks burned the forests. The spirits and the Hauflins ran north over the mountains and into Lithe, the animal spirit kingdom, and Mearas, the spirit kingdom. Some of the elves charged at the tanks led by Louisiam, Halir and Haladin. Alewan ran into lake Aranelenna and escaped. All the elves that charged at the tanks were killed or died on their way because their trees had died. Louisiam, Halir and Haladin were taken as prisoners and brought to Peter as he had requested. The screams of the people who were burnt alive were heard in the souls of every person on Melda Cemmen except for the humans'. Twenty-four hours later the fire had crossed the entire forests. Some trees had survived the fire but were very weak as were the elves connected with them. Most of the young trees had died instantly. The elves and the Hauflins had lost the brightness of their eyes and started to look as old as they were. The two capitals had been destroyed. Their beauty would never be as much as it had been before. The land seemed to have been visited by Dedum, protector of Death. The humans had now three kingdoms. They're ego grew bigger.

CHAPTER 10
THE THIRD FRONT

In Saeros, the Demon kingdom, the Demons were anxious to complete their purpose. They knew they had to do it now or they would never get a chance to do it again. Their swords and crossbows were ready to kill them. The Dwarves were waiting with their axes for the first sight of the Humans. They were ready to help. The Dragons were standing behind them. They were only there to destroy the planes if they ever came. Some Wizards and Witches were standing beside the Dragons ready to fight the Humans. Meanwhile, the humans were getting their tanks and planes ready. Paul was giving a final speech to Ty, Sarah, Luc and Ed about what this battle meant to the humans and why they had to win this. He also told them that Peter had ordered that all kings and queens be brought to him. On the border, the humans were loading their guns. When Paul gave the order. The tanks accompanied by some soldiers moved into Saeros. As soon as the humans looked at the Demons, fear filled their bodies. Each Demon was different. Some were very tall and some were normal size. The Demons charged at the humans followed by the Dwarves. If the tanks would not have accompanied the humans they would have all perished in the first hour. While the Demons were busy, Ty managed to bring a battalion to the protected forest. It was a forest surrounded by mountains. In his mind, if Malerk had placed mountains all around that forest it was to protect something. Ty and his gang explored for a few hours before finding the opening of a cave. They entered and found what Malerk was protecting. They found blue crystals and black iron. Ty grabbed a sample and brought it back to Paul. When Ty arrived beside Paul, he said to him:

- Paul! I've found something.
- What? Asked Paul.
- I found a mountain...
- Ty, I don't need a mountain.
- I wasn't done. That mountain could make us rich. Inside there is black iron and blue crystals like these.

Ty took out the sample and gave them to Paul who was hypnotized by them. Paul then turned to Ty and asked:

- Is there a place where we could land the planes?
- There is a forest but no field.
- That will do. Luc!
- Yes sir. Said Luc.
- Send your planes inside the triangular mountain chain. There you will find a forest. Land there and go into the tallest and blackest mountain and bring me as many of these as you can find.

Paul showed the crystals and the iron to Luc who looked at them in wonder. Luc looked at Paul and said:

- I will bring all I can.

Luc left and went to the airbase. Fifteen minutes later, 18 750 planes took flight. They flew towards the Merelyn

Mountain. When the dragons saw them coming, they took off to meet them in the battle. Twelve thousand dragons went towards the planes. To protect the hand-to-hand fighters, the wizards made a shield around them that would stop the debris or the dead dragons. The fight started between planes and dragons. The dragons would target the fuel tanks and the humans the hearts. The battle lasted at least five hours. Eventually, the humans gave up and returned to their base. When Paul saw the planes returning, he asked Ty to go in with a battalion of elites. They were trained to sneak in everywhere under whatever circumstances. Meanwhile the dragons were landing in Saeros. A silver dragon landed beside Deimos and told him:

- "I saw something terrible. I saw the elfin forests going up in flame."
- The elves have fallen. Let's hope the Hauflins and spirits will keep defending Melda Cemmen from the spirits' kingdoms.

The silver dragon agreed with the king and returned to his kin. For the next few days, the humans only defended their territory and did not try to get more. They were keeping the attention of their enemies so that Ty and his guys could get the iron and crystals. At the Merelyn Mountain, the humans had just arrived. They slowly entered the mountain that trembled in fury at the sight of the intruders. When the humans arrived at the core of the mountain, they opened some bags and started to fill them with all they could carry. The next day, when they came out of the mountain, someone was waiting for them. Someone who did not like people who took his things without permission. Malerk was standing in front of them by himself. Ty approached him while looking at him. He thought Malerk was stupid to be carrying a sword and not wearing any armour. Ty asked Malerk:

- Can I help you?
- I don't need help. I'm here to take back what belongs to me. Said Malerk.
- We haven't taken anything from you.
- You have taken my crystals and my iron.
- It does not belong to you. We found it first so it belongs to us.
- This is your last warning. Give it back to me or go place it where you found it.
- No. Now move out of our way or we'll kill you.
- "Dark-angels come to fight along my side."

Thirty dark- angels arrived with their swords in hand ready to help Malerk. Five minutes later, Ty and his battalion where lying lifeless on the ground. Malerk and his soldiers returned the crystals and the iron to the mountains before leaving. The Demons eventually pushed the humans back into their kingdom. The humans had lost that battle.

CHAPTER 11
THE SECOND FRONT

Kim, Amy, Carlos, David and Danny were trying to figure out how they were going to get their troops across the Maratulde River. There was only a 25 km stretch that was dry land right beside Anoriel. They had to find a faster way to get across. Kim went to see her engineers and scientist. She asked them to find a way to cross the tanks over the river without having to build a bridge. It had to be quick but solid. The engineers and scientists got to work immediately. Danny decided to send one thousand troops across the river. As they moved farther away from shore, many of them where pulled under water and never returned to the surface. The water dragons did not like people who disturbed the water. Instead of crossing the river the humans then decided to lure the Vampire into crossing to their side. But a day later, they gave up because it was not working. The Vampires protected their homes but did not wish to destroy those of others. The next day, Janele, general of the fourth army, arrived at Edain and reported to Peter. When Peter saw Janele come in the mansion, he asked her:

- Why are you here?

- There is no enemy at the fourth front. They do not want to cross the ocean.
- Then you will protect the capital. Do not let Edain fall.
- Yes sir.

Janele ordered her troops to spread around the capital. A few days passed and no shot was fired. But as the sun rose on the next day, a man arrived from the west. Alexandre saw him first and noticed he was wounded. Alexandre approached and caught him as he fell to the ground. It was a Sindarin-elf. The elf looked at Alexandre and said:

- I must speak with queen Eos.
- Hold on. Mother!

Eos looked at her son and when she saw the elf, she ran to them. When she had approached, Eos saw who it was. Eos asked the Elf:

- Alewan, what happened?
- They destroyed the forest. They burnt it. The spirits have escaped but many of the Elves and Hauflins are either dead or very weak. Louisiam, Halir and Haladin have been taken as prisoners. You must save them.

Those were his last words. His eyes closed forever. Alexandre placed Alewan on the ground and looked at his mother. Eos looked at Alexandre and said:

- We're going in.
- No we're not. Said Malerk and Lydia.
- Why not?
- Because that's what they want you to do.
- Then we keep on waiting until they die of old age.

- That's not what we meant. We have to make them come to our side. Said Lydia
- That's a good plan. Said Malerk. You keep on perfecting it and I'll be back later.
- Where are you going? Asked Eos.
- I have to protect what belongs to me.

Malerk left in a hurry to go to mount Merelyn. Alexandre, Eos and Lydia were left alone. Alexandre then turned to the girls and said:

- Why not use the necklace of immortality and the crystal of power to make them come.
- Good idea Alexandre but we do not have the necklace of immortality with us. Said Lydia.
- I can get it for you.
- How?
- Watch and learn.

Alexandre closed his eyes and concentrated on what he wanted in his hands. Five minutes later, the necklace appeared in his hands. Eos looked at Alexandre and asked:

- How did you do that?
- I found out a few months ago that I only had to think about the object I wanted and not have to see it to make it come to me.
- Lets get started.
- Wait. Said Lydia. We need one more person.
- I'll go get William.
- No. I already had someone in mind.

Lydia pointed to the sky towards the south where a shooting star was coming towards them. The star was heading for Lydia, Alexandre and Eos. As it approached the ground it turned into a wood-elf who landed on his feet in front of them. Lydia made the introduction:

- This is Lumos, protector of light, and my twin brother.
- Your what!? Said Eos.
- My brother.
- Why do they not mention him in the history of Melda Cemmen?
- Because I have not done anything that changed the world. Said Lumos. Most people don't know I exist.
- This is Eos, queen of the Vampires, heir of Malerk. Said Lydia.
- A pleasure to meet you. Said Lumos while bowing to her.
- And this is Alexandre, prince of the Vampires.
- Nice to meet you also.
- The pleasure is all mine. Said Alexandre.

Lydia turned to her brother and explained to him what they wanted to do with the necklaces. Lumos blew on the necklaces that started to shine immediately. A spell was then put on them so that any human of the second front could see it. On the other side of the river, the humans were very quiet. Carlos, David and Danny were talking together when they saw the necklaces. They all turned to see where the light was coming from. They were hypnotized by them. It would take half an hour for all the humans to fall under the spell. When Kim had seen the necklaces, she returned to the scientists and engineers. When she entered the room and asked them:

- Have you found a way to cross the river?
- We have. Said one scientist. You will also like to hear that we found something else that could help you by accident.
- What did you find?
- We found a way to make silver bullets. All we have to do is bring the silver to its melting point of 962°C or 1761°F and

then mix it with uranium. It keeps the silver liquid even if it goes under its melting point. We placed it in a silica glass shell. It can be fired from any standard gun.

- Very nice, but what about the way across the river?

- It's very simple. We have designed these rubber tubes hooked to harpoons that keep going until they find dry land. On one side of the tubes, there are little holes that will let some eladrium, which is a metal that solidifies in contact with hydrogen, out. The guns, which we designed to shoot the harpoons, will then be hooked to the eladrium that will be blasted to the end of the tubes and will then escape from the little holes. Be careful to always place the tubes on the correct side or it will not work.

- Thanks. Load them up. I am taking them to the second front.

The engineers and the scientist loaded their inventions on sport utility vehicles(SUVs) that brought the weapons to the troops. The silver bullets had once been invented by Liv but the technology had died with her. When Kim arrived at the front, the bullets were handed out to every soldier. The eladrium bridges were then made one kilometre apart. In total, there were fourteen hundred bridges. The troops, marines and tanks started to cross the river.

As the harpoons crossed the river, they made noise as they skidded on the water. At the bottom of the river, where the light of the sun did not reach, something had been woken by the noise. A few dozen water dragons were waking. They started to make their way to the surface. When they reached the water that was blue because of the sun, they saw the bridges that had been made. The humans were going to pay for intruding their homes. The dragons waited patiently for the humans to be at least half way. When the humans that were on the bridge that was the closest to the Demon kingdom had arrived half way, one of the dragons made his move. He jumped out of the water and brought the bridge in front of the soldiers with him under water. One of the soldiers that was on that bridge contacted Kim with his radio and said to her:

- There's something in the water. It just broke the bridge in front of us. We can't get across.
- Stay on the bridge and kill whatever is down there.
- Yes ma'am.
- As for everyone else, get across the river as fast as you can. We cannot let the creature of the water defeat us.

On every other bridge, the humans were hurrying across the river. The other water dragons each took a bridge of their own to destroy. After the front of a bridge had been broken, most humans returned to shore. But some were either too afraid to move or wanted to die bravely. The humans remaining on the bridges had water on one side and soon water dragons broke the bridge on the other side as well. The water dragons then showed themselves to the brave humans before pulling them under water. They would join those who had been pulled under when they first tried to cross the river. Unfortunately, the dragons did not succeed in destroying all the bridges before the humans got to Yaviere. When David saw that the bridges had not worked, he sent the planes.

Meanwhile in Yaviere, Malerk had just returned with his dark-angels from Mount Merelyn. Eos approached him and asked:

- Where were you?
- At the bottom of Mount Merelyn to protect what belongs to me.
- How many did you kill?

- About... Malerk paused. He had seen Lumos. What is he doing here?
- Long time no seen, dad. Said Lumos.
- My name is Malerk.
- I'm your son.
- I wish you weren't.

Malerk walked away from Eos and Lumos towards William. Before following him, Eos turned to Lumos and said:

- I'm sorry.

Malerk approached William who was talking with Drew and asked them:

- What did I miss?
- Not much except some waiting. Said William
- What did I miss? Asked Eos.
- I told you already. Said Malerk.
- That's not what I'm talking about. I meant between you and Lumos.
- I don't like people who are purely good.
- I know but there's something else.
- No that's it.
- You don't' let him call you father yet you let everyone else do it. What happened?
- Seven thousand years ago, he...
- He what?
- He threw me a star.
- That's it?
- Eos. Screamed Malerk. You wanted to hear the story so listen to it.
- Sorry.
- That star was the brightest one so it sucked all the evil out

of me. The only way to save myself was by letting Nature torture me until I didn't care. I let her do it because I didn't want to die.

- It must have been hell. Said William
- Hell for everyone else because I didn't care about anything good. Since then Nature has never been the same.
- What happened to Lumos?
- He was forced to never enter Melda Cemmen again unless he was called to it. Eos!?

While Malerk had been talking to William, Eos had walked away. She had gone to the forest at the northern edge of the Vampire kingdom to be alone. But she wasn't alone. Simon was there also. He approached Eos without being seen and said:

- Why did you come here?
- To be alone. Said Eos.
- I will leave then.
- No, wait. You can stay. I need your advice.
- What's wrong?
- Why is it that Malerk and I are so alike yet so different?
- You've both suffered more then anyone should, you've both been betrayed by your own children, you've both been rejected by your fathers and you both understand humans more then they understand themselves.
- Then why do I feel like I don't know him?
- Don't worry about it. You're the one who knows the most about him. You're the first one outside of his children who has met his protectors.
- You can't be serious.
- Maybe Nature knows him more then you but no one else.
- Thank you
- You're...
- Shut.

- What's wrong?
- I hear a machine.

Simon listened to see if he could hear it. As the sound got clearer, Eos began to remember what it was. The noise was being made by tanks. Eos turned to Simon and said:

- Machines of war are coming.

In the first tank, the aimer had spotted them. He told everyone else that was with him in the machine and, one minute later, a shot was fired. Eos heard it coming so she pulled Simon to the ground and the missile passed right above their heads. Simon then said to Eos:

- We should get out of here.

Eos agreed with Simon who helped her get back on her feet. Simon then said to Eos:

- You go warn the others, I'll buy you time.
- Are you sure?
- I can't feel pain.

Eos ran to the army that was in the Vampire kingdom while Simon got the attention of the humans. When Eos returned form the forest, William asked her:

- Where were you?
- I have no time to explain. The machines are in the forest.

At that moment, David's plane flew over their heads. The dragons went after them. Meanwhile in the forest, Simon had been hit by the explosions of two missiles. The human who was shooting turned to Carlos who was with them and said:

- Missiles don't kill him.
- You mean those kind don't kill him. Bring me a white missile.

The white missile was brought to Carlos who loaded the gun with it. The aimer locked on to Simon and Carlos fired the missile. Simon was hit right in the stomach and this time he felt it. The white missile had been designed for spirits. It reconnected them with their bodies and so made them mortal. Simon collapsed in pain. While Carlos took care of Simon, Danny led his troops that had gotten across the river towards the Vampires. When the humans saw the Vampires Danny fired the first shot. The bullet left the shadow of the forest and entered the centre of the heart of the one it was aimed at. The Vampire collapsed under the pain of the silver. William was dying. When they saw that he had been hit, Eos, Alexandre and Scott ran to him. When Alexandre realized what had hit his father he turned to one of the wizards and asked:

- Could you protect us from the bullets?
- You will be protected as long as you don't cross the place were we are standing.

All the Wizards placed themselves in a line and hit their staff on the ground at the same time. A transparent shield appeared to protect the Vampires. No bullets could cross it. Eos kneeled beside William and said:

- I'll pull out the bullet.

Eos tried to pull out the bullet but there was nothing but broken pieces of glass. Eos knew that most of the silver had already been circulated by William's heart and that his veins were probably full of silver by now. It would not be long before the silver eliminated the blood. Eos looked at William's face and said:

- It's liquid silver in a glass shell. The glass is broken and the silver has entered your blood stream.
- I know. I'm dying.
- You can't die without me. You can't leave me alone.
- You won't be alone. You'll be with Alexandre, Scott and Malerk. Eos, I will love you until the end of time and I will wait for you even if it takes eternity. I love you Eos, forever.

The silver had now eliminated all of William's blood. He had died looking up at his true love. Malerk and Dedum approached eos and the body of William. Eos looked up at Dedum and said:

- Please don't take him, I beg you.

Dedum kneeled to be at the height of Eos. He looked into her eyes and said:

- He received a liquid silver bullet in the center of his heart. How could I possibly save him?

Eos looked up at Malerk to make sure that Dedum wasn't wrong. Dedum was right. Eos held back her tears and wiped those that had already fallen. Eos closed his eyes and got on her feet. She placed Yar on William's stomach and Tari in the ground beside William. She then said the sending phrase of the dead "Spero *the stars* et *the winds* amant vos satis *to guide* vos ad tuas *next* vitas(I hope the stars and the winds love you enough to guide you to your next life.)" Eos then looked at Alexandre and said:

- You are now ambassador to the crown. You rule the Vampire kingdom until you have a daughter.

Eos then got on her knees and looked to the sky while saying:

- I ask Vira and Dedum to take care of my life and my death as they should be taken care of.

Eos got back on her feet and turned around and started to walk toward the forest where she had left Simon. When Malerk saw where she was going, he said:

- Where are you going?
- I'm going to get my protector.
- Don't go get revenge.
- I'm not. I'm going to get Simon.

Eos crossed the shield and started to run. When she got close to the river, she whistled. A water dragon appeared and Eos jumped on his back before it started to make its way across the river. When Eos was half way across the river, she took her bow and started to shoot at the humans who were on the river bank. When the humans saw her, they started to shoot at her. By the time she got close to dry land only two bullets had touched her because of the speed of the dragon. Eos could feel the silver but she was so angry that it did not stop her. She put away her bow and took her father's swords. She jumped on the land and started to run towards the humans. Eos killed the humans that were standing in her way before continuing to run towards Edain. As she got closer to the capital, more and more people fired bullets at her. When she was five kilometres away from the capital, Eos was in so much pain that she lost control of her body. Her eyes turned red, her wings appeared and she flew 500 meters away from the ground. When she was in the sky, lightning came down to destroy the machines before Eos turned into a ball of fire. A few minutes later, the fire around Eos turned into an explosion and killed everyone in a radius of a kilometre. When the explosion was over, Eos had no more strength so she fell to the ground. Before she lost consciousness, she saw four black figures lean over her.

CHAPTER 12
THE DECISION

Nature called for an urgent meeting with the council every king or queen that could make it. Alexandre, ambassador of the Vampires, Hobbes and Clarwena, prince and princess of the wizards, Guenevieve, queen of the witches, Octet leader of the banished, Nora, princess of the spirits, Deith, king of the Demons, and Stephen and Mickeal, guards of Nature's prison, had all agreed to come. Nature had used some of her magic to transport them to her castle to save time. When everyone had arrived and sat down, Nature started to explain why they were there:

- An hour ago we found out who was destined to save Melda Cemmen. It is Eos and not Clarwena as I first thought. The battles started, as it should have like the prophecy had said. The king of the Vampires then died which pushed Eos to complete the rest. Nature paused. Something went wrong. I was not going to get involved in this war but now I have no choice. Eos is stuck inside.
- What!? Said Alexandre and Clarwena.
- I knew one day she'd destroy herself. Said Guenevieve.

- She did not destroy herself. Said Stephen. She saved us all even if some of us did not deserve to be saved.
- He is right. Said Octet. She of all people deserves to be saved once more.
- But how are we going to get in if she can't get out? Asked Deith.
- Peter will bow to me. Said Nature.
- What if he doesn't? Asked Hobbes. What if he's like Eos?
- Then he will bow to Malerk.
- Wouldn't it be wiser to banish them again? Asked Iire.
- We've already tried that. The Blackhoods resisted us. Said Oia.
- I think what Iire meant was to send them somewhere else. Said Hui.
- Council members, find a way to send them away and a place to send them while we go save Eos.

After everyone had left the room except for Mickeal and Stephen, Stephen turned to Mickeal and said:

- She's a good liar.
- She wasn't lying. Said Mickeal.
- She does want to go in the human kingdom. It's true that she wants to get rid of the humans. But she doesn't want to save Eos. There is someone else who is trapped inside.

Eos opened her eyes. Her head hurt, one of her wings was broken and she was very weak. Her veins had turned silver with a hint of red but because of Malerk's powers it wasn't going to kill her. Peter, Mary, Ben and Max were sitting at a table at the feet of Eos. Eos looked around and saw that she was attached by chains surrounded by a force field so they could not be broken on an operating room type bed. When Peter saw that Eos had woken up, he got on his feet and approached Eos before saying:

- It's about time you woke up. Of course compared to him it didn't take you much time.

On another bed beside Eos was Simon still unconscious. His flesh was almost completely destroyed. The white missile had hit a bull's-eye. Since the pain was so intense, Simon's brain had shut down. Peter then continued:

- And in the prison cell, we've got those three.

In the prison cell on the other side of the room, there were Louisiam, Halir and Haladin. They seemed very weak but still managed to smile to Eos to say hi. Peter got to Eos and placed his hand on her stomach where most of the bullets were. Peter then said to Eos:

- I see you all know each other.

A tear of pain ran down Eos' face and she then spit out the blood that had come to her mouth. Eos then looked at Peter and asked him:

- Are you a descendant of Liv?
- No. Said Peter. I'm a descendant of Guillaume. Why do you ask?
- You behave more like Liv then Guillaume.

Peter did not like when someone insulted him or his family. He pulled out his gun and fired another silver bullet into Eos' shoulder. Max couldn't take it anymore. He got and his feet and said to Peter:

- Stop it! Why do you insist on making her suffer?

- I want her to suffer as much as the people she burned alive. Said Peter.
- I want you to suffer as much as the persons you burnt alive. Said Eos. But no matter how much we try we will never be able to do that because we do not know how much they suffered. But if it makes you feel better, do it.
- Are you giving me the permission to torture you?
- Do your worst.
- Eos, don't. Said Louisiam.
- Shut up Elf! Screamed Peter. Let's get started.

Peter aimed the gun at Eos and stayed that way for five minutes. After a while, Mary looked at her brother and said:

- Are you going to shoot or are you going to stand there all day?

Peter dropped the gun and moved away from Eos. An hour later, Peter was still sitting on his chair looking into the emptiness. Mary was tired of his silence so she asked her brother:

- What's wrong?
- She's right.
- About what?
- Everything. Ben, remove the bullets from her body.

Ben approached Eos who opened her eyes when she heard him. Ben approached his hand closer to Eos' body with fear. Eos looked at him and said:

- Don't be afraid or you'll make me want to kill you.

Ben took all the courage he had and pulled out the pieces of glass from a bullet from Eos' shoulder. Eos' breath accelerated and she tried to free herself. Ben backed away from her and Simon woke up.

Nature and the others that had come to the meeting had just arrived in the Vampire kingdom where Malerk was helping the others kill the humans that had crossed the river. Nature approached Malerk and asked him:

- Where's Lydia?
- Over there fighting against that machine. Said Malerk.
- Do you know what happened to Eos?

Malerk lifted his shirt and turned around towards Nature. Malerk had all the wounds Eos had on his stomach. His body was filled with bullet wounds and stained with blood. Nature then asked Malerk:

- How could that be?
- Do you remember the black hand I use to put on the ones I made? Asked Malerk.
- The one that made you feel their pain. You didn't do it to Eos, did you?
- I did when I gave her wings.
- Malerk, you've doomed yourself to death.
- I've doomed myself to save her life.
- You can't die while she's not with you.
- We have to save her.
- Let's go.

Meanwhile, back in the human kingdom, Simon was trying to free himself to help Eos. Eos' pain finally dissipated and Simon calmed down. Max turned to Simon and said:

- I think we've found your weakness. How are you two related?

Are you her boyfriend, husband, best friend or is it something else?
- Something else. Said Simon.
- Which would be?
- I'm her protector.
- So you've failed. Said Mary.
- I will only fail when she dies of an unnatural way.
- Are you a Human?
- No. I'm a Spirit.
- I know that. I meant before you became a Spirit.
- I was a half-blood.
- Of what species?

Simon did not want to say what species he was. He looked at the elves and at Eos but no one wanted to stop him. Simon took some courage and told them:

- My mother was a Witch and my father was a Vampire.
- You're a banished! Said Eos. How did you end up being a protector? Usually, they don't let them be protectors.
- My mother begged Nature to save my soul. Nature loves my mother so she made me a Spirit and I later decided to become a protector.
- Your mother is still alive!? Said Ben.
- Yes. She will never die.
- Your mother is Nessima!? Said Eos. And you were banished!? What happened?
- I wanted to live in the Witch's kingdom and I guess I put to much trust in my title. They asked me to leave their kingdom and I didn't want to so they banished me. I know how Merrill feels.
- Why didn't you go live with your parents in the castle of the council?
- Would you want to live with the council?
- You've got a point.

Silence took the room. There were no more questions from the humans. The elves were still silent and Simon did not wish to say anything else about his life. But Eos had something to ask the humans:

- Why did you capture all of us?
- You all have a gift that could help us. Said Peter. The elves live young all their lives yet they are thousands of years old, the spirits can separate themselves from their body and you hold the secret to the purest form of immortality.
- I should have known.
- What does that mean?
- You've lived so long away from the rest of the world that you no longer care about us.
- I do care.
- You care about what we possess but you do not care about us. If you really cared you would not have gone to war against us. You would have taught the Humans to live in peace with us.
- I tried but humans don't want new friends, they want new enemies.
- That's exactly why your memories were erased.
- Get her on her feet.

Max approached Eos and removed the chains that were holding her down. He then helped Eos sit on the bed and let her go. Eos fell forward but Max caught her. Ben approached them and handed a pill to Eos while saying:

- Take this. It will numb your body while we remove the bullets from it.

Eos took the pill and swallowed it. Max approached his hand and removed the pieces of glass in one of her wounds. Eos felt his fingers but not the pain. An hour later, half of the pieces of glass had been removed. A knock was heard on the front door. Mary got up and went to answer. Nature and Malerk were standing outside the door. When Mary had opened the door, she asked them:

- Who are you?
- I'm Nature and this is Malerk.
- We wish to see our granddaughter. Said Malerk.
- I'm afraid I can't let you in.

Malerk pushed Mary aside and entered followed by Nature who apologized for what Malerk had done to her. Malerk and Nature then made their way to the room where everyone was. When Malerk saw Ben and Max with Eos, he thought they were torturing her. Malerk made lightning come down towards them. When Eos saw the lightning, she pushed Max and Ben and took the hit. Eos then collapsed but was caught by Ben and Max who helped her back on the bed. Peter looked at Malerk and said:

- I think you have the wrong idea about us.
- I don't think so. I use my feelings to make a judgement.
- We gave her a pill to numb the pain but not her body before we removed what was left of the bullets.
- Hand her over.
- Just her?
- We want the others to. Said Nature
- Could I ask you a question first?
- Go ahead.
- Who are you?
- I'm Nature queen of Melda Cemmen.
- I'm Malerk, Lord of all evil.
- You're Nature and Malerk!? Said Peter. Then I have another question.
- You said one.

- Go ahead. Said Nature.
- Why didn't you give the humans a special power?
- I did. I gave you inventive brains, which unfortunately led you to your doom.
- "Nature!" Thought Nessima which nature heard.
- "Yes Nessima."
- "You have fifteen minutes to get out of the human kingdom before the portal to their next world opens."
- "Will you erase their minds?"
- "It will be done in fourteen minutes."
- I'm sorry but we must go.
- Think again. Said Peter while they were surrounded by Humans.

The Humans were not about to give up the things that could help them become immortal. Malerk was ready to kill them all with his black sword but Nature was worried this was going to take too much time.

CHAPTER 13
THE LONGEST FIFTEEN MINUTES

The humans took out their swords because they knew they could not kill them with guns. Malerk took out his black sword and Nature, even if she thought they had no time for this, took out her magic weapon. It had the appearance of a small piece of branch and it was decorated with jewels. It could take the shape of any weapon that already existed in the world. Before they started to fight Nature turned to Malerk and said:

- We have thirteen minutes before we have to leave.
- You found a way to end their world.
- No, we've found them a new world.
- Let's get this over with.
- Malerk, don't kill them please.
- I'll try.

Max and Ben got Eos and pulled her into the next room where they watched over her. Malerk and Nature started to fight against the humans. In the room, Eos looked up at Max and Ben and said:

- Why did you bring me here?
- We have to finish removing the glass. Said Ben.
- Why are you helping me?
- Because you once lived with us and you will always be one of us.

Eos pushed Max's arm that was taking care of the wounds away before saying to them:

- I was never human and I will never be one of you. So leave me to die like I deserve.
- We can leave the glass but you can't die. Said Max.
- I wish I could.
- Why? Why would you want to give up immortality?
- Because when the first silver bullet was fired, it killed my husband and soul mate.
- We're sorry, very sorry.
- Don't let it weigh too much on your conscience. In ten minutes, you won't remember it.

Back in the other room, Malerk had not listened to Nature. In four minutes, he had killed two humans. The first had been killed quickly; Malerk had broken her neck. The second had suffered; he had two cuts on his left arm, one wound on the stomach and his main artery had been cut open. Malerk's only plan was to rescue Eos. Nature's plan was to rescue Simon and the Elves without killing anyone. When Peter realized that this would not end well, he left followed by his sister. Seven more minutes had passed; only three remained. Nature then had an idea. She separated Simon from his body who then got up to help her rescue the elves. They then all disappeared leaving Malerk alone to rescue Eos. He knew, because Nature had left, that there was not much time for him left to rescue Eos. He pushed aside the only human standing between him and the door to Eos, which he then forced open. Ben and Max were still with Eos. Malerk looked at the boys before taking Eos in his arms and disappearing. The other humans ran in only to see Max and Ben by themselves.

Nature placed the elves on the ground in the Vampire kingdom and a minute later, Malerk appeared with Eos. Just after Eos and Malerk had arrived, blue lights started to rise to the sky. Eos looked at Malerk and asked:

- What are those?
- They're the memories of every living human.
- What will happen to them?
- They will be destroyed.

A minute later, white light started to rise and a portal opened above them to greet them and bring them to their next home. The white lights were the souls of the humans.

CHAPTER 14
THE NEXT CHAPTER OF MELDA LEMMEN

The sky darkened; the white lights had disappeared. Eos approached Malerk and gave him a hug. Malerk placed his arms around her but his attention was on Nature. He could still not believe that she had left him and Eos in the human kingdom. Eos let go of Malerk and said:

- Thank you for coming to get me.
- I couldn't have left you to die.
- I was hit by so many bullets yet I did not feel the amount of pain I should have felt.
- You had adrenaline and anger in you. The two things that make you forget pain.
- It should have hurt more than the time I was shot by two normal bullets.

Malerk backed a meter away from Eos. He had the same look on is face he had before he collapsed in Eos' bedroom. Eos then felt her wounds close. At that moment, Malerk's shirt was stained with blood. Malerk fell backwards but Eos caught him. She sat on her knees and placed Malerk's head on them. Eos looked at him and asked:

- What spell did you use this time?
- Do you remember the black hand on your chest?
- Yes. What did it mean?
- It meant that I took your pain as my own. When you asked me to remove it, I hid it under your skin.
- You're dying because of me!?
- No. I'm dying to save you.

Malerk closed his eyes and reopened them. Nature was still taking care of the elves and of Simon. She had not even noticed that her husband was dying. Malerk looked at Eos and told her:

- Don't ever trust Nature.
- I never have.
- I know. You should know that it was her idea to go into the human kingdom and that after rescuing the elves, she left us to die. Malerk paused. I love you. Don't ever trust her. Don't ever agree to what she says. Don't let her in your heart. I will always be with you.

That warning was his last words. His eyes closed and his soul was lost forever. The "gang" had finally found Eos. They all lowered their heads when they saw that Malerk was dead. Nature finally approached and looked at Eos while asking:

- Is he dead?

Eos did not answer Nature's question. She got on her feet after gently placing Malerk's head on the ground. Eos looked at Nature before turning to her brother and saying:

- Could you bring William's and Malerk's bodies to my new castle?
- Of course. Answered Scott.
- There their body will be burned and we will have a funeral.
- As you wish Eos.

Eos walked away from the battlefield and went to the black castle where a new life awaited her. She had no emotion. Her face was empty. She felt too many things to react to any of them. Scott and Drew placed William on a portable bed. William's veins were still grey from the silver. Drew placed Yar on his stomach and placed his hands on the handle just like Eos had done. William's crown was brought and placed on his head and a black rose was placed on top of his sword as a sign of love and death. Karl and Gabriel placed Malerk on a portable bed and placed his black sword on his stomach with a black rose. Two days later, outside Malerk's castle, all the royalties of Melda Cemmen came to pay their respects to the dead. Two stacks of wood were being made on which Malerk and William would be placed. While everyone placed themselves around the dead, Daniel, king of the Animal Spirits, approached Eos and said:

- I'm sorry they died. He was a great father figure to both of us.
- What do you mean? Asked Eos.
- Malerk was like a father to both of us.
- He was a great one to.
- Why do you not show sadness? You have lost so much yet you do not cry.
- Sometimes we are in so much pain that crying would not make us feel better. Right now, I feel like screaming as loud as I can.

- You should scream if you want to. It is better to let it escape then keep your feelings inside.
- Thank you.

Daniel bowed to Eos and returned to his family. A few minutes later, Guenevieve approached Eos. She just stood beside Eos looking at the Dark- Angels who were stacking wood. After a few minutes, Eos asked Guenevieve:

- Do you have something to say to me or are you just trying to annoy me?
- I have something to say to you. Answered Guenevieve. I'm sorry for your lost.
- Thanks for your concern. Said Eos with an empty voice.

Guenevieve left Eos alone. The bodies of Malerk and William were brought and placed on the wood. Everyone then stopped talking and looked at the two bodies. Eos looked around to see who was there. She saw all the kings and queens with their families, the council, Stephen and Mickeal, the "gang", the dark angels, the protectors, Nature and Lydia. Eos did not know why the good protectors were there but she would ask questions later. Eos then saw Nature approach the dead with a knife. Eos approached Nature who was now beside William's body and asked her:

- What are you doing?
- I'm going to empty his veins so he can have a chance at becoming a spirit. Said Nature.
- You decide who becomes a Spirit. Are you really going to save him from death?
- Of course not. He is doomed to go directly to hell.
- After his soul leaves Melda Cemmen, you have no saying on where he goes. Now get back to your place.

Nature and Eos returned to their place in the circle. Scott approached Eos and held her in his arms as both bodies were burnt. Everyone looked at the bodies burn in sadness except for Eos who showed no emotion. She just looked at the flames and thought of their last words.

CHAPTER 15
THE TRUTH

Two weeks had passed since the bodies of William and Malerk had been burned. Eos had been sitting on the black throne ever since. She had fallen asleep for short period of times but immediately woken when she had heard a noise. Eos was looking into the emptiness. Valir was beginning to worry about her. Dedum eventually approached her to ask her a question:

- Your highness, could I ask you something?
- Go ahead Dedum.
- During the battle, why did you put your fate in Vira's and my hands?
- I wanted you to decide if the Humans were going to destroy me or if I was going to destroy myself.
- Did you get your answer?
- Yes. I let myself get destroyed by the things that were happening in my life.

Dedum left Eos by herself after her phrase. The next day, someone arrived at the castle and asked to see Eos. The guards did not want to let him in but Valir insisted that it would do some good to Eos to see people. He entered the hall and his footsteps resounded. When Eos heard him, she lifted her head to see who it was. When she saw who it was she returned to the emptiness. The visitor stopped in front of her throne, looked at her and said:

- I have come for the truth.
- Aren't you supposed to be with the stars?
- No. My banishment was an agreement between Nature and Malerk. Malerk is dead so my banishment is cancelled. Said Lumos.
- What do you want to know?
- Every secret about your life.
- Ask a question and I'll see if I can answer it.
- Where to begin? What really happened to your mother?
- She killed herself.
- Then how did you end up in the past?
- How should I know? I was three days old. Why do you want to know everything about my life?
- Because I was supposed to be sitting on that throne.
- You!? Protector of light. You're not evil enough.
- You don't have to be evil. Look at you.
- You must have suffered.
- But why you? He could have chosen any of his evil children.
- Valir! Bring me the black book called "Ways to kill the immortal and to prevent the mortals from dying".
- As you wish. Said Valir.

Valir left the room and came back ten minutes later with the black book that Malerk had used many times to help his children and Eos. Eos took it and opened it at the first page. She then read the words that were written by hand to Lumos:

- One day, my son, you will have to choose an heir. You will have to choose her wisely. Yes her. I know that the rulers in our kingdom have always been men but you will change that. I know that you do not believe in the future but that I have seen has clearly as I see you. You will search many years for her because she will not be your daughter. You will find that she is exactly like you yet different. But she will not be easy to have. You will have to rescue her from many dangers and some life threatening situations. This book will help you protect her life. But be careful for you might give your life for hers. Have a nice life on your new planet. But be careful about Nature. Don't ever trust her. Don't ever agree to what she says. Don't let her in your heart. Be brave, I will always be with you. Your loving father, King Vile.

Eos closed the book and looked at Lumos. He was terrified at the idea that it was already decided that he would not get the throne even before he was born. Lumos then looked at Eos and said:

- One day I will know the truth about your mother's death and I will punish the one who killed her and destroyed my chance at the throne.

Lumos bowed to Eos, as he had to do and left the castle in a hurry. Eos gave the book back to Valir who brought it back to the library. A few hours later, someone else came to see Eos. Nature entered and said to Eos:

- I have two things to ask you?
- What do you want?
- First, what did you tell my son to make him that angry?
- I read him a passage from Malerk's book that said that it was decided even before he was born that he would not get the "evil" throne. Now, what was your other question?

- I want something you have.
- That is not a question. But what would you like that I have?
- I want Simon.
- You are not aloud to have a protector.
- I want my grandson.
- Your grandson is dead.
- What did you do to him?
- Nothing. He was dead when he became my protector.
- Give him back to me.
- I'll make you a deal. You can have him if you tell me the truth.
- About what?
- Did you really want to save all of us in the Human kingdom or did you only want to save the Elves and Simon?
- I wanted to save all of you.
- Did you abandon Malerk and me in the Human kingdom?
- I would never abandon Malerk.
- Did you ever love Malerk or were you just using him to make you feel more at home?
- I loved Malerk with all my heart.
- You're not getting Simon.
- I answered all of your questions.
- You lied about at least two of the questions. You did abandon Malerk in the Human kingdom and you never wanted to save me. You just didn't want everyone to hate you because you had not participated in the war.
- That's not true.
- Then tell me the truth or the truth will be what I said.
- I was jealous of you.

Eos looked in the eyes of Nature. Nature was telling the truth. Eos got off her black throne and approached Nature. Eos then asked her:

- Why were you jealous of me?
- Because you had everything I wanted.
- What did I have that you did not?
- Malerk's love. He protected you as if you were the only thing keeping him alive. He loved you more than he loved his children or me. I'm certain that if you would not have been his granddaughter, he would have wanted to marry you.
- I'm sorry I destroyed your marriage.
- No you're not.

Nature pulled out her stick and transformed it into a sword so fast that Eos did not have enough time to move out of the way. A wound stretching from one side to another of Eos' stomach appeared. Nature then grabbed Eos by the throat and said:

- How are you going to get out of this one without Malerk?
- First my wound will close by itself.

Nature looked at Eos' stomach. The wound was now only a red line. Eos then continued:

- Then you will say...
- How could that be?
- The healing powers of the Vampires, Elves and Malerk combined as one make any wound disappear in seconds.
- I am not done with you.

Nature let go of Eos and left the castle after putting her weapon away. Eos made sure she had left before returning to her throne. After Eos had sat down, Valir approached her and asked:

- Can I bring you anything?
- A glass of blood please and lock the door.

- As you wish.

The front door was locked. Eos drank her glass of blood before going to bed. She had gotten her answers. A week later, an Elfin-Dragon brought a message for Eos. Valir took it and brought it to Eos who was with the "evil" protectors. Eos took it and read the message.

Dear Eos, Queen of Evil,
We wish to see you at the Oracle's castle immediately. We have urgent business to talk about. The protectors also want to meet the new ruler of Evil. Don't bring the evil protectors. Come to us or we will come and get you.

Sincerely, Lydia

After reading the message, Eos gave it to the protectors because they wanted to read it. After they had read it, Frice approached Eos and said:

- You can't go alone.
- Why not? Asked Eos.
- Because everyone knows that when it is written, "bring no one" or anything that suggest you to come alone it means it's a trap.
- It does mean that for evil beings but it does not mean that for good beings. It only means that they wish to speak to me alone. You haven't spent much time with your "good" brothers and sisters have you?
- No. We have spent fifty hours with them.
- That's it. You each spent around fifty hours with them!
- No, we mean fifty all together. Personally, I spent about two hours with them.
- I'm going alone and I will be fine.

- If you need our help, just close your eyes and call us.
- I will.

Eos left her black castle by herself and went to the grey castle of the Oracle. When she arrived at the front door, the two Elfin-Dragons that were there let her in. When Eos entered the hall, she saw Lydia sitting on her throne. Someone was leaning against the back of the throne looking towards the wall. Eos heard the front door slam shut and started to be nervous. Lydia nodded down and the others protectors surrounded them. They were placed from Eos' left to right in the following order: Pera, Giorno, Mythra, Vira, Soara, Niam, Lez, Lily, Planctus, Pois, Typhon, Ahuale, Ceri, Chinook, Dido, Lut, Sout, Luna, Clorus, Lyco, Solano and Lumos. After everyone was in place, Eos looked at Lydia and asked:

- What do you want?
- I don't want anything but my sister does.
- Which one? You have eleven sisters present.
- Fate, protector of the future.

The girl that had been leaning on Lydia's throne since Eos had entered turned around and walked around the throne to be on the left of Lydia. Her skin reflected everything like a mirror except it showed what would happen to it according to her. Fate looked at Eos and said:

- You are the first one who is not a member of my family to see me.
- Well technically you are part of my family. You're my aunt because my father is your brother.
- Do not correct me, do not insult me and do not interrupt me. Is that understood?
- As you wish. Said Eos in a sarcastic voice.
- I asked you to come here because I need to know the truth

about something. I need to know what truly happened to your mother.

- Did you ask the council?
- Yes. They told me that they were under an oath of secrecy and that if I wanted know the truth, I had to ask you.
- Did you ask Pera? She's after all the protector of the past.
- Pera makes sure we do not lose the past. She does not know everything about the past.
- All right then, I will tell you. Lyco asked Lydia to kill him because he was afraid of my brother and me. Three days later, my mother died of sadness because she thought her husband was dead and not locked in her children's bodies. That's how my mother died.

The protectors started to talk between each other. They could not believe that Eos was blaming Lyco for what had happened to Selene. After a few minutes, Fate asked everyone to stop talking and then said:

- You are lying.
- How would you know?
- We are protectors of truth.
- I am protector of lies. Which makes you able to see when someone says the truth and me able to see when someone lies. But if that is true than you can also see when someone lies and I can see when someone tells the truth.
- It still makes you a liar.
- Perhaps.

Eos turned towards Pera and approached her. Everyone kept an eye on Eos because they did not know what she was going to do. When Eos was a meter away from Pera, she stopped moving forward and started to walk towards Giorno still keeping the same distance. She continued doing so until she was in front of Lyco where she stopped and got closer to him. Eos looked in his eyes and Lyco did not move his gaze from her. The silence lasted for five minutes before it was broken by Eos who asked Lyco:

- Why were you afraid of my brother and me?

Lyco did not answer the question right away. He was thinking of how he would answer it. The other protectors where anxious to hear his answer as well because they did not know why he had done that. They had never asked him that question. Lyco then finally opened his mouth to answer:

- Everyone is afraid of what is new to him or her.
- That's the reason why you wanted to die when you saw us for the first time. Because you were afraid of what we were capable of doing. Said Eos. I'm going to guess that you were also afraid of what would happen to you because you had not married Clorus as Fate had told you to do.
- Yes.
- Everyone tried to talk you out of it but you wouldn't listen. It's your fault that Selene is dead. It's your fault that my brother will never like elves. It is your fault that I lived twenty human years of my life living as a human. But you brought good things to my life. It is because of you that I married William instead of Louisiam and that I became Malerk's heir
- I'm sorry and you're welcome.

Eos walked back to the middle of the circle and turned towards Lydia and Fate. After a few minutes of silence, Eos asked Lydia:

- Can I go?
- I am not done with you. Said Fate. You still haven't told us how you ended up in the past.

Eos stood there looking at Fate. Eos was determined not to tell the truth to the protectors. She knew that no matter what lie she told Fate, she would know it was a lie. Eos was tired of this conversation so she closed her eyes and called Chaos, protector of fire. A few seconds later, flames enveloped Eos and she disappeared from Lydia's hall. Fate would never know the truth about Selene's death.

CHAPTER 16
LAST CHANCE

A month passed and Eos managed to keep the truth from Fate. For a week now, Nature had been preparing herself for a trip but no one knew where she was going. She had packed all her clothes and her books. Nature had named Lydia as Queen of Good. Two days later, something happened that amazed everyone in Melda Cemmen. A small ship that had capacity of two landed between the black and the white castle. Everyone that was in the two castles came out to see what had landed. Nature came out of her castle in a hurry and opened the door of the ship to put her things in it. Eos approached her and asked:

- What's going on?
- This is a ship that came to bring me back to my planet.
- You called it here. Because you knew it was coming a week ago.
- Yes I did.
- You called it after Malerk had died yet you could have done it before.
- No I swear. I only figured out how to contact them a month ago.

- Promise me one thing then.
- What?
- You will go to the black kingdom and tell Malerk's father about what happened to his son.
- I promise.

Nature was serious. She was not lying. She climbed inside the ship that left a few minutes later. It blasted off in the direction of the next galaxy. It would take it six months to get back to Aura. When the ship arrived on the planet, it landed on the limit between the black and white kingdoms. Queen Peridot and King Oric were waiting on the south side and King Vile and Queen Audrey were waiting on the north. Nature was in the ship by herself. She was going to step on the north side. She would be the first one of the white kingdom to step in the black. The doors opened and Nature got out of the ship. She walked up to King Vile while his people stared at her. When she was in front of him, she bowed to the King and Queen before the king asked Nature:

- Why are you on this side of the planet?
- I come to give you news about your son. He died a few weeks ago in a great battle defending his heir.

The queen could not believe that her son was dead. But the king looked at Nature as if to say that he already knew what she was telling him. Prince Rekor and princess Laurie who were behind their parents could not believe that their brother was dead. King Vile then asked Nature:

- Who was is heir?
- Eos, queen of the Vampires, and also his granddaughter.
- What are Vampires?
- They are one of the creatures Malerk and I made when we were on Melda Cemmen. They were made to be creatures of

the night that drink blood but they made a deal with witches and became creatures of the day like everyone else.

- So these creatures are your children!?

- Not all of them. Only 97 of them are our children. But one of them is dead.

- How many were there?

- Tree billion one hundred and ninety million one hundred and thirty-five thousand and ninety-seven.

- I do not believe you. I must see it for myself. Prepare a ship! I am going to Melda Cemmen. Nature, you are coming with me.

- Father. Said Rekor. Let Laurie and me go as well.

- Yes you can come. We will bring Queen Peridot and King Oric with us.

A bigger ship was prepared for Nature, Vile, Audrey, Rekor, Laurie, Peridot, Oric and Sapphire. They all climbed aboard and left their planet to go see the new one that they had found.

Six months ago, after Nature had left, the news that Nature was gone had traveled the land. The dragons were now living on the main land with everyone else. Mythra and Typhon along with the elves had restored the trees that were still alive after the fire to their original beauty. Everything that was man made had been destroyed and replaced by vegetation. The animals had returned to the forest and continued to live as they had always done. The following year passed very peacefully. Until, one day, a ship landed on the hills in the Hauflin kingdom that was close to the council's castle. Some Hauflins gathered around the ship. The door opened and the royal families stepped out. When King Vile saw the Hauflins, he asked Nature:

- What powers do these tiny creatures have?

- They have a lot of courage and care for all the little things of the world.
- I didn't think they could care for the creatures that could eat them in a bite.

Nature went down the ramp followed by her family towards her old castle. The Hauflins followed her who were followed by Malerk's family. When they reached the council's castle, the royals entered while the Hauflins returned to their homes. When the council members saw her enter through the front door they all bowed to her. Nature told them that it was not necessary and presented her children to her parents and to Malerk's parents. She then explained the characteristics of each species. After meeting the council, Nature brought them to Nature's old castle where Lydia now lived. The outside looked the same but inside each bedroom of the castle had been changed to the desire of a "good" protector. The protectors now all lived in the castle. Nature was well greeted by her children. The protectors in Nature's castle did not impress Malerk's family. King Vile thought that many things that they protected were unnecessary. After an hour with Lydia, they left the white castle and went to the black one. They all entered Eos' castle but there was no one in the hall. They listened to see if they could here anything but they heard nothing. Meanwhile, in the fighting room, Eos and her protectors were fighting each other to see who was the best. Thor stopped and shivered. He turned to everyone and said:

- Everyone stop fighting. I feel the steps of eight people in the hall.
- I will go see who it is. Said Bora.

Bora transformed herself into the north wind and went to the hall to see who had entered the black castle and disturbed them. Bora came back thirty seconds later and told them that

Nature was downstairs with other people. Eos turned to the protectors and said:

- Let's go see what she wants.

Eos went to the hall followed by all the "evil" protectors. When they entered in the hall by the door that was the closest to the throne, they all turned towards them. The protectors placed themselves around the room while Eos approached Nature. Eos stopped in front of her and asked:

- Why did you come back?
- Mom, dad, Vile, Audrey, this is my granddaughter and your great-granddaughter.
- Why did you bring your parents?
- King Vile wanted to see who was replacing his son and what empire he had built.
- She is the heir of Malerk. Said King Vile while turning to Nature then back to Eos. What species are you?
- I am half Vampire and half wood-elf. Said Eos.
- Malerk chose a half blood for his heir! In my kingdom all half blood are tortured then killed. If you were in the black kingdom, Malerk would have killed you because it is a tradition that the next general kills the half bloods to prove himself worthy.
- Be careful what you say King Vile for you are in my kingdom and I decide what happens here.
- This is my kingdom more then it is yours. You wouldn't be here if my people wouldn't have discovered this planet.
- It was not your people who discovered this planet nor was it the people of the white kingdom. It was an accident. The ship carrying Nature and Malerk crashed on this planet and you never came to rescue them so they decided to make this world their own.
- I've had enough of your remarks.

King Vile pulled out his sword. The protectors all moved forward to help Eos but she told them not to do anything. Eos changed her blue eyes into her red, her black wings came out, she turned into a ball of fire and electricity appeared in her hands. King Vile could not believe that Eos had mastered all the powers of his people in so little time. Eos looked at Vile who soon put his sword away. Eos then returned to her normal self. King Vile bowed down to Eos. Soon after, everyone else of Aura did the same. King Vile looked up at Eos and said:

- Please forgive me. Let me grant you a wish.
- There is nothing that I want that you can give me.
- Perhaps you do not know what we can do. We can bring anyone back from the dead for an entire day. That person will either stay the entire day or will leave before if you wish her to. Maybe we could bring back William or Malerk.
- Do not ever mention those names in front of me. If you insist on doing this for me, I would like to meet my mother.
- Can you describe her to me?

Eos closed her eyes and tried to see the first three days of her life. It took a few minutes before she got a clear picture of her mother. When she saw her mother, Eos described her to Vile:

- She had dark brown hair as long as mine and her eyes were hazelnut. Her skin was soft and her voice calm with a small hint of fear. I cannot tell you how tall she was because she seemed like a giant to me. That's all I know.
- Do you permit us to do this magic? Asked Vile.
- Go ahead. But just tell her that her daughter wishes to see her and don't tell her my title.

Vile and Rekor face each other and placed their hands together. They whispered words to each other. A few seconds a later a frigid wind entered the castle and formed a tornado between Vile and Rekor but it did not make them move. The wind warmed as it slowed down and when it stopped it turned into Selene, tenth queen of the Vampires. Vile and Rekor moved away while Selene opened her eyes. After Selene opened her eyes, she recognized the "evil" protectors and Nature but no one else. She noticed that Eos was wearing the dark blue crystal of Malerk and immediately thought that Eos was evil. Selene pulled out her sword that she had been buried with and charged at Eos. Bora turned into the wind and returned to normal in front of Eos. Selene stopped in front of Bora and said to her:

- Move out of my way, Bora. She killed Malerk. And she has the courage of wearing his Necklace. I did not like him but the balance of this world depends on it.

Bora stayed where she was and did not move a muscle. Everyone else looked at the scene with great interest. Was Selene going to believe Bora or was she going to kill Eos? Selene asked Bora once again to move out of her way but she did not. Selene lowered her sword and asked Bora:

- Why do you protect her?
- She replaced Malerk a year ago when he died. He sacrificed himself to save her, to save your daughter.

Selene looked at Bora and at Eos. She didn't seem to understand that the Queen of all evil was her daughter. A few minutes later, after Selene had passed every hypothesis trough her head, she put her sword away and asked Eos:

- Are you my daughter?

Bora moved beside Eos to let her approach her mother. Eos moved closer to Selene and answered her question:

- I am Eos Anoura, daughter of Selene.

Selene grabbed Eos and gave her a hug. She was so happy that her daughter had survived. Selene then let go of Eos and asked:

- Where is Louisiam? I want to see my son-in-law.
- Louisiam is in the wood-elf kingdom and your son-in-law was killed by a silver bullet.
- You did not marry Louisiam!? Why did you disobey the Oracle?
- I fell in love with someone else before I met Louisiam.
- That's impossible. The Oracle predicted that you would marry Louisiam.
- She was wrong. After you died, I was sent to live as a human in the past. I was found and brought back when I was twenty years old. It was then that I met William Henulka and fell in love. I married him and had a daughter who now rules the wizard's kingdom with her husband and a son who his now ambassador of the Vampire throne.
- I did not die. Said Selene while turning to Nature. I was murdered.
- By whom? Asked Nature while Eos started to think of how she could stop the truth.
- By Jonathan, my protector.

It was too late. The truth was out. Jonathan's life was in danger. Nature and the others from Aura looked at each other and knew they had to punish him. Murderers where not tolerated. Nature sent a message to the "good" protectors who soon arrived. Eos looked at her protectors and they knew what they had to do. In the chaos, Selene had not noticed that Lyco was there. Chaos and Bora disappeared and appeared in Jonathan's room. When he saw them appear, he stopped speaking with Simon and looked at them. Chaos said to Jonathan:

- You have to get out of here.
- Why? Asked Jonathan.
- Selene was called back by Eos from the dead for the day and she told Nature who is back with her family and Malerk's family that you had killed her. In a few seconds, they will be up here and they will want to make you pay.
- Where should I go?
- To the Dragon kingdom and go with Simon. When they calm down, you will be able to come back.
- Is Eos releasing me? Asked Simon.
- I don't know. All she wants is that you protect Jonathan instead of her for the moment.

Jonathan and Simon where ready to leave when Sout, Lut and Dido appeared in the room and stopped the spirits from escaping. Frice then ran in the room and froze the wind protectors that where holding the spirits. Jonathan and Simon freed themselves from the frozen fingers. Chinook then entered the room and freed the frozen protectors and made Frice leave the room because it was getting to hot for him. Downstairs, Eos was trying to talk everyone out of trying to kill Jonathan. But no one would listen. All the protectors were already on their way to Jonathan's room. Eos was draining herself to stop them. The dark-angels arrived to help Eos. Selene eventually managed to get out of there and joined the protectors. Upstairs Vira entered the room followed by Dedum who was trying to stop her. Vira touched Jonathan's arm and was pulled away from it by Dedum. Jonathan's arm returned to life and he was now unable to disappear as he would usually do. After Dedum had gotten rid of Vira, he approached Jonathan and "killed" his arm. Jonathan and Simon then teleported themselves in the dragon kingdom before anyone else tried to stop them. Outside the room, Lumos illuminated himself and entered. The "evil" protectors immediately hid themselves while the "good" ones stayed where they were. When Lumos saw that Jonathan had disappeared, he returned to normal and the "evil" protectors could now come out. A few seconds later, the protectors went downstairs where Eos was still trying to keep Nature away from Jonathan. When she saw the protectors, she let them past. Dedum approached Eos and told her that Jonathan and Simon had escaped. Eos then looked at Nature and said:

- Take your family and return to your home.
- We will not go unless Jonathan is dead. Said Vile.
- This is my home. I make the rules. Leave and never come back.

Queen Peridot, King Oric and Sapphire left the black castle and returned to the ship while the others insisted on staying. Eos could barely stand straight but she forced herself to because she knew that if she showed weakness they would stay. Rekor approached Eos and asked her:

- He murdered your mother, why do you protect him?
- If he wouldn't have murdered her, I would have been another slave of Nature and her two daughters, Lydia and Fate. I would have married Louisiam because that is what they would have wanted me to do. Instead, I followed my heart and got to meet and marry my true love. I got all I wanted.
- But you lost it all.
- I didn't loose any of it. I realized that after seeing my mother. I have the memories. I have the past, the present and the future. Beside, the people who gave their lives to save mine will follow me everywhere until I die and I will lead them and watch out for them as long as I live.

CHAPTER 17
THE END

The Auriens left Melda Cemmen and would never return to it again. Eos didn't want her mother to stay after she had almost caused the death of Jonathan. Selene had left a few minutes after Nature and her family. The land itself was now different. There were no more humans and so there was peace. There would be no more wars between any species for they had learned to live as allies. The banishment of the dragons was now lifted because they had come to help the others even if they were not wanted. The Demons were now free to live normal lives without worrying about their purpose. The elves that had survived the fire had found all their strength.

Louisiam and Ilya had a daughter a year and a half after the war called Oreel. Alewan, king of the Sindarin elves, who had died in the war, had now been replaced by his son, Numen. Octet, leader of the banished was now king of the banished. Hobbes replaced his father and became king of the wizards and ruled with his queen Clarwena. Alexandre married Arabella and they both ruled as ambassadors. Nathan had married Aura, and his twin brother, David, had married Coiva. Jak had married Ilmen a month ago. Jonathan had managed to escape death. Now that Nature was gone, the "good" protectors were too afraid to approach Jonathan. Scott and Juliet had left the castle and had gone to live in Nenime, Juliet's birthplace. Marty had gone to live with the spirits because Clarwena no longer needed him. Gabriel and Essie were living in Lithe. Merrill and Drew returned to Namaarie, Merrill's birthplace, where she was accepted. Karl and Lecksha were still living in Tindome where they now lived in a small house. Ashka decided to take a trip around Melda Cemmen to try and find out more about her family's history.

After these time no major event or war occurred and so no one bothered to write down the history of their kingdom. I died a few weeks later. In the battle against the Humans I had received a silver bullet threw the arm. It had not burst but their must have been a crack in it because my cause of death was silver poisoning. With my death came my birth in a new world as a Human. I spent my last life hating them and now I am one of them. After twenty years of living with them, I still do not fully like them but I have learned to understand them. The stories I narrated were of my queens, my kingdom and world. I will forever remember the 7132 years I lived in Melda Cemmen.

THE END

To those who followed this story from the beginning, hope you've enjoyed it. It was pleasure to make your imagination soar. Until we meet again.